LAND OF HEART'S DESIRE

D1645787

LAND OF
HEART'S DESIRE

Alexander Cordell

PAN BOOKS

This edition published 1998 by Pan Books
an imprint of Macmillan Publishers Ltd
25 Eccleston Place, London SW1W 9NF
and Basingstoke

Associated companies throughout the world

ISBN 0 330 37725 6

The first world edition published in Great Britain 1995 by
SEVERN HOUSE PUBLISHERS LTD of
9–15 High Street, Sutton, Surrey SM1 1DF.
This first edition published in the USA 1995 by
SEVERN HOUSE PUBLISHERS INC. of
425 Park Avenue, New York, NY 10022.

British Library Cataloguing in Publication Data

Cordell, Alexander
Land of Heart's Desire
I. Title
823.914 [F]

All situations in this publication are fictitious and any resemblance
to living persons is purely coincidental

Typeset by Hewer Text Composition Services, Edinburgh.
Printed and bound in Great Britain by
Mackays of Chatham plc, Chatham, Kent

For my friend
J. Iorwerth Davies

ACKNOWLEDGEMENTS

I am grateful to Mozart's librettist for the words of the song "When a Maiden Takes Your Fancy" (Il Seraglio), also for verses from *Songs of Travel*, by Robert Louis Stevenson.

I am indebted to many people in the writing of this novel, not least to the old gentlemen of the industry whom I meet in my research travels, and who know what it was like in the Welsh valleys before the so-called social order we enjoy today: they who knew the colour of the flame before the furnace was tapped; or stood on the Farewell Rock before the coal ran out.

To such as these, and to Mrs Margaret Griffiths of Mid Glamorgan County Libraries, Bridgend, who helped me in research, is offered anything they consider worthy in this book.

In conclusion, my gratitude to the late Mr Brinley Richards for the assistance of his book *History of the Llynfi Valley*, and to its publishers Messrs D. Brown and Sons Ltd., of Cowbridge, South Glamorgan.

Alexander Cordell
Rhosddu, Wales 1994

Wales is a poem written in blood.

Anon

Ah, Love, could thou and I with
Fate conspire to grasp this sorry
scheme of things entire: would we
not shatter it to bits and then re-
mould it, nearer to the heart's desire?

Omar Khayyám

Book One

Chapter 1

1860

Had I known the fatal outcome to my family, I would not have visited the city of Carmarthen that day.

The March day was splendid, with just enough nip in the estuary wind to freeze a baby's bubble, and Wales was all over green and russet brown, spring having just booted wailing winter out of it; and Dai Dando, our coachman, was in fine voice, bawling his bass oratorio over the rears of the big, brown horses, his words drowned in the clattering of the wheels.

All this I later recorded in my *Diary of Events*, for a new life is not worth living, said my father, unless it is meticulously set down in a man's own hand, as had earlier been done, apparently, by a chap called Samuel Pepys, and what he put down was enough to make your hair curl.

Therefore, soon after my mother, the Princess Durrani, brought me to Wales from Afghanistan, I began this diary by writing in the front of it in English (much corrected as I got older):

This is a diary of events recording the life and times of Tom Mortymer, aged six, not to be confused with Suresh Ali Fusta Mahommed, known otherwise as heir to the throne of the House of Barakzai in Afghanistan. So please understand, all who read this, that my name is Tom and that, although my mother is an Afghan princess, I am the son of Iestyn Mortymer of Cae White Farm in the

Welsh County of Carmarthenshire; therefore I am Welsh, and have no intention of sitting on the Afghan throne in Kabul or any other foreign place.

That having been made clear to the world, I sat nibbling the end of the quill and staring out of the broad window of my father's study to the sunlit acres stretching out to the banks of the River Towey.

A shadow fell over the doorway.

"Are ye comin', youngster?" demanded Dai Dando, our bruiser, "or are ye sittin' there moonin'? Your ma and pa are outside in the coach, waitin' for the off."

"Don't you order me about," I said, "or I'll show you the four corners of the room!"

"Aw, come on, Maister!" and he raised a gnarled fist at me.

Old now, he was once a mountain fighter, this one, with five guineas of a gentry purse every Saturday night in the yard of the Black Boar tavern, he told me, and I didn't know a right cross from a left hook until old Dai came into my life.

Because I moved slowly, he swore at me in Welsh, a language I didn't understand, and he added, prodding me out into the shippon, "Stop playin' games and move your backside, or your mam will get her rag out and throw one of her tantrums."

I did not reply to this; silence always came over me when my mother was mentioned.

"One day," she said, as I got into the coach and sat between her and Dada, "you will learn the virtue of punctuality, one observed in Afghanistan, but non-existent in this appalling country."

A word about Mother while on the subject.

Four years ago back in Afghanistan, the courtiers there called her "The Pearl of the Age", and I can well believe it.

Black was her hair, lying like a wreath either side of her dark and lovely face, then falling in tight ringlets over her shoulders; she was small, only coming up to my father's

4

ears, and her figure had been most beautifully designed by the God who made ladies; her limbs (for once, by chance, I saw her in the bath) were delicately proportioned, and when she danced for the dirty old viziers in the foreign courts, their wrinkled eyes rolled in their sun-black faces. Possessing eyes that slanted seductively at strangers, but not my father, hers held the tenderness of a young fawn's, until something upset her, and then they were the eyes of a bitch, said Old Bid, our cook, "and a common young bitch an' all," she added, "so don't talk to me about the Mistress, for I'm 'aving no truck wi' the likes of her, for all her fancy airs and graces, and ye can tell her that to her face. Can ye hear me?"

"Woman, they can hear you back in County Cork, so stop your palaver," said Dai Dando as I came into the kitchen.

Now the pair of them looking at the floor, mainly Biddy.

"Biddy O'Shea," I said to her. "Please do not call my mother a bitch."

"It weren't for your young ears, Maister," said she.

"Nor for my father's. Supposing he had heard you?"

And she warmed to me, sniffing and snuffling. "Forgive me. It's just that I'm so sorry for your pa, that's all . . ."

"Do not worry about my father, he can take care of himself."

We stood in silence, and I added, "And another thing. My mother may be your mistress, but my father is the master here."

"That's what he thinks," murmured Dai.

But that was then, and this was now – sitting between my parents in the coach swaying along the road to Carmarthen for our meeting with the County Commissioners, the representatives of the Home Secretary in London.

"They tell me that the important one will be the one in the middle," said my father, "and that he is a very unpleasant piece of work."

"But he is not your God Almighty," replied my mother, and from the coach window there came a little gust of wind, bringing to me her perfume, a scent of musk, and she

5

added, "Did you mention, in passing, that I happen to be the Princess Durrani?"

"The cure of all ills?" asked my father, and she did not reply to this. "Frankly, I doubt if it will impress him in the least."

Dai took the coach into the middle of the city, tethered the horses, got an urchin by the ear with the promise of a penny to mind them, and handed my parents out on to the cobbles.

Here is a sight for sore eyes, this Carmarthen!

Almost instantly we were surrounded by pleading beggars, the ragged community of Welsh poor: soldiers in faded red jackets, still clutching at unhealed wounds, were there in scores; legs off, arms off, their empty sleeves and trousers tied up with string, they beset us with fierce cries for alms; this, the refuse of Victoria's Colonial wars, from Waterloo to the Crimea, jigged and jogged and pulled at us; some down upon their spindly knees begging for bread. She, our noble Queen, said my father, who promised before her coronation, "I will try to be good", had become the perpetrator of an evil ambition and the massacre of national innocence that would stand to the end of Time. My father was a man of few words, which befits true manhood, but his was a very high horse when it came to God bless our noble Queen; "for I have been in the thick of it," he told me, "and have seen men die cursing her name."

In the middle of the beggars he stood now, the tallest there, emptying his pockets of coins into their grimy hands; something he always did, I noticed, when we came into a beggar town. And Dai Dando, when each had had his share, handled them gently aside with the indulgence he showed when dealing with people of lesser intellect, although he himself was solid rock between the ears.

While this was going on, my mother stood in her lace and finery like a sunlit goddess of beauty, shrinking away from the grasping hands, and the beggar women in their rags touched the hem of her skirt with awe and whispered exclamations.

*   *   *

6

Mind, it do always beat me how many moulds God uses when making people; in His workshop He must have racks and racks of them, each one numbered and designed, male and female; to suit the needs of the population at the time, I suppose. And apart from the special mould He uses for the Welsh, Iberian or Brythonic (such being special for very special people, says Dada), some moulds, especially for females as beautiful as my mother, have to be of classical lines: silk-lined, I expect, for royalty and aristocrats; yellow moulds for Chinese, black ones for Africans, and white for the likes of my father; but for the likes of my mother and I, I expect He has a few moulds coffee-coloured, which He leaves in the midday sun until He cooks them right.

Beyond the fringe of the beggars a girl was standing; about my age was she, and did not beg, but stood there gripping her mam's skirt and staring in my direction.

It was her eyes! Large and bright they were, like jewels in her dark-skinned cheeks: indeed, it was because she was the same colour as me that I continued to stare back at her. Her mam, tall and slim in the body, was possessed of long black hair: proof that she was of gipsy blood, her plaits were tied with red ribbons.

"Damn me," exclaimed Dai, steering me out of the crowd, "there's a beauty!" and he elbowed me in the ribs to bring me back to life.

Pushing a path through the crowd he led us along the quay.

"Did you see the Romanies, Tom?" asked my father, and I noticed the unusual glance of recognition he gave to the gipsy mother, the meaning of which was to become clear later in my life.

I nodded, still looking at the girl, and at that moment she lifted her chin in a small petulance, turned, and walked away. But still I looked, following her movements.

"Little Jenny Wildflower's taken ye legs with her, has she?" whispered Dai into my ear.

"Who?" I asked.

"Jen Wildflower, the Romany!"

"Come on, come on," said my mother, pulling at me. "You can always stoop to pick up nothing."

7

"Nothing?" Dada gripped my hand. "They are the aristocrats of the gipsy tribes – red bows in their hair, Tom, remember?"

Yes, it was her eyes. And I think I knew in that moment, that at some time, now or later, this girl would become a part of my life.

"This way, sir," said Dai, and ushered us up the steps of the Immigration Office.

Jenny Wildflower . . . eh?

It was like the name of her soul.

Chapter 2

The great hall in which we were interviewed was lofty with pillars, a marble floor and echoing Corinthian columns tinted with gold, yet a blue-bottle, buzzing desultorily against a high-paned window, held me with fixed interest; flies on walls, I thought, must surely hold the plans of the Universe, so stuffed are they with the secrets of Man.

My bottom already ached on the mahogany chair and my high-buttoned boots were killing me. Three aged Immigration Commissioners sat opposite us behind a polished desk; I sat between my parents, already dozing in the blue-bottle's song.

"Your name," asked one of the three, "is Iestyn Mortymer, sir?"

My father smiled a reply.

"And you reside, it says here, at Cae White Farm, in the County?"

"I do," said Dada.

"With your wife and son, the boy sitting here?"

"Correct."

"Not quite correct," interjected my mother. "I am his common-law wife here: in my country, which is more advanced, I am his wife through the joining of hands; it is as Allah wills it."

"Let me make something clear, madam," said one of the commissioners wearily. "The laws of Man are the only authority here. As a token it may appear of small importance; as a fact it is the law which here applies. When one is in Rome, madam . . ."

"Please continue, sir," said Dada.

A commissioner rustled papers. "Doubtless you are aware,

9

Mr Mortymer, that now peace has been restored between our country and Afghanistan, our Ambassador is now again in residence in Kabul?"

"Of course."

"And this Ambassador, representing the Crown, has, upon the instruction of your King, madam . . ." and here he bowed, "interceded upon your behalf and obtained from our Home Secretary a pardon which absolves you, Mr Mortymer, from continuing with your prison sentence here, which normally . . ."

He faltered, and my father added, "Which normally would have caused my arrest and further detention in this country. Yes, I know it, and am deeply obliged to the Ambassador."

Another said, "The tragedy of the 'Afghan Promenade', as it is called here in military circles, is still with us, Mr Mortymer. Any who survived it are entitled to the understanding of the nation."

My mother again interjected, "Would it not be more accurate, sir, to assume that had not my King intervened upon my behalf and sent me to join my husband here, he would by now have been arrested, tried and sentenced as a deserter, if unjustly. Enough of this bumbledum!"

"Durrani," whispered my father, "for God's sake . . . !"

A commissioner raised a pale, lined face to her. "Possibly, my lady, but it will do little to advance the reason for your visit to this Court, which is for us to give consideration to your husband's application for your son, here present, to be granted British citizenship. Is that not the case?"

"It is," answered Dada.

Adjusting his pince-nez spectacles, the man said, "Since it would appear that your King, lady, the Dost Mahommed, is so concerned with the welfare of your family . . . I am a little surprised to receive from the office of the Home Secretary the following message which has recently arrived from Kabul." He raised his eyes to us. "I fear you will find the content displeasing."

"What message?" demanded my mother.

"Shall I read it to you, sir?" This to my father.

"Please do."

Picking up a paper, he read, "'Be aware, at local and diplomatic level, that while political circles at the Court of Kabul emphasise the need for the family of the Princess Durrani to enjoy the protection of the British Crown, the King of Afghanistan refuses to sanction the granting of British citizenship to any male issue of the Princess, either now or later, she being of the Royal House of Barakzai. Instruct the applicants accordingly.'"

My mother shouted, getting to her feet, "That is insulting! More than that, I shall not acknowledge my grandfather's authority! This is my son, and I shall order what nationality I like for him!"

"Alas, madam, that is not so," said a commissioner wearily.

"You mean that you accept the jurisdiction of Barakzai without objection?"

Another opened his hands at us. "We have no alternative. The Foreign Office has no power to intervene in what is so evidently an Afghan matter."

"But on what grounds does the Dost object?" asked my father.

"On grounds that your son, like his mother, is an Afghan national."

"But are there not other cases of our nationals requesting British status?"

"Naturally, when normal restrictions are adequately met, such status is granted. A most friendly state now exists between our countries. But this is a Royal intervention."

Moving away, my mother said vehemently, "Understand this, I shall not accept this interference without the most indignant protest to your Home Secretary. When I return to the Kabul Court, I shall do so unencumbered by a son who is recognised neither here nor at home; to be stateless in this world is a living death. Inform your superiors that I shall raise the matter with your own Royal family."

"In which we wish you profitable success," came the cold reply.

"So what happens in the meantime?"

11

"I suggest we all go home," said my father.

In the coach, my mother asked, more placidly, "What can it mean, this Afghan intervention – God, we have been over three years resident in this damned country!"

Dada did not reply to this, but put his arm about me.

Later, coming into my bedroom with a lamp to wish me good night, he said, "Do not worry. I care little if you are granted British citizenship or not."

"Mother cares," I replied.

"Nor does she, in reality. It is simply that, being Durrani, she insists on being perverse. Do you understand?"

I shrugged, and he added, "Princesses, you see, are rather different from ordinary folk; one has to make allowances."

Chapter 3

I suppose, looking back on it, Old Bid, our cook-house-keeper, had supplanted my mother in my affection; for whereas Mam was cold and stiff in her affections, Bid was soft in all the places where a woman ought to be for a boy, and had a breast for weeping on.

Unfortunately, I wasn't alone in fancying her, for Dai Dando wasn't behind the door when Biddy Flannigan of County Cork was loose and mirthful, which was often: brown hair bunned at the back was she, and like a ship in full sail when off to Whitland market, with a cameo brooch pinned on her front like a gargoyle and a behind on her like the Mountains of Mourne. Which appeared to send Dai Dando demented, for he was never the same come Monday after Biddy had shown him the door on Sunday.

"It ain't a question of knock twice and ask for Bid Flannigan," said Dozey Annie, our new maid, "for she's her own woman is that one, an' a maiden lady, too, and twice to Church Feast Days and Michaelmas, being Church of England Irish."

This new maid of ours, too, was a sight for a young man's fancy, for what she lacked in the top storey she made up for in other directions; and since she was too young for Dai and too old for me, I naturally took to her like a duck to water; being prepared to sacrifice myself on the altar of womanhood the moment I turned fifteen, which was about Annie's age at the moment.

Therefore, while in search of a female in place of a mother, it was natural to latch on to Biddy, until Dozey Annie turned up and replaced her in my filial affections . . .

13

Dozey, a London cockney who had wandered into Wales, was a great girl when it came to bedtime stories, when she would sit and tell me (while tears streamed down my face) of poor children being starved in the workhouse by a sod called Dickens: also, there were servant girls like her being visited in their bedrooms by randy young masters who deserved to be horse-whipped; none of which I really understood, except the *Farewell Blighted Love* song, which was good for a howl at any time, especially the last verse with Dozey practically breaking down. So there I was in my nightshirt, smoothing and patting her convulsive sobs, and if my pa had come in on one of these functions there would have been hell to pay.

All of which was excellent for my puberty but bad for my morality, for Dozey finished up on my pillow in magic dreams of adolescence, and it took me a couple of years to get her off. With Dozey in full flight and me after her with the worst of intentions, I was the dirtiest young master in Carmarthenshire.

Lithe and quick was Dozey, swatting the dust from one place to another and making big eyes at me while brooming out the corridors, with promiseful winks after I reached the age of thirteen.

Dreams, all dreams. Where is she now? I wonder.

But, mark me, compared with my pa they can keep the lot.

See him outside at the tub, lathering up for a shave; summer or winter, first thing, he washed in the shippon.

Six foot up was he, then some, with a fine brown body on him and a muscled chest like Atlas: plunging his hands into the icy water and flinging it over his black-curled head. Some men have door-mats for chests and hair over their backs, which they say is a sign of strength, but that's all balls, says Dai Dando, for Samson, whom he knew personally, had a body as white as a woman's. And such was the body of my father.

"Masculinity, that's it," said Dai. "Look at his ears." But even he did not possess my father's prized deformity, a gorgeous cauliflowered ear, the trademark of a man handy

14

with his fists. "Must 'ave done a bit in his time," Dai concluded, "you don't collect a thick ear pansying around with the poofs, and even were I twenty years younger, I'd not tangle with 'im, so you treat him decent."

See Dada now, weekdays, with the fields of Cae White bright gold with corn and the labourers coming in from Trimsaren with the scythes on their shoulders for the reaping. And my father leaning on his scythe in the middle of them, giving instructions to the three-man teams: fine he looked standing there stripped to the waist, the only master south of Carmarthen who worked alongside his men, sharing the heat of the sun in summer and the estuary winds come winter, for when the breezes came over the roof of Black Boar tavern in December it was enough to freeze your teeth in their sockets.

God, I love the world when our house is at peace with itself and Old Bid's kettle is singing on the hob, and Dozey Annie stitching her sampler in memory of her grandpa who died a week last Sunday; Dai with his hands on his chest in his big armchair in the kitchen, and my mam safe in bed at a reasonable time, for she was a devil of a woman for staying out after midnight; especially when the moon was full, apparently, though what the moon has to do with a wife's behaviour I do not know.

"She's a princess, remember," Dai observed. "I reckon they come different from ordinary folk."

Aye! As usual, I thought. The same old excuse!

Biddy at the hob on dumpling stew, sweating like a puddler and patting and wheezing. "O aye? Sure to God, He made the pair of us in the same image, save that she's got less of it than me. How that man puts up with it I do not know."

"His business, woman. Loose up!" said Dai.

This turned Bid in her wrath. "His business, is it? And isn't it the business of the whole house, us included? For if she carries on the way she's goin' these last few months, she'll 'ave the lot of us scratching beggars' backsides in Carmarthen workhouse, which means you, Dando – last in, first out, remember?"

15

"Aw, stop sheddin' blood, woman, it hasn't happened yet," and moodily Dai spooned up his stew and sucked it out of his whiskers.

I've never seen a pair of whiskers like Dai's on any man, with the ends turned up like a Prussian aristocrat, stained with blackcurrant pie in summer and Biddy's gravy in winter, with potato and onion bits hanging on to the sides; a most insanitary article, protested my mother, and if he doesn't get rid of it I'll get rid of him – the big stumbling oaf.

"Ach, leave him be, *cariad*," replied Dada, going Welsh. "A man is entitled to his whiskers without female interference, and our Tom is safe with Dai around."

"Safe?" And my mother swept us up with her skirts and said disdainfully, "That's the last word I'd use since the Dost's interference. My grandfather thinks big; a refusal to grant this naturalisation sounds more like Karendeesh."

Dada eased himself down into an armchair and began to fill his pipe, his eyes narrowed to the light of the window.

Rooks were having their annual parliament in the trees fringing the river, I remember, and the air was filled with their circling antics: always a sign of bad things to come, I'd heard the old ones say.

Karendeesh . . . ?

Karendeesh, *Karendeesh*! It was a name that haunted my childhood. Here's a bit of history that requires explanation, for it was with this fella in mind that I began to write my diary. One of the earliest entries being written soon after our visit to the Carmarthen Immigration Authorities:

April 20th, 1861. Cae White.
This evening, soon after I had got into bed, Dada unexpectedly arrived in my room, saying that he wished to discuss with me the day's happenings, and how it might possibly affect my future. My father was not given to outward demonstration, and had I been as old and as wise as I am now, I would have realised that on this matter he was clearly affected.

"Are you asleep, Tom?"

At which in the light of the window moon, I sat up to receive him.

He entered in vast shape, like a bear feasting, and sat on the bed beside me.

"You are too young to realise it," he began, "but what happened at the Immigration Office is of great importance, and it is necessary that you know why."

I laid back on the pillows.

"There is much concerning your mother and I which you have not been told," he continued. "You know, for instance, that England transported me to Afghanistan as a convict for my part in the Chartist attempt to overthrow the British government? I explained that to you, remember?" I nodded, and he went on, "You know, also, that later, having assisted your great-grandfather, the King of Afghanistan, in the production of his armaments, I was given the title of Court Engineer in his service; that while holding that appointment, I fell in love with your mother, and, because of this, was banished from the Afghan Court?"

"Yes."

Reaching out, he gripped my hand. "You also know that, as a result of a man and a woman falling in love, children are born to them, which is the way God usually blesses such unions. You understand so far without a doubt," and I nodded.

"Excellent. And how much do you know about this business of sending for babies – apart from the stork and all that rubbish?"

"Not a lot."

"Well," said he, double bass, "it is a subject on its own, and I do not intend to start it at the moment. Meanwhile, because of our loving, which was forbidden by your great-grandfather, the King, your mother and I were banished by him – myself on pain of death, your mother soon after. Are you following this?"

"Yes."

Rising from the bed he walked to the window and stood staring out on to the moonlit countryside.

I asked: "And because she was not wanted by Dost Mahommed she brought me to this land?"

"To be with me and to live with me as my wife, also that I could begin to enjoy you as my son."

"Thanks for telling me, Pa," said I, which I sometimes called him in moments of warm affection, and turned over.

"But there is more to it than that," said he, and returned to the bed.

"An official of the Afghan Court, an important man named Karendeesh, who also loved her, escorted your mother and you across half the world to this small farm. Some say he did this because commanded by the Dost: others claim he did so out of his unselfish love for your mother. It is enough to know that he did it, and I shall always be grateful." He peered at me in the moonlight. "You are half asleep?"

"No, Dada."

"Well done, for it's the usual tale of human stupidity and typical of humans who manufacture complications where none exist. Only this morning the Commissioners officially informed us by letter that your great-grandfather, as King of your mother's country, has officially refused to allow you to become a British subject." He swore softly.

"You explained that in the coach," I said.

"Which, in turn, must mean that he has also changed his mind about her banishment, and wants her to return home; you also."

"I do not want to go to Afghanistan, I want to stay with you."

"Of course, and so you shall. But it is necessary, Tom, for you to know the truth about kings. At the best of times they are persistent, and this one is no exception."

We sat silently and in that moment a cold emptiness stood between us.

"Tom," said Dada, "facts, like Truth, are best faced square on, when they can prove cowardly and insignificant if handled properly.

"The danger to you is real. I do not know for sure, but I sense that your grandsire is planning that one day you will

18

sit on the throne of the Afghans; blood-ties being more important to Afghan aristocracy than life itself . . ."

"But you are not of royal blood, are you?"

It brought him to silence, then, "Ah, that is is another story, but one which will not save you if it is ordained by God that you return to Afghanistan."

I asked quietly, "What has God got to do with this?"

"Nothing, if He is a God of justice, and I make this promise to you . . . Whatever the years bring with them and whatever the commands of kings and clowns like Karendeesh, nobody will ever take you from me."

From somewhere out in the country a cockerel crowed; faintly at first, then louder: three times it crowed in the night silence.

An astonishing thing happened then. Tears glistened in my father's eyes, which terrified me.

I had never seen my father weep before.

Chapter 4

School was something I hadn't set my heart on, like you sit there and behave yourself and I stand here and give out history and arithmetic, all of which goes in one ear and out of the other.

Up to the age of eight I'd got away with this, having been taught by private tutors, and by my father when it came to the important things like down with the Queen and off with her head, and put bishops and their three-cornered hats into the nearest nut house.

But, later, Dada got hot under his apron, as the people here say, and decided that a Prince of the House of Barakzai should attend the nearby Dame school to mix with the vulgar-tongued Classes, as my mother called the locals.

Mind, if she'd had her way I would have been packed off to Eton, Harrow or some other such snobby old place, there to learn about algebra and how many wives Henry VIII knocked off; all of which is useless in the world of commerce, a profession Dada had got lined up for me.

In this I agreed, especially since the afternoon I took my rod and line down to the river and came across a fish I had met once before: the Romany girl of Carmarthen.

The one with the eyes.

How to tell of her with only words available?

The first thing I saw near my favourite pool was smoke standing in the clear summer air, then a caravan, red and white, its brass glinting in sunlight, with a tufty old nag grazing nearby. A woman I recognised – the Carmarthen Romany – was at a tin bath, washing out her smalls.

" 'Mornin', missus," I said, coming up, which was not the

20

way I usually spoke, but that understood by the locals; for if you speak beautifully refined around some of these parts you can get an eye filled up.

"Ay ay, young Maister, 'afternoon to you an' all," came the reply. "And a fine an' wholesome day it is, to be sure!"

Black was her hair, now hanging down either side of her gipsy-dark face, the plaits still tied with red ribbons. Happy as a lark was she, with no uncertain thoughts about being on Cae White land without permission, and if my mother got to hear of it, she would have ended with a high-buttoned boot behind her, and old Bullens's policemen called to shift the caravan.

"You from Cae White then, young fella?" she asked.

"Aye, Mrs Wildflower." I glanced at my watch. Soon my mother would come riding along the river . . . even now I fancied I could hear approaching hooves, for April, our young mare, put them down very heavy when the going was soft; but I stood there like a goof and the Romany's red hands paused on her washboard; there was no sound but the trilling of larks and wind-whisper in the grasses of the river.

She said, "Reckon I saw you and yours up Carmarthen way, though I ain't certain sure." Raising a soapy hand, she made a face and wiped some off the end of her nose.

"That's right, my father and I . . ."

"And your mither, the traders say, and I anna seen the likes of her in a month o' Sundays. A princess, they say, and Gawd, she looks it! That makes you a prince or some'ut, don't it?"

"No. My father says I'm just like any other lad."

She sang then, smiling at the sun, and went on scrubbing. "Ach well, I suppose he's right – we're all God's creatures when ye peel the clouts off. Seen our Jenny, 'ave ye?"

"Jenny?"

"My girl, 'afore me old man took to the stars. The one you cracked your neck for a look, remember?" And she glanced upward. "Nigh four o'clock – she's due home from school," And she looked at me very old-fashioned, adding, "Young as ye are, me son, if you've got an eye for the women, she's the prettiest little sparrow you'll find around here for all she's a Romany."

"My father says that the birth doesn't matter. It is how folks behave that counts."

"Is that a fact? He wants to tell that to Bullen's peelers, he's always movin' us on – sprag his own coat, that sharp he is, and I expect he'll shift us from here, half a chance. Could ye speak for us, young 'un?"

"I will talk to my father," I said, and stood decently for her.

"For we don't touch the snares nor poach the buns, and my Jenny don't feed gin-peas to the pheasants to get 'em drunk, like some round here I could mention. Just give us water from the river, and we'll bring him Romany luck."

I bowed, and left her still singing the discordant gipsy song I had heard before from caravans: and in some haste, too, for out of the corners of my eyes I could see a girl in a white dress walking the river bank and there'd been enough palaver in the last ten minutes to last a fortnight.

"That's her comin' now, young Maister, but I'm certain sure she don't go a lot on gentry breeches, not since her pa earned their money and they killed him down Ogmore."

"Killed him?"

Her hands paused on the washboard. "Crushed under coal and gone to the stars. In fact," she added, smoothing back her hair, "we ain't that neighbourly when it comes to strangers, lest you're a Romany, so I'm a'warnin' ye, she'll likely put her nose up."

Which is what the girl did.

I've heard my mam say that clothes make the man, which is mainly when she's got me in front of a mirror in my Sunday best, pulling me out here and pushing me in there, and flicking off the dust to make me decent; but that doesn't apply to real men, says Dada, and certainly not to women – leastwise, not the kind I saw coming along the tow-path now.

A ragged old white dress frayed at the knees on this one, a bright red tattered jacket, and her legs and arms, as brown

22

as walnuts, were bare: clogs for this Jenny Wildflower, looking ludicrous as she stood before me tapping her foot, and making no eyes to speak of.

"Good afternoon," said I, and did my little Afghan bow, which is usually enough to get the females going, but it didn't have a lot of effect upon this one.

Then I noticed that she was carrying a little cloth bag hitched to a belt at her waist, and in the bag something was moving; probably a poached rabbit, I thought. And all of a sudden, consternation struck her face, which changed to horror as the air moved, bringing the sound of hooves.

My mother, I thought, best get moving; then came the faint wail of a hunting horn.

Hearing this, the girl made off, with me after her along the river bank towards her caravan; breathless, I caught up with her within yards.

"What's the hurry?" I asked. "It's only the Hunt!" And for reply she opened the top of the bag at her waist and out came a little face, blinking at the sun.

A tiny fox cub.

"They anna having 'im," said she, and the hatred of them was in her eyes. "I got 'im lame. Last week they tore his mam to bits and two cubs like him, but he ran to me, so now he's mine. They anna having 'im!"

"They will if we hang around here," I replied, for the cub was struggling to get out, and the stink of his terror was rising between us; doubtless this was already in the nostrils of the hunting pack. "Look, give him here," I commanded, and pulled the thing out by the scruff. "Follow me," and we went off.

The Trimsaren Hunt was right behind us as we ran into Cae White's shippon, and some horses were already milling around the out-buildings, and hounds baying furiously at our kitchen door ten seconds after I'd got the girl inside.

My father had just come in from the fields. As usual, nothing disturbed his outward composure; he just stood there while the Romany and I panted breathless before him, and I blurted out, showing him the cub, "Dada, the Hunt dug out and killed his family!"

23

"Don't let them 'ave him, please . . . ?" The gipsy had her hands out, her eyes bright.

"One thing at a time," came his reply. "Stay here until I call you, and leave this lot to me." Saying this, he opened the door and strode out into the shippon, taking his shot-gun off its hook as he went.

"He be daft. He's got the smell o' the fox on him, and they'll tear him bad," whispered the gipsy, looking out of the window, for the big hunting mares and their bloody-clad riders were clattering, wheeling and bundling at my father, pushing him about, and all the hounds were collecting in the shippon, sniffing at his clothes and baying . . . until the gun went off, an explosion that silenced the clattering hooves, the baying, the indignant protests.

Everything ceased; birds again began their music.

"And now get off my property before I pepper the backsides of the bloody lot of you, you barbaric bunch of hooligans!"

And they went.

"Dear me," said the gipsy, still staring. "I 'ad a pa like him once, till he walked up to the stars," and she made a little lamenting sound in her throat. "I ain't never seen the Trimsaren Hunt done that good before. He's some man!"

"You can say that again, missus."

"You realise, I hope," said my mother later, "that had I not been out riding this afternoon with Jason Llewellyn of Top Hill Acres, I could have been with the Trimsaren Hunt?"

"Of course," answered my father.

"Which means, I suppose, that you class me with those you called barbaric hooligans?"

"Naturally." He picked up his whisky and examined the ornately cut glass, then dismissed me with a glance. Outside the door I paused to listen.

"Yet I am the Princess Durrani, whose son is in line for the throne of Afghanistan," shouted my mother. "How dare you!"

Then I knew more of the barriers between them; of rifts that would never be healed, for the quarrel got louder still:

"And another thing," said Dada, his voice raised. "You're spending too much time over at Top Hill Acres with that milksop Jason Llewellyn. It has got to stop!"

"You will not tell me what to do! I am Durrani and do not take orders from a guttersnipe!"

"A guttersnipe who gave you a son, remember?"

She shouted back, "But never again, and I will tell you something more . . . I left my country to come to this heathen place to give you that son. But if Allah wills it and the King demands it, I shall return to his Court, and I will not go alone, mark me!"

There was a long silence; then my father said, his voice trembling, "Go when you like, Durrani, but you will never leave here with Tom. Understand it!"

My mother laughed then, her voice shrill. "Dead or alive, take your pick. We Afghans have our own way of changing the minds of irresponsible husbands. Meanwhile, stay out of my life!"

Up in my room I sat on the bed and watched the moon sailing on misted air: all that night it had rained, as if the world itself was in tears; for the rain, Old Bid once told me, "is only really the weeping of quarrelling wives and husbands, which is why I stays a maiden lady, for I ain't havin' no fella in this life tugging at me shift one moment and belting me the next."

I do think it very sad, this behaviour, and I can recall the days when first I came to Cae White, when the pair of them downstairs were billing and cooing like a pair of daft old turtle doves, with kissing good mornings and going up the stairs arm in arm at night, but this occurs mainly, I have noticed, when the moon is bright and the stars in God's grinder sprayed out to make the Milky Way.

Very strange is grown-up behaviour I have noticed when moonlight is upon them, but when the moon comes skinny it brings them to a hungering, and nothing feeds 'em full; and I put this theory to Jen Wildflower when we were lying in a haystack one Sunday, saying:

"I reckon they go daft with thin moonlight, for when the thing's a crescent it's all shouting and insults and kicking the cat, and you sleep in your room and I'll sleep in mine, and see how you like that!"

"I know," she replied, "I've had that, too. Mind you, my pa was an invalid for as long as I can remember, so he and Ma spent a long time hitting hell outta' each other, and his mates used to come with a litter and take 'im down to Betsy Ramrod in Black Boar tavern, who used to fill him up wi' ale; then when they brought him back home he were pixilated, cursing and shouting because his back was broken and the pension only two-and-six a week. Like it was Ma's fault." She sniffed, her eyes brighter.

"Yet," she continued, "it were his fault, mainly, because before I was born, Ma said, an inch o' petticoat used to drive him demented, so perhaps that's the trouble in your house, Tom Mortymer; usually hops or petticoats are at the bottom of it, I've found."

"Didn't she wear petticoats? Your mam, I mean."

"Oh aye, but he weren't that interested in those."

I considered this, and said after some thought, "There's that old Jason Llewellyn over at Top Hill Acres . . ."

"Oh well, if he's knockin' on doors, that's an end to it, for Ma said she wouldn't trust him wi' a Whitland Fair monkey."

Jen looked at me; then added after a moment:

"That right you'll be leavin' here soon?"

"Ay ay," I answered, lying back in the hay.

The wind came sipping up out of the valley and kissed my face, and distantly I heard the braying of an ass and the gentle bleating of sheep: all Nature seemed set up to perfume that day, I reckoned, when I planned to kiss Jen Wildflower or die trying to.

"Where you off to, then?"

I shrugged. "Don't know. Dada won't tell me, says it's a secret place far away. Might even be back to Afghanistan, from what they were whispering. Bloody hell!" And I thumped my fist into my palm.

"Don't swear, Tom. You're the only Welsh fella I knows who don't swear."

"I know some terrible words, mind, once I get going. Anyway, who says I'm Welsh?"

26

"You said you were once."

Tuk, the fox cub, ran around in little circles and she picked him up and kissed him; fine for him, I thought, but nothing for me. Then she laid back and smiled at the stars, not knowing that the top of her dress was rumpled, and it's all right for the likes of Dai Dando to say that this petticoat business isn't worth a good winter sneeze, but it's different when you're lying within inches of it; and Jen Wildflower, as if reading my thoughts, said, "Time I was gettin' back, Tom Mortymer . . ."

"Please don't go."

This turned her with such a smile that I reached out and touched the curve of her under her pinafore, and this closed her eyes and she lay unmoving, and the air seemed to tremble between us.

"Dear me, Jen Wildflower, you're beautiful," I said.

It stirred her and she said, eyes still closed, "My pa went to the war, Ma told me. Something about lots of Turks our lads went over the sea to kill.

"But he told her, Ma said, about our soldiers, ill and dying, and how our nurses went over there to help them, and something about ladies with lamps who used to come down the rows of hospital beds at night."

"Yes, Florence Nightingale took nurses over there, didn't she?"

"Aye, some'ut like that. And in the straw next to Pa was a young soldier wi' frost-bitten hands; some of his fingers had gone, Pa said, an' he was holding 'em up like claws and crying with pain, and down the beds comes this lady . . ." Jen faltered.

"Tell me."

"An' when she got to the bed of the soldier, she did something he will always remember, said Pa. She put down her lamp and knelt on the floor beside him and opened the front of her bodice and put his hands between her breasts. And he stopped moaning after a bit and listened, while she whispered to him like a mother. My pa said he'd never seen anything like it."

"Dear me," I said, and with that she suddenly opened the

27

top of her dress and reaching out, took my hand and put it down the front of her, saying:

"That lady were a woman, of course, and I ain't got much here to talk about yet, but you're welcome to what there is, for ye spends an awful lot o' time lookin', Tom Mortymer."

"Dear me, Jen Wildflower, that's gorgeous!" I said.

Later, she spoke again, but I did not hear her, and then she said:

"Tom Mortymer, if you want to know some'ut important about women, don't go clobberin' among the village skirts, eh? You just come to your Jen Wildflower, an' ask – anything, mind."

"*Diawch*, no," said I. "I've had enough to last me a fortnight, missus."

Whereupon she put up her face with her lips pursed up against the sun, so I kissed them.

A time to remember; Jen and me. Our first loving.

Chapter 5

It is queer how memory sticks like glue on to some daft old things and rubs out thoughts of others.

For instance, looking back I recall little of my mother's features, though she turned the heads of men from the moment she arrived in Wales.

Indeed, even at the age of ten it was a shock to me to discover this, for mothers are people who aren't included in such behaviour: the fellas can look, of course, but one doesn't expect them to be invited to tea: neither are mothers expected to look seductive, like mine does, since they belong mainly to sons.

I was a little surprised, too, when Dai Dando told me that he had been brought up by his pa, and that his ma was a goof right from the start; nor did I like this much, for the last thing a man does is criticise his mam, I told him, the lady who gave him his life, and, according to my father (and he said this while wagging a big finger at me), ladies can do no wrong.

From the word go, said he, one must hold them in the highest respect, such as walking on the outside of the pavement in case their skirts are splashed by passing carts, and always taking off one's cap when meeting a lady; and it was more than a fella's life was worth, apparently, to come out with a "damn" or a "sod it" when one of the skirted variety was within earshot; while such words like bums and bellies apply solely to the male of the species, and ought never to be confused with females.

Even Dai Dando subscribed to this, and he had been in the Navy.

I was a little in the dark, too, when it came to productive organs. I know I have got one because it becomes more apparent as time goes by, but ladies, it seems, were behind the door when God handed these out; and no reference to the subject should be made by anyone, especially by boys.

Therefore, I was interested when my father called me into his study one evening, to talk with me, he said amiably, on the subject of procreation.

"At ten years old you have found a lady friend, it appears," said he, and sat down and began to fill his pipe, always a sign that it was going to be an important session.

"Yes, Father."

Procreation, eh? This was a new one.

"Little Jenny Wildflower, the gipsy girl in the Big Field caravan?"

I nodded.

Diawch, I thought, there's a lovely word out of the dictionary – *procreation*: it rolled off the Iberian tongue and covered a multitude of sins, especially when it came over in English, for they, said Dai, are beggars for putting up the birth rate. But, sober serious was my father, and he was about to get going on how to keep your emotions in check until you're knocking seventy, when Dai Dando came in with an envelope in his hand.

"This just arrived from the penny post, Maister," he announced, and gave me a sly wink and went out again, which could have meant anything. But one thing was sure, it put an end to the business of procreation, and just when I was becoming interested.

Taking the envelope, Dada opened it.

Its contents put a spell on the Mortymers for the next two generations.

"You are old enough to understand it for yourself, Tom," and giving me the letter, I read:

"Honourable and esteemed friend, Durrani.

This message comes to you with all the wisdom of the elders of the Afghan Court and the blessing of the Royal

30

House of Barakzai. Greetings to all beyond the seas, especially to relatives who embrace the true Faith, whom God for ever preserve. Now take note.

Most gracious person, I pray you be aware of the royal line to which by birth you are indebted and of the noble Afghan blood that courses in your veins: of Islam, and your pious submission to the will of Allah; you who, banished from Court, now dwell in the tents of the infidels.

By decree it is now decided, that the ten-year-old son of your loins, sired by Mortymer, one of a royal line, is also a Royal by Christian standards; wherefore your son exists in direct line to the throne of Afghanistan, and, as such, will be returned to the country of his birth, by you escorted.

Fear not the King, who has granted his forgiveness.

Signed by me this day as Grand Vizier, for he who rules with the benediction of Barakzai.

Ever your most felicitous friend, Karendeesh."

I lowered the letter, saying, "But it is for Mother."

"Perhaps," came the reply, "but the letter is addressed to me, and clearly the intention that I would read it first."

"What does it mean?"

"That you and your mother should return to the country of your birth, to be in service to her people."

"Has this man Karendeesh the power to do this?"

"No, and if he thinks he is going to get away with it, he has another think coming. I'm telling you again, nobody is going to take you from me."

I said, "He writes that you are also of royal blood. I have never heard that before . . ." At which point my mother entered, dressed in riding habit, and said sarcastically:

"Then it was time it was told, for the blood of Islam, believe me, child, is very small fry compared with your father's line, once known as bastards." With this she sprawled on a chair before us in the attitude of a man, her riding boots thrust out. "Listen, and I will enlighten you . . ."

31

Dada interjected. "You know of this?" he asked, showing her the letter.

"Of course. Are you in the habit of reading other people's correspondence?"

"It was addressed to me."

"In order to keep you informed. I received the original a week ago."

"Yet didn't think to mention it?"

"To await the reaction of higher authority," and she winked at me. "A princess in Afghanistan is but of minor importance here; you make all the decisions."

"Especially in respect of my son. You are going to reject the invitation, of course."

"It is not an invitation, Iestyn, it is a command, and one which the Dost expects to be obeyed."

My father rose and poured whisky into a glass.

"What makes you believe this is the King's wish – it is signed by Karendeesh."

She fidgeted impatiently. "My God, how little you know of the affairs of our Court! The Dost commands, all obey; and his Grand Vizier speaks for him."

Old Bid knocked at the door, entered with a menu for next day and left again, dismissed by my mother's imperious wave.

Dada said, "Years ago you were banished by Afghanistan – in Tom's memory he has no knowledge of the place, and by my blood he is Welsh. Write back and tell them so."

My mother stared at me in token surprise. "You see, my son, how pride of birth pops up in unexpected places when it suits them? Is that not so, Husband?

"Did you not know of the Mortimer line that influences our house? As I entered, I heard you asking, Tom, for information concerning it, so now I shall tell you.

"It appears, though I have reason to doubt it, that your great-grandmother, Lady Jane Mortimer – her name spelled with an 'i' and not a 'y' – was the daughter of the Mortimers of Llandovery, not far away from here. And she could trace her ancestry back to Edmund Mortimer. Shall I continue?"

"He is entitled to know – carry on," said Dada.

"All this happened about four centuries ago, so it is scarcely relevant, which is why your father rejects it. Also, there are some black sheep around, are there not . . . ? For Edmund Mortimer abandoned a lady of the Welsh court when she had a child by him and, to avoid a scandal, its bastardy was hushed up in polite circles; this was the beginning of the Mortymer dynasty, for your aristocratic forebears insisted that the child should be named a Mortymer, to differentiate it from the royalists who fought at Mortimer's Cross. Have I got it correctly?"

My father nodded. "You are correct."

"Therefore, I am correct also in informing you, young Tom, that while on one side, mine, you are impeccably a Royal, on the other side of the line, your father's, you are sprung from bastardy; indeed, since your father and I are not married, according to the Christian faith, you are doubly so!"

Dada said, staring into his glass, "My God, Durrani! You are speaking to your son, remember!"

She rose, gripping herself. "One that I birthed in joy, but whom I now deplore." She indicated the letter on a table before her. "Now this has come, why not face facts, Iestyn? This is not my country, neither am I wanted here! Better to have it out now than face a future of misery for us all. Let me take him back to Afghanistan."

Dada said quietly, "You may return when you like, I have always made that clear; but not with Tom." And he added, "Not that I give a damn about royal lines and the perversions of aristocracy, yours or mine, but isn't it strange that the Dost himself gives credence to the Mortimer line?" He drank slowly, watching her.

"That," came the tense reply, "is for the convenience of the aristocrats, and I tell you this . . ." – her eyes were narrowed and filled with animosity – "If the Dost is prepared to accept my son, and me also, I shall take him to his rightful people, and neither you nor anyone else will stop me! I have told you this before."

"It remains to be seen," said my father, and drained his glass.

33

It is a devil of a thing when a house is at odds with itself, people saying one thing and meaning another, with one lot telling you to shoot off in one direction and the other saying, come back here. Also, the more I think of it the less I understand this baby-birth palaver, too; one lot in wedlock and the other out of it.

"Much better, I think, to be born at the bottom of the heap rather than at the top, for folks with crowns and coronets appear to make a sow's ear of everything they touch," as Dai Dando used to say.

"Better by far to be the son of a labourer and born in straw, as Jen reckons she was born, than put up with all this complication 'If you're a commoner and I am an earl', or suchlike, for we all end up in the same old place," said Dai.

"Ay ay, he can say that again," said Biddy.

Within a day or two, however, I came to learn what the future had in store for me, for I saw my mother under unusual circumstances.

The Towey River was in a terrible way with herself that summer, for floods had come over the pasturelands and she was in full spate, driving the swans and coots demented as she roared along within inches of Jen's caravan.

So it happened that skirting Black Boar tavern to avoid the wetness I found myself with Tuk, our fox cub, along the lane that led to Top Hill Acres farm, and the home of Jason Llewellyn, the local squire.

At the end of the lane was an ancient outbuilding in which was stored the harvest overflow; built long before Squire's Reach, the old ones said, and once burned down by the Rebecca Rioters. Seeking shelter from sudden rain, I ran towards it.

It was here, in this deserted building, that the Rebeccarites used to meet, according to history: further more, and this excited me greatly, my Uncle Jethro was one of their leaders, and a dab hand at burning hay-ricks and toll-gates and generally playing hell with the gentry . . . an *enfant terrible*, to put the right name on him, and long gone over the sea to Philadelphia to work in Andrew Carnegie's ironworks, I gathered.

"He were some man, according to the locals," said Dai. "After me own heart was he, and handy with his fists, as a man ought to be: so handy that he took on a sixteen stone dragoon one night when cornered and saw him away to Kingdom come."

"He killed him?"

"Ach, he didn't mean to, but left him unconscious, and he rolled down a bank and into a stream and drowned: that stream still runs today."

"Murder?" I gaped at Dai.

"Aye – the soldiers tracked him to Saundersfoot, but he got away; like your pa he were, a man and a half."

"Got away to America?"

"An' they anna seen hide nor hair of 'im since."

Murder, eh? I was overjoyed at the thought, having heard of folks being hanged for sheep-stealing and transported overseas for rabbiting; but to have a relative guilty of murder!

"And in the first degree an' all," added Dai with gusto.

So I approached the old barn with trepidation, the crime having been committed in close proximity.

With Tuk scampering before me, I went with care; pushed at an old, rusted lock, and entered; the broken door, groaning on rusted hinges, slammed shut behind me like a coffin lid.

Silence: nothing moved in the sun-shafts from a solitary window high above in the loft, and even Tuk stopped to listen to the nothingness that pervaded the quiet of this ghostly place. I knelt, and he leaped into my arms, panting against my face.

"Quiet, you," I whispered, "or we'll have the goblins out."

Queer, isn't it, when anticipation becomes a threat and the threat loosens into fear? Weird and palpitating are the tales Dai Dando has told me, and the wind, rising outside, brought rustling within like the *tylwyth teg*, the supremely fair and terrible Welsh fairies: the females of this species would have the nuts off you without so much as a blink, to say nothing of flying vipers and suchlike wriggling out of the Towey, and where they end up for inconvenience don't bear thinkin' about.

I fought for calmness, listening to the wind; and then the sun suddenly blazed, bringing the whole place to golden light. A rickety old ladder beckoned, the loft above it seeming to offer a haven against apprehension, and with Tuk under my arm I climbed upward, crawling along the hay-strewn boards to lie down, looking through little cracks in the slates at the rolling clouds of approaching dusk.

Was it really in this isolated place where Uncle Jethro and his fellow conspirators had met to plan their attacks upon the gentry? I wondered. Was it beside this gurgling stream where he had killed the soldier? If so, I thought, then surely the soldier's ghost walked in this lonely dusk . . . ? Tuk, now bored with the suddenly pervading quiet, yawned, curled up on my chest and slept.

I was about to move when I heard a faint drumming of hooves. A horse was coming . . . no, two; then the sounds merged into a staccato rattling as they clattered on the outside cobbles.

Panting horses now, whispered words: tense, I heard footsteps approach the barn door below me. Tuk twitched an ear, yawned again and lay warm against my naked chest. The door hinges shrieked like a vulture as someone entered; darkness had fallen like a witch's cloak over the day, and I peered down at two indistinct shapes standing together within the barn.

It was so quiet that I swear I heard birds rustling in the trees.

"Shall we go up . . . ?" It was my mother's voice.

I froze, my heart thumping madly against my shirt; and Tuk, as if in recognition, raised his little snout and gazed at me in mute inquiry.

"Not this time. Mice up there last time, remember?"

I peered down from my hiding place above them, one moment cursing myself for a peeper, the next wishing that

God would strike me dead. And then, in a last shaft of the evening sunlight from the window beside me, I saw him clearly . . .

Jason Llewellyn.

Even as I recognised him, he took my mother into his arms and drew her down into the hay bales.

Trapped, I lay above them and listened to their love-making.

White limbs I saw in the fading light; a gyrating whiteness that moved from the barn darkness into form and shape: breathless gasping I heard; the suppressed exclamations of those who snatch at lust in secret places. Now the swift intake of stolen kisses, the mouthing idiocy of lovers; and I saw my mother's outflung arms as Llewellyn's big white body enveloped hers in the obscene rhythm of their love-making: while in my ears beat the sounds of swine at the troughs.

Turning in the straw, I pressed my face into the hay to obliterate my mother's defilement, and the betrayal of my father beat about me.

Chapter 6

A few interesting things happened in the year I was eleven years old, the first being that Mr Jason Llewellyn of Top Hill Acres was absent at the Hunt Ball up in Carmarthen, being in bed with a broken jaw and both his eyes filled up, poor soul, and nobody could think who had done it; which happened about the same time that Dada caught his hand in the shippon door and had to go to a doctor to have it sewn up. About then another old randy called Major Jon Bloor, up for the day from Kidwelly, was seen out riding with my mother and the Carmarthen Hunt.

"Mind, she do get about a bit, it seems," said Jen.

"Ay ay, she likes a bit of company," I replied.

"Handsome is as handsome does, they say, and beauties like her should stay at home with their men-folk, my ma reckons."

"She's a princess, remember; they're not like other people," and I added, "Dada says she's making the most of her friends, but we're away from here as soon as we sell the place."

"You're leaving Cae White?"

About this I had been timid, not wanting to tell her dates lest she cried.

Sometimes in the villages I saw women cry, rocking themselves to and fro with their sack aprons up to their faces, their cheeks tear-stained and their eyes red, and I didn't want Jen to look like that – she of the laughing eyes and bright smiles. And sure enough, just what I'd been dreading, she turned it on like a tap and stood there before me in her ragged dress, howling.

"Soaking me you are, Jen," I said, and held her, which was the first time I had ever held a woman in my arms, save Old Bid, and she doesn't count; nor Dozey Annie either, come to that, though with her I didn't dare, for she was grown up. And just as I was drying her out with my arms about her, who turned up but my father, and I don't know who was the more surprised of the three of us.

Getting off his big stallion he said, "What has he done to make you cry, Jenny?" and this mopped her up quicker than light, and she smoothed down her apron and stood decent for him.

"Said we were going away," I explained, "and this turned her on."

"Goin' to miss you bad, Mr Mortymer," said she, still wiping. "You mainly, for most farmers see off the Romany folk round these parts."

"Won't have them on their land, you mean?"

"Sure enough. Said like we're all that tinker-trash – cheap old boyos selling pegs an' that, and snitchin' the eggs when their backs are turned, but we be Romanys."

Smiling, he listened to her musical voice, his head on one side. "Romany people, tinker folk, they're all the same to God, Jenny. Is it well with your mother?"

"Fine dandy, sir." And she curtsied.

"Give her my regards. Perhaps we go, perhaps we stay, tell her, but wherever we land, here or elsewhere, there will always be grazing for your pony. You tell her that?"

"For certain sure!"

My father did not turn to go, but leaned back against the horse as if awaiting our pleasure, and I took the hint.

I would have kissed her then, had my old man not been hanging around to get the size of it, and I could tell he'd been weighing us up by the look on his face.

"A word with you, Tom," said he, and we were off, walking the stallion between us.

The evening was gorgeous, I remember, with the sky a sea of

mackerel clouds all snow-white and billowy from St Peter's weekly wash; curlews were shouting from the estuary far away, and a ring dove popping the question to his mate from the great oaks of Squire's Reach.

"How much do you know about girls, Tom?" Dada asked his boots.

"Like I said before, not much."

"You know about boys and girls and babies, and all that stuff?"

"Oh, aye!"

He stopped in his tracks and stared down at me, and he was so big that he shut out the sun. I was going to ask him if there was something he was doubtful about, but decided against it.

"You do?"

Bass is the voice for me when I grow up!

The wind kissed us from the estuary, bringing a tang of salt and ships.

I thought, Oh God, keep this moment best for us, my pa and me, that I may cherish it: a little time away from a troublesome mother, and the dirt of the world.

"Aye aye," I repeated. "I know how babies are sent for and how they arrive."

"You are proficient in the subject?" He was trifling with me now.

I wagged my shoulders and made a face.

He pondered this, then said, "I ask this, not because I am concerned about you personally, but as to how you stand in the business with Jenny."

"I do not know what you mean."

His eyes, I thought, were incredibly blue in sunlight; something I had never noticed before. He said gently:

"Women, in this world, get a poor share of favours when it comes to men, Tom. While love to us is something removed, to a woman it is her whole life. Are you listening?"

"Yes, Dada."

We walked on with the horse snorting between us.

"Yet, it is women, whom God formed from the rib of Adam, who give us life. Being the weaker sex, a man never takes a fist to a woman, so pick a man if you want a quarrel. Raise a hand to a woman and God will turn His back upon you.

"Take Jenny, for instance – how small she is, yet the emotions within her are probably stronger than yours. The same with her purpose in life, which is to mate and bring forth a child from her womb, in her own likeness; a child most intricate in design and beauty since it belongs to God. Yet we poor fools, with the world of science and engineering at our disposal, cannot make a baby's fingernail. You are following me?"

I nodded assent.

"Take the great artists – Leonardo da Vinci, Michelangelo – the great Cellini swaggering through the sixteenth century, yet producing statues and carvings which are beyond mere inspiration. Where do you find women in such company? You do not. Search the archives of the classical universities and their names and histories are absent, nor are they mentioned among the great intellectuals, either of today or in the past. Likewise, however, do not expect to discover them among the butchers – the Alexanders, Genghis Khan, Akbar Khan – to whom you are unhappily related – and Wellington, our noble Duke who does his blood-letting for our pious Queen.

"No, you will not find the guilty among womankind, for they are the givers of life, not its takers. God ordained this from the start of Time: indeed, it has been said that since He couldn't be everywhere at once, He decided to invent mothers."

We walked on back to Cae White and the day was splendid. Dai came out from the stables, saw us, came running and took the horse. My father said:

"I did not intend to give you a sermon, but to indicate to you the value of women, one of whom one day you will take as your wife. The military conquests of men, their romantic assignations, their poetry and their songs are as nothing to the value of a good and faithful woman, as your mother is to me. And it is our task, Tom, to uphold women in their weakness; to protect them from bawdy whispers and so maintain their purity, for a pure woman – who is as good or bad as a man chooses to make her – is above her weight in jewels. Remember your Bible?"

"Yes, Father."

"No sniggers in dark places with young Jenny, Tom. No roaming hands to discover her secrets, for they belong to her: and remember, the first kiss you give and take from a lover is the one she will remember. You have no sister, but had you one, would you lie with her in a cornfield, as once I saw you lying with Jenny, even in innocence? No, you would not. This girl is your mother, your sister, your companion and your friend; treat her as such until your heart tells you otherwise."

I nodded, my eyes lowered.

"Right," said he, "this has taken more out of me than you, let's get going."

Did my father know what my mother was up to? I wondered: it appeared that he did not.

So who, I speculated, had done up Jason Llewellyn? The poor soul had mislaid his front teeth, too, apparently; and had eyes he wouldn't see out of for weeks, according to reports.

I looked at my father while he buttered toast with his bandaged hand, and he fluttered a wink at me while my mother, at the other end of the refectory table, looked daggers.

Mystery, deep and pure, lay in my father.

If he knew what was happening between Mam and Jason Llewellyn, he was not giving the slightest indication.

"You did it," I said to Dai Dando. "It was you who filled up Squire Llewellyn's eyes, wasn't it?"

"Don't be daft, young Maister," said he.

That night I wrote in my secret diary:

September 5th, 1866. Cae White.
Soon we are going to leave here and go to some secret place, to get away from letters and threats arriving from

42

Afghanistan, for Dost Mahommed, my great-grandfather, is demanding that I return to his country and sit on the throne in a place called Kabul, when my mother, he now says, would become Regent, or some such thing.

Dada says over his dead body and my mother says yes, very likely.

I go to the Dame School now, which Dada says is good for me and have to sit among the village lads, some of them call me the "Nigger in the wood-pile" because of my dark skin. Dai said to lay one of them out and then it will stop, so I did, a great heaving oaf aged thirteen. So school is better now, though I still hate it. I hate the teacher, too; her name is Miss Ira Jones and she has spots on her face like Dozie Annie, and she calls me The Prince. I am not a prince, except a Welsh one, and I do not intend to return to Afghanistan.

After the confrontation about procreation with my father, I began to wonder if I had gone wrong somewhere in handling the situation, and found it under the carpet runner in the middle of my bedroom.

Now, it happened that some time in the past a lad sleeping here had realised that his bedroom was smack above the servants' bedroom on the floor beneath, and, finding a convenient knot in the floorboards, had prised it out.

Now, although it was furthest from my intentions, I discovered that if you got under the carpet and put your eye to the knot-hole, you got a prime view of the double bed where Old Bid slept (at night I could hear her snoring), also the narrow bed in the corner where slept Dozie Annie and, when in operation, the big tin bath they kept in the middle of the floor.

It didn't do a lot for my constitution; indeed, it took a lot out of me to lie with that carpet over my head and my eye glued to the knot-hole, while Dozie was getting undressed for bed.

Saturday night was usually bath night, and calling myself all the swines in creation, I'd lie there watching her take things off, which was enough to send a healthy male berserk at the best of times.

For a single chap to watch a woman get in and out of a set of whalebones is a phenomenon not to be missed, and Dozie, although a herring in boots, was no exception.

First off comes the white dress, then the camiknickers, and she is there in stays; after which comes a scratch, lifting things up and down while making astonishing faces at the ceiling. Now off with the breast plates – for decoration purposes, in this case, for Dozie had nothing much to boast about – and she is there in black stockings: this had such an effect upon me that I very nearly fainted. Down on a stool now and peel them off, one leg in the air at a time, and she's there as bare as an egg.

My interest naturally subsided when once she was in the bath.

After this performance of uninhibited lust, I was so upset by my caddish behaviour that I went to Chapel twice a week to pray for my soul; swearing to God that never would I do such a thing again, until a week next Thursday when I heard Dai Dando coming up to the servants' quarters with pails of hot water.

This coincided with the arrival of another female, the niece of Old Bid, and one of very desirable proportions; so I lay upon my bed thinking about Satan and how I'd feel if somebody was doing this to my sister, and I'd just got the better of the Devil when I heard this new arrival gasping and bubbling in the old tin bath, making enough palaver for a woman drowning; betimes singing in a cracked soprano, *The Lass With The Delicate Air*, which shot me out of bed and under the carpet.

At first, such was the swirling steam in the room below that I couldn't even see the bath; then, to my horror, there emerged out of the suds no vision of Aphrodite loveliness but Old Bid herself with two arms outstretched to me as if in greeting, one hand clutching a flannel, the other a brush. Scarcely had

44

I recovered from the shock when she turned her back to me, and bent looking for the soap, my world deteriorating into a backside of such proportions that it put all my dreams of feminine symmetry to flight.

Next day brought Dada's further pronouncements about procreation; and that night, suspicious, I peeled back the bedroom carpet to find that somebody had nailed up the knot-hole.

Slyly, I accosted Dai Dando while he was brushing out the stables. "You been in my bedroom lately?" I asked him.

"Me? For why? Got a bedroom of me own, ain't I?" And he grinned wide. "An' next door to Old Bid an' all, remember?"

As if I could forget.

And he was welcome to it, I thought: the very thought of anyone procreating with Old Bid put me off women for life.

Chapter 7

My mother constantly complained about my speech, saying that she had done her best to bring me up as a gentleman, but that after years in Wales my vowel sounds had degenerated into the sing-song articulation of the Welsh; "God knows what they will think of you in the Afghan Court," she added.

"Face facts, Durrani," interjected Dada. "He will never go to the Afghan Court."

"I will tell you again," said she with finality, "you do not know my grandfather. Any time now you will receive another directive."

She was right, being possessed of the oriental intuition known to the subjects of Allah.

"Another letter from Afghanistan, Maister," announced Dai, and brought it in on a salver. Dada opened it.

"As I thought," he said to me. "Make ready, Tom, we will be leaving here within the week."

"Within the week we could all be kidnapped," Mother observed.

She was dressed that day in robes of saffron, the lovely orange hues of varying textures, silver-lined silk here, gold-lined there, enhancing the beauty of her dark, Afghan eyes. Her profile was refined, the features delicately chiselled; she moved with exquisite grace, soundlessly, on upturned slippers of red and gold. Strangely, and I had heard my father remark more than once on this, the intemperate Western air seemed to have distilled the hue of her flawless skin, and I can see her now at her toilet before the great mirror of her bedroom, her light-brown arms moving grotesquely in lamplight so that the rest of her small figure appeared disembodied; a strange apparition.

Usually, she wore a bodice of plain silver, the edges trimmed with green for Afghan (though sometimes, and mainly on Afghan feast days, the bodice was yellow). And there exuded from her small person a perfume so delightful that even as I write this I am aware of it in my nostrils.

Let me be clear on a point: the men of Carmarthenshire, Welsh to the backbone and raucously sexual in hunting pink, were more to be pitied than blamed. She really was a most delightful creature.

Her womb, said my father, was small; "indeed everything about her is a miniature: therefore it must have been that you were changed at birth, for it does not seem possible that she brought you forth. Indeed, Tom, I was not around to substantiate this! You of the strong hands and large feet speak of the Mortymers, for my father was six feet three and I am only one inch less. Also do not allow your mother's gibes about your speech to upset you, for in your throat lies the music of Wales, and neither Wales nor I want you any different."

"Are you ready, Dai?" I asked the coachman.

"Aye, if I knowed where I was goin'."

"Don't you?"

"Maister don't know where himself."

"What about Old Bid and Annie?"

"Them's the same; they'll come, they do say, but don't know if it's Tenby or China."

I asked my mother, "I know we are going to move, but to where?"

All that day there had been a commotion of removal men coming and going, but where to? Dada was tight-lipped on the subject.

My mother said, "It is all highly dramatic, Iestyn, but are you not overdoing the military precision? Details of such domestic manoeuvres are known to the Afghan Court the moment you decide upon them!"

47

"Don't overrate them," said he, packing a briefcase.

"I would never overrate Karendeesh. Of all the viziers to the Dost, he was always the best informed. His task in life is kingship, his own security at Court depends upon it. He will be watching, make no mistake."

"No doubt. Meanwhile it is ridiculous to sit around here waiting for them to act against us."

My mother shrugged disconsolately. "Husband, see the practicality of it. The Dost demands our son. We live in Wales, but our destiny is Afghanistan. Here my life is bare; in my own country the three of us could live like kings. As regent to my son we could own the East from Kabul to Jahore."

Strong men, I have noticed, are often prey to the whims of women, and so it was with my father; but not this time; this time his only son was involved.

"He will trace us, you know," Mother said.

Dada's hands paused on the packing. "Who?"

"Must I keep repeating it? *Karendeesh*, of course. Wherever we go – north, south, east or west – he will trace our whereabouts, and his secret police will haul us back for interrogation and justice; my grandfather can be merciless."

"He has got to get us to Kabul first!"

"Do not doubt that ability."

"For God's sake, woman, get about your business!" Dada shouted. "You're either painting up your face or giving me the length of your tongue about your bloody grandfather," and, snatching at her in a sudden rage, he pushed my mother out of the room and slammed the door upon her.

Dozie Annie, hard at it in the hall with brooms, lifted her shanks, and fled: tumult always hit the house when Dada lost his temper.

Mind you, what with one and the other, he had something to put up with; and didn't know half the story when it came to his wife.

I recall the years when first she brought me to Cae White; as I said earlier, at first they were all bills and coos, and butter wouldn't melt in their mouths; but after a while my mother seeed to get bored with this, and began to decorate the place for Hunt Balls and afternoon soirées and tea on the lawn.

Most of the dignitaries of Carmarthen City were coming and going, their horsey wives giggling behind their fans and giving the men saucy eyes; in chattering groups they vied with each other for the latest London fashion, while having each other over as to who had been sleeping with who.

Their menfolk were like hunting animals, of spurs and military barks, their medals clattering on their chests (the fat ones with cummerbunds around their bellies to stop their guts falling out): their talk mainly of hunting, military victories (never defeats like Afghanistan, said Dada) and God Bless Queen Victoria, though she had removed more arms and legs from the bodies of innocent British soldiers and blinded more eyes, said he, than Napoleon in his retreat from Moscow.

Ay ay, men of blue jowls and commands were these, and gin and bitters before tiffin; and never could remove from their peanut brains the proposition that Great Britain owned the world by the grace of God and the Archbishop of Canterbury.

But, such was the life my mother loved; with the great and good paying her tribute, the latest debutantes curtseying before her and giving her the homage of a queen at court. Princess this and princess that it was, below glittering chandeliers, and the music of the minuet and military gallops floated over the fields to Black Boar tavern where Betsy Ramrod, the landlady, held a very different kind of court for the locals. And it was here (for I saw him through the tap-room window) that my father often sat alone with a pint of old and mild on the bench before him, and his brow furrowed in thoughts of what might have been.

What was actually happening was twice worse than he knew . . . Or did he know, I often wondered afterwards, and keep the secret locked in his heart?

Go back a few years.

"Tom, are you awake?" This from my mother, bending over my bed.

I was about four years old when first she began this secret

message palaver, which I understood at the time was nothing to do with courtship, and everything to do with Allah.

"The old hollow tree, Tom, my darling – remember you took a letter there for me once before – from me to God?"

"Yes, Mother."

"And you will take another? Remember you promised?"

"Yes," and I hauled myself out of bed in my nightshirt and took the little scented envelope from her hand.

"And you will remember, too, Tom, that it is a secret between you and me? Nobody else must ever know about it. Promise?"

"I promise," I said, shivering.

"Cross your heart and hope to die, like you say?"

"Cross my heart . . ."

They were summer nights with owls hooting their ears off around the fields of Cae White, and the old Towey shimmering under the moon as I tiptoed like a wraith of sin past the ghostly trees that fringed Squire's Reach. Hag-ridden nights these witches of summer: and sometimes ferrets and weasels were hunting as I went and little things dying, their screams threatening.

Sometimes a ferret will trap a bun down a burrow and eat from the back and he will scream and scream, calling for his mam, but still the ferret goes on eating.

Dai told me this, and the picture he had conjured filled my nightmare dreams.

"Eaten from the arse up, Tom – can you imagine it?"

Imagine it? I used to think the ferret was eating me.

With the letter clutched in one hand I would go, slipping and sliding through the refuse of dead autumns, with the lowering branches of Sin-Eaters' Wood flowering above me, and thorns and catch-me-kill-me nettles snatching my nightshirt.

In a living terror I would go, taking the message to the hollow tree that stood alone in a little clearing, and arrive in a bath of sweat before it. And it would stand, this blasted oak, as if in judgement of the small boy before it, and stare down at me from its lofty height.

See this crippled tree in daylight with the sunlight making gold patterns on the forest floor and it is frightening enough. But see it in moonlight in all its ghostly apparition, or on nights of tempest when the wind is wolf-howling and lashing it into a fury . . . and it is enough to stop the heart of a man, let alone a child.

"Please," I would say, my face turned upward, "I have brought this message from my mother, for you to give to God."

And in the nightmares I had about these excursions , the tree would reach down a withered branch and touch my hair in fatherly benediction – the signal for me to climb its knotted trunk and put the envelope in its crippled heart.

Soon, I thought, when morning came (for this my mother had told me) Allah will reach down his hand from Heaven and take the message into his bosom. For this, she said, was the way we poor mortals speak to the Great Almighty. "And not a word to a soul," she whispered, "or the Prince of Darkness, he who dislikes children, will strike you dead."

She was right, for the sod was after me now, breathing fire and brimstone in my wake as, the letter delivered, I raced through the trees back to Cae White and the solace of my bed.

There was only one moment, a solitary occasion, when I was tempted to pour out this terror to another human being: the night my father heard me return from the forest. Racing up the stairs he followed me to my room, threw back the bedclothes, and held me.

"Tom!"

And I flooded the pair of us with tears and incoherent exclamations.

"But you're soaked and covered with mud – where have you been?"

His panic was as real as my agony. But I shook my head and buried my face in his shoulder.

"Now come on – tell me!"

I wailed and struggled in his arms.

"You have been out of the house. Tell me, Tom, where to?"

Beyond him, wrapping her dressing-gown about her, my mother stood in the lamplight, a wraith of darkness. Hearing her, Dada looked over his shoulder.

"This child is ill. I'm taking him to the doctor."

"The child is perfectly well. Did you not have nightmares when you were a boy?"

Next morning, with the starched white of the breakfast cloth between us (Old Bid washed very white), I met my father's eyes.

"It's a new day, Tom," said he, "and everything is beautiful. Later, we will go down to Squire's Reach and fetch out a salmon."

"Please, Dada, not Squire's Reach!"

"But why not? It's the most beautiful place in Tarn, and the salmon are so thick they're rubbing their fins off!"

With speech impossible, I lowered my head.

"Tom . . ."

I raised my eyes to my mother's voice and her smile was beautiful, her teeth white between the curved scarlet of her painted lips. "Now come, darling, do not be silly! Tell your father that you would love to go."

I turned to him. "Yes, Dada," I said.

"Of course you will!" He answered with what I thought later was forced jocularity. "Face your fears, Tom – never turn your back. Is it the Squire Wood forest that's bothering you? You were in there last night, were you not?"

The Prince of Darkness. "Oh, *God*!" I thought.

"Of course he wasn't!" said my mother. "It's a nightmare. You'll grow out of them, won't you, darling?"

"You were not in the forest?"

"No, Dada."

It was the first time I had lied to him.

By the look upon his face then, it would be the last.

Yet, within the terror of it there always arose within me pride in this new responsibility; not to everybody is given the chance to be in service to God.

These frightening journeys to Squire's Reach came on

occasions when my father was due to go to London on business, and suchlike. More, they were usually followed by increased social activity in the house, such as visits from officers of the King's Own Grenadiers and, on one occasion, a captain in the Shropshire Light Infantry.

These, highly decorated heroes, usually home on leave or before embarkation to go to fight the Riffs, arrived to receive a blessing on their activities, or, if real luck accompanied them, a soldier's farewell; a department in which my mother was proficient, a fact I soon discovered, most of such patriots being more accomplished in the bed than on the battlefield.

All this culminated in witnessing my mother's adultery with Jason Llewellyn at the seasoned age of eleven; and although leaving Cae White would mean losing my new friend, Jen Wildflower, it also meant that my mother would lose a legion of lovers . . . of whom Dada appeared completely unaware.

I could not have been more mistaken.

Now came the morning when we left Carmarthenshire.

What is there about leaving a house, I wonder, that brings such chaos to the heart?

First I put Tuk on the lead and went down to the caravan in the Big Field, bowing to Mrs Wildflower. I stood decently by for her while she said I was a nice young gentleman; this while pushing me in here and pulling me out there and smarming up my quiff with spit-fingers as usual, and behind her I saw shining cups and saucers – real china, said Jen – and a painting of Queen Victoria; also china dogs on the mantle above the van's big red wheels. Romany, perhaps, but as clean as a new pin, and the harness of the little grey pony was burnished bright.

Now, in the shelter of a big oak beside the river, we stood, Jen and I, and I don't know who was the shyest of the pair of us. The wind wafted the water into deep grey ripples and there was a shine of blackbirds in the branches above us: from

distant pastures came the sounds of sheep and from Top Hill
Acres the smell of udders scented the wind.

Behind us the Cae White animals clustered about a
five-barred gate, waiting for the drovers to drive them to
Carmarthen market for slaughter, and spittle from their
expectant mouths crisscrossed the ferns of the roadside.

"I do fancy they know," said Jen. "I tell you what – be
there buggy-bo's or marsh goblins around, they knows about
them, too, and they dursen't cross the bogs to Black Boar
tavern if there be drunkards around, nor corpse candles."

"Corpse candles?"

"Ay ay, they be buggers. My grandfer, when he was alive,
told that the sight of a corpse candle under a harvest moon
was a sign of a comin' death. And he knew all about
animals, too."

So I said: "Tell me about your grandfer, and corpse candles
and his animals, Jen Wildflower."

And she frizzed up her hair in thought and made a face at
the sun, adding, "My grandfer was a queer old chap, mind,
but he knew all about them cows and what goes on in their
hearts," and she squatted on the grass with me beside her
and I listened to her quaint music, which is the sing-song of
the true Welsh Romany, and she said:

"Like they knows when they're be goin' to die – nor we
don't know, Tom, neither today nor tomorrer, but them old
cows, they do. And my grandfer said as how, when he was
too old for farming, he had to drive his herd to Carmarthen
market for the slaughtering, and outside the slaughterhouse
the killing men put up squares of canvas on poles, so the
cattle couldn't see what was happening to those going in the
front, like . . .

"And he stood, my old grandfer, with the tears rolling
down his cheeks while his Daisy and Gert and Mary and
Hannah were driven up to the chief slaughterman, but one
old cow there called Tizzy, she stopped short when she got
near the knife, and turned to my grandfer standin' there
cryin'. And d'ye know what happened then?"

"Tell me," I said like a man.

"Well, this ole Tizzy, she stood her ground and every time

one o' the killers came close to her she downs with her head and gives him a butt, sending him arse over tit, till they all comes sick of it, and came at her with clubs to beat her back for the knife; but no! That Tizzy turns her back on them all and crosses the road and pulled down the canvas sheet until she got to my grandfer, and there was he sobbin' his heart out: and she stops before him and looks into his face, so that the slaughtermen look, too, wondering what was going to happen . . ."

"Go on."

"Well, this ole cow, she moos once just like saying goodbye, then slobbered all over my grandfer's face in kisses, then turned and went back to the slaughtermen and stood before them, waiting for the knife.

"Animals know about death, an' tell it all the time. You want to know about corpse candles, they speak of death an' all."

"Who lights corpse candles?" I asked.

Jen shrugged and I saw that her sack dress was torn at the throat.

"God, I reckon. Ain't you seen them burning on witchery nights? It's the peat gas, mainly," she said. "The peat farts off and God lights it by the stars, and it do go runnin' like zig-zag, dear me. Frit I be of them corpse candles."

"I love you, Jen Wildflower," I said.

It was out. All that day I had been saving it up. Sweat grew on my forehead.

Standing sideways in my boots now, I examined her for the effect, but all she did first off was to bow her head! Then she raised her face to mine and her eyes, brown orbs in her high-boned face, grew bright.

"Reckon I loves you, too, Tom Mortymer," and she forraged in her dress pocket and brought out a cherry stone. "Reckon I've loved you since the day we met; see, here's me first cherry stone."

I took it and held it in my fingers; a hole had been drilled in it. She explained.

"Mind, it don't work proper in the wane of the moon, and only two stones I've got to date, but when I've done them

55

I'll have ten, one holed for each year of me age. Then after you're gone and left me, I'll thread them on string and sleep with them tied round me knee for a fortnight, to bring you back to me."

"It don't need cherry stones to bring me back."

"And after you're gone to some foreign place, I'll smooth you over with a magic nutmeg to mak us fall in love."

"*Jawch*, how about now, then?" I said, going Welsh, and I ran in a little circle about her with Tuk after me squealing, delighted, and catching her by the waist swung her down beneath the tree and the fox leaped upon us both, trying to lick our faces, while I did my best to kiss her.

Mind you, it isn't much fun to kiss a gipsy girl aged ten, for mostly they've got wrinkled crab-apple knees and carroty hair, unlike the black-blue sheen of my mother's; and tufted, too, like a hedgehog, while Mam's hair, her crowning glory, is down to her waist. Nor is Jen's mouth like my mother's, full and red like a summer rose, but winter-cracked and colourless; and while my mam's teeth are like pearls, the teeth of one aged ten came sideways, and gapped, like a suckling baby's. All in all, looking at Jen Wildflower, I do wonder why I got the nibbles, for you could pick her up at the Whitland Hirings for five pounds a year of any farmer's money.

Later in life I noticed other things of course – things that add up to her being a woman instead of a girl.

The hair, usually straight, became waves of black; the cracked lips became rose-buds, mostly parted in expectation; the broken teeth are straight, and the smell of her, once cough-drops, changed to the perfume of the woman, which is a smell of summer, as if she has gathered the flowers of the honeysuckle and put them between her breasts.

Like this my mother smells, and I think it is terrible that she smells like this for others, and does not save such perfume for the likes of Dada.

"What you thinkin' of, Tom Mortymer?"

"Don't matter. Jen Wildflower."

56

"Would you like to kiss me proper before you go?"

"I anna that all particular," I answered, using her language.

"Please yourself, mind, but you won't get no nutmeg."

I was wishing her to the devil because while she was bothering me about cherry stones and nutmeg there had started within me a strange and marvellous feeling in my loins: an ache that snatched me up and made her a part of my being; very strange.

This I told her.

"I know," said Jen. "Same thing's happenin' to me."

I looked at her then and knew a wish to lie close to her and, were she willing, to touch secret places.

"What's wrong with us?"

"Could be the nutmeg. What time is it?"

Later, I walked hand in hand with her back to the caravan and old Joe Stork was standing on one leg in the river shallows and corncrakes were crying above the estuary.

"Can I kiss you goodbye now?" I asked her.

Her mam was within the van, sewing something pink by the light of the lamp, and her features were like those of her forebears, the sorcerers who inhabited the earth before the Flood.

"If you like," said Jen, so I did so, but her lips were not like the softness of my mother's, nor was her perfume one that I remembered, but the dinner smell of her stained pinafore.

"Goodbye," I said.

"Goodbye, and Romany luck," said she, and this time did not cry.

Ah well, I thought, there's a lot more fish in the sea.

Chapter 8

Although the beds were packed, the big brown furniture loaded and Old Bid's kitchen utensils stowed aboard the second cart, and all was ready for the off to Somewhere, we didn't go for a week.

We didn't move off until the buyers of Cae White arrived, and this they did in style.

Here's a dandy – Lord Lieutenant of the County by all reports – an ex-Eton fop of a man if ever there was one.

My father greeted their coach with his usual candid demeanour: prince or wayside labourer, all were treated the same.

I was landed with the son of the family, a high-collared snob of the usual variety, home from half-term with Christmas coming up. And we stood together in the Cae White shippon, this fancy boyo and me, stamping and blowing on frozen fingers in a late November frost with all the paraphernalia of the move around us.

But, had I known the fate that soon would be his, I would have treated him decently. Later, in manhood, I registered the son of Sir William ap Tristan-Evans among many of my life's regrets.

After introducing himself, he said, "They tell me you're the son of the house, Old Fish, that right?"

I took his limp hand with resignation and the knowledge that soon he would be past tense, anyway. Perhaps, I thought, this was how they always began conversations at Eton.

"Any good hunting down this way?" he asked next.

He possessed the profile of the inter-bred aristocrat; a chinless wonder in a morning coat and striped velvet trews, and his high celluloid collar under his chops was there, I learned later, to keep him in an autocratic posture: rather like the serfs in olden times who kept their hair bobbed by order of their masters, to keep their eyes downcast when their betters rode by. There are some who accept idiosyncrasies in humans, but I am not one of them: this new arrival I disliked on sight.

"They tell me that you are a prince, or something," said he.

"They say so, but I am not."

"And that soon you will be travelling to the East."

"If my father says so, not before."

"Any pretty tarts round here?" His pale blue, aesthetic eyes wandered about him, to settle on Dozie Annie who, with her mop cap crammed down over her ears, was taking her seat beside Dai Dando.

I replied, "There's Billa Jam Tart recently arrived from Merthyr Tydfil, living over at Tarn, they tell me."

"What-O! Jolly good!"

"Got ten kids, and she's knocking fifty."

The mundane talk went on; if this was a sample of what they turned out at Eton, I thought, thank God my father kept me away from public school.

Dada and Sir William were talking earnestly together, rustling official papers; a breeze was getting up over the bogs where a Mortymer grandfer, three sheets in the wind, had stumbled in and died years ago, his body never recovered; this I put over dramatically.

"They say his ghost haunts Cae White," I added.

"Oh, golly, you don't say!"

"And there's a gipsy girl living in a caravan over by the river. Keep clear of her or you'll get the Evil Eye."

"Dear me," said he. "Pater never mentioned any of this."

"You're welcome to the place, rather you than me."

He was a fool, but that was all: he didn't deserve my coarse behaviour, and years later I was still sorry.

Such was the terrifying end he suffered.

*   *   *

What is there about a house that leaves such a stain upon its owner's soul?

Here the stone floor of Old Bid's kitchen and the rush mat she used to stand on at the oven; there the rows of hooks where hung her hundred and one pots and pans; Dai's old rocking chair we left behind, to creak away the years under another such retainer; there is the peg upon which Dozie hung her mops.

The tears glistened in my eyes as I looked around the bare kitchen, and fell upon my cheeks as I remembered those of whom my father had spoken, and had once lived within these walls: the beautiful and fiery Morfydd, his eldest sister, being one; she who had laboured down the now derelict Gower Pit and died in a roof fall: of others, too, I'd heard of from old Betsy Ramrod of the Black Boar tavern – she spoke of my grandmother on my father's side – a comely woman of cherubic face and manner, who, widowed when her man was killed in a town called Blaenafon, came to Cae White with her brood and wedded an Eastern Valley preacher.

As for my uncle Jethro, he who was wanted for murdering an English dragoon, Betsy knew him well, apparently, and he was a maverick; with a fist on him for flattening a mule, and a *romeoantic* if ever there was one: and handsome! Dear God, said Dada, he set 'em swooning.

It is my opinion that a house, especially when lonely and deserted, does not part with its memories and ghosts easily.

I have been told, and believe it, that the toys of one's childhood come out to play together at midnight while one sleeps: that the wraiths of beloved people, their bodies buried and gone, move hand in hand together among the silent furniture; and walk in lonely places like Sin-Eater's Wood.

Indeed, I heard that the ghost of Cassie Scarlet, after whom the wood was named, had often been seen with a baby at her breast when funerals were around, waiting for her shilling for eating the sins of the dear departed, and the baby's name was Tramping Boy Joey later in life . . . he who fell into a limekiln, and died.

*   *   *

Now, with the Eton lad wandering after me, I walked the rooms of Cae White for the last time, and turned in the winter sunlight when we ended back in the shippon, knowing that tears of that parting were hot on my face; seeing them he could have chanted some jubilant nonsense, but did not, and I liked him better.

"Hard cheese, old man," he said.

Where is he now? Algernon, the son of Sir William ap Tristan-Evans? I wonder . . . he who was destined never to return to Eton . . . Under what dark sky does he wander in the dusk, seeking the manhood to which he never aspired?

I say it again; bitterly do I regret my behaviour.

"Come on, come on, young Maister!" bawled Dai above the wind. "Shake a leg, we're off."

The boy from Eton bowed to me as I left.

"When Adam delved and Eve spanned, who then was the gentleman?"

They had the makings of one at Eton School, at least.

Book Two

Chapter 9

I see that I wrote in my diary (after various addresses to put the Afghans off the scent):

December 1st, 1868. Cefn-Ydfa House, Maesteg, Nr. Bridgend, South Wales.
My father, mother and I arrived at this strange address with Dai Dando, Old Bid and Dozie Annie, and with Tuk (my mother holding her nose) curled up on my knees. Behind us, loaded on to two big carts came the furniture, not nearly enough for this large mansion.

My mother was in what Dada called a "tiz" during our last house removal was either crying or bursting into fits of temper, saying that had she been in Afghanistan she would have been travelling by elephant in a regal caravan with *pukkah wallas* fanning her instead of shivering in the bitter cold of this filthy country. My father maintained his usual cool serenity, treating her tantrums with smiling disregard.

"This," said Dada, alighting from the coach, "is one of the most sought after mansions in the county."

"Which presumably is why it is empty," said Mother.

"It is empty because it is being let to us."

Inside its vast room everything was bare, the previous tenants having shifted anything movable, and it was as cold as a Spanish prison.

Later, I learned that my father had secretly made contact with a Maesteg solicitor with a view to obtaining rented accommodation in the town, and had received the following cutting from *The Cambrian* newspaper:

"Glamorganshire. Cefn-Ydfa House, near Bridgend, to be let with immediate possession, for a term of years if desired.

This genteel residence, set in eight acres of arable land: rates and taxes being moderate, the house is ideal for a family of distinction, having ample accommodation. The South Wales Railway is but five miles distant, as is the market town of Bridgend; outbuildings include Stables, a Coach House, Pleasure Grounds and all the usual offices, and a further 200 acres are available, well stocked with game for the pleasure of sporting gentlemen.

Mrs Catherine Maddocks, living in the adjacent Farm-house, which is included in the rental, would be pleased to show prospective tenants around."

What my father later discovered was that the mansion he rented had once been the home of Anthony Maddocks, a local solicitor now deceased, who had married Ann Thomas (known later as the Maid of Cefn-Ydfa) against her will in order to possess her substantial family fortune; further, that the reason why the old mansion had remained empty for years, was because legend had it that its rooms were haunted by the unquiet spirit of an exploited girl, whose soul could not rest.

"Wonderful," said my mother on hearing this. "Now we're landed with an official ghost, that's all we want."

As usual, she was overstating the situation, said my father.

For once, it appeared that she wasn't.

This, the Llynfi Valley, delighted me, for it was shot with history.

Here, in the broad valley which ran from Caerau to Bridgend, a pulsating industrial life existed, one removed from the quiet pastures of Cae White; if a toe was stubbed on a farm gate there, it was known all over the county.

But here, where once the Roman legions had cast their sandals, the past, like the present, was vividly alive, the landscape being riven with ancient fortifications. Active and

66

progressive communities existed here before the coming of Christ.

After Tuk and I had explored the rooms of the house we set out together to discover the camps of the Roman legions: together we climbed the ridges of Bryncyneiron and Garnwen mountains, and identified the earthworks of the ancient Britons, flung up to halt the invading Romans.

How many, I wondered, had died in those lonely places; they whose courage has resisted the passage of Time and whose dirt monuments remind us of their sacrifice?

Where, I wondered, was the body of Bodvoc, said to be the last British chief killed in battle against the Norse sea-rovers . . . He, a martyr of the sixth century, whose valour is still remembered!

I knelt, with Tuk snapping at my fingers, in that isolated place on Margam Mountain and saw Bodvoc in the eye of my mind, skin-clad, bearded and ferocious, defiant to calls for surrender, and put my arms about his humble monument in stone.

Here also tramped the Norman hordes and the Celtic tribes who opposed them. Robert Fitzhamon was here in the eleventh century: the very air about me echoed to his exultant shouts of conquest and the groans of the vanquished; the very petals of the dandelions, my favourite flower, appeared splashed with blood; but the land had also been savaged by more civilised speculators.

Did not the Squire of Margam, in later years, obtain through his ancestors (after the dissolution of the monasteries) loot sufficient to bequeath an estate valued at six million pounds!

Imagine how much that is today!

Better by far, I think, to learn of the tribal wars of the past, when people fought for freedom and honour, for the true cannibals of history are not so much the conquerors of the past, but its speculators of the present.

Later still I discovered that the history of the house that changed my life was a perfect example of greed personified.

*   *   *

The name of this house, Cefn-Ydfa, paid tribute to its ability to grow corn over its acres, though when we arrived everything was snow-white, being in the grip of winter.

At this time, for me, the name meant something else; a local farmer having named the area *The Ridge of Wailing*, and this I can believe; it being said that a great battle had once been fought here.

At night, in my small room at the top of its winding staircase, I would lie and listen to the wind, and no wind wailed like the wind of Cefn-Ydfa, being at its best on wolf-howling nights like babies under torture.

Even Tuk, in his flannel bed beside mine, would raise his mask at me when this wind got up its tonicsolfa, till I put out a hand to soothe him.

Dai Dando and Dozie had discovered in an outhouse painted portraits of Cefn-Ydfa's ancestors, and these they had hung on the walls of the vast oak staircase, each board creaking like the lid of a vampire's coffin as I went up. And I used to mount the stairs in heart-stopping trepidation with a lighted candle on my way to my bedroom; and pause to examine the haughty faces of men long dead; the plump, corseted females in their stuffed-up bodices, and the angelic expressions of their well-fed children.

This air of deadness, a past stupefied by the ancient and decaying, was possessed of its own symbolic perfume: that to be found in the air of a family tomb.

The eyes that so meticulously followed my upward progress were those of long-gone but strangely motivated corpses . . . dusty relics of a dead once very much alive.

Industry came to the pastoral Lynfi Valley in the 1820s, the beginning of its Industrial Revolution which had begun earlier in other Welsh areas.

The early Spelter Works being followed by "Yr Hen Waith" (The Old Works): known afterwards as Maesteg Iron Works, which began in 1826, but these were not the first.

Old place names tell us that Margam monks mined coal four hundred years earlier, and that a smelting furnace was discovered east of the River Lynfi at Cwmdu, while parish records confirmed that in 1682 Henry John was killed by "a fall of coal".

Coal seams and ore levels abounded in the valley, limestone and timber providing rich returns for the ambitious speculator, and soon ranks of houses began to spring up to house workers who, following the magnet of employment, flooded in from every corner of the compass.

Mass limestone deposits, however, necessary for iron-making, were a rare commodity in the valley and had to be brought in from other areas. It was in transportation that my father found his first employment, by buying a small directorship in the failing Maesteg Transportation Company, a position he soon abandoned in favour of a seat on the Board of the Garth Iron Works, which had opened in 1847.

Dada said, "We are going into iron, Tom, back to my old trade. And you, in the course of time, will follow me into it."

"Not before he goes to boarding school," interjected Mother.

"Any school he goes to will be in this town," came the reply.

"And what quality of education do you expect to find here?"

"There's plenty of retired intellectuals around the place: I am not letting him out of my sight," said Dada.

This was in the following March, with spring stealing over the land.

Within weeks the hedgerows were in bloom and the blackthorn a shower of white blossom. Down the middle of the valley, from Nantyffyllon to Coetrehen via Maesteg, the river had sparkled in earlier times, but became dull-water as it collected the refuse of the industry from the twenty blast furnaces which had sprung up along its banks since 1826.

New tramways thundered along with wealth bound for the ports of the world: goods for Turkey via Bridgend, sheet iron for Norway, coke for the furnaces of the north, smelter goods up to Sheffield; and coal poured out of the Llynfi pits for the fires of Britain.

Along Bowrington Street to Cefn-Ydfa Lodge went the horse and mule trains; from Smokey Cot Weighbridge, Pyle and Nottage puffed the wealth of Wales to empty into the maws of Porthcawl Docks: never had there been such a bonanza on the graph of progress.

That was one side of the coin; the other side was that which belonged to the labouring poor.

Here terraced houses had been flung up haphazardly by industrialists in search of quick profit; and the incoming migrants, attracted from their impoverished smallholdings and farms by full employment, flooded into the valley from all the corners of Wales.

They came in tattered clothes, holding together the last vestige of their dignity before the onslaught of actual hunger.

They came in families from north of the Conway River and in scarecrow groups of women and children, organised from departure to arrival by the rising Benefit Clubs and the outlawed Unions. From overseas, as usual, came starving Irish in their droves, with Paddy this and Bridget that on our street corners begging for a decent living wage.

Some came, as did the Abergavenny community, which had links with the Gwent Top Towns and sick to death of names like Crawshay Bailey, the Pig of Nantyglo. With drums and fifes, marching to merry tunes and with banners these arrived, shouting the defiant songs of Ernest Jones, their Chartist poet. With sticks and cudgels they threatened local employers with the old Merthyr yell of, "Bread or Blood, *Bread or Blood*!"

"This is going to be worse than the Afghanistan slaughters," said Mother.

"It is the signal of a nation again in revolt," answered my father. "Can you blame them? They have starved under the landed aristocracy, now they starve under Parliamentary democracy."

70

See us now, the three of us, sitting at table; and what a table! It was the one piece of furniture the outgoing tenants couldn't get through the door.

At one end of it sat my mother in queen-like dignity, dressed in the yellow and green silken colours of the House of Barakzai; at the other end sat Dada, his evening coat bulging to the breadth of his shoulders; the white cravat he wore at his throat enhancing his quiet demeanour. Dark-handsome in his youth, his bronzed features vied with my mother's arresting beauty.

I sat between them with my chops just above the tablecloth, which was snow-white and of Afghan silk, for I could never boast of my size; though now aged fifteen, I was still a herring in boots.

In a dim recess of this baronial room Dozie Annie stood waiting at table, with her black homespun dress down to the floor and her lace cap on sideways; aware always that if she came within reach of me I would pinch her under the bustle; she usually emitting a soprano exclamation before I'd even touched her . . . which lifted my mother's eyes in unspoken inquiry.

This ritual I had to perform with care, for another, a most observant servant had now arrived at Cefn-Ydfa; an English butler brought from London by Mother; as handsome as Lothario, he rejoiced in the name of William Bumstead.

Stiff-starched and pompous, this one, he paid obsequious attention to all my mother demanded. Bowing regally to my every mood, he treated me with the patronising politeness due more to a Prince of the Realm than an adolescent, spotty Welsh boy whose ambition it was to get a leg over Dozie Annie.

Bastard, as I named him, was possessed of the Evil Eye; an eye, I soon discovered, that was aimed at my mother.

Therefore, with the prospect of another suitor, this time in the house, and further attacks upon my father's dignity, I invented suitable deaths for Bastard, while the ghost-ridden mansion creaked its agreement: such as lacing his cocoa with spirits of salt and suspending him by his goolies from a meat hook in the basement.

"I have been thinking, Tom," announced Dada complacently, "that in gratitude for our safe delivery from Dost Mahommed, we ought to attend Chapel next Sunday."

"I trust I am not included in the invitation," interjected Mama.

"Of course not, but it would be a preamble to getting to know members of the Maesteg community, and take advice on obtaining a private tutor again."

"For me?" I thumbed my chest, appalled.

"Who else? Apart from intermittent education by your mother and the private tutor you had at Cae White – your short period at the Dame School can be forgotten – your learning has been completely neglected."

"Dada, you said you'd take me into a firm."

"At fifteen?" asked Mother, and narrowed her eyes over her wine glass. "I've said it before – Eton or Harrow is the place for him."

"We've been through all that," came Dada's reply.

I thought, Oh God, not Harrow or Eton! And Dada, as if reading my thoughts, announced with finality, "Durrani, understand something. Even if there were no political threats coming out of your country, I would not send a son of mine to a public school in today's moral climate."

"What do you mean by that?"

My father did not answer

My mother smiled beautifully, "Enlighten me!"

"You know exactly what I mean."

There was a silence; distantly came the thunder of new railway and the clatter of the horse-drawn tramways.

"I do not, Iestyn; when it comes to the vices of this world I am singularly uninformed. Or could it be that such information enlightens the lower classes, who are so proficient at it! Now come, do not begin a delicate subject and then dry up emotionally," and she smiled at Bastard.

As for me, I didn't know what anyone was getting at, and sat there dumbly, watching my father's face. But of one thing I was certain: if the moral degeneracy was better than anything Dozie Annie had to offer, I was prepared to give it consideration.

Dada said, his serviette to his lips, "I apologise for raising a subject I am not prepared to discuss further, Durrani," which put the bottle on my revived ambitions, for if Eton, Harrow or any other boarding school had anything better than Maesteg I wanted to know about it.

A week later, however, an end was put to any suggestion that I could safely leave the environment of Cefn-Ydfa; news that was horrible, to say the least.

Having known the son of Sir William ap Tristan-Evans for little over an hour, I wrote in my diary:

May 3rd, 1870. Cefn-Ydfa House, Maesteg, Nr. Bridgend, South Wales.

Today, in a newspaper, was a terrible report. It read:

"James, the only son of Sir William ap Tristan-Evans, of Cae White House, Carmarthenshire, was yesterday found shot dead by members of the Trimsaren Hunt in the vicinity of a place known as Sin-Eater's Wood, not far from his home. The Coroner's verdict has not yet been announced, but the police from London state that, to date, foul play is not suspected; the unfortunate young man, heir to the family fortune, was found with a shot-gun in his hand. It is said that the family, distressed beyond measure, are nonplussed at the apparent suicide of their relative, a particularly happy youth who was down on half-term from Eton."

Chapter 10

Often I wondered how the economics of Cefn-Ydfa were run on such generous terms: my father lived the life of a retired country gentleman, while my mother, with monthly unescorted visits to Swansea or London, was a fashion plate when it came to her wardrobe; some of her adornment, the latest silks and laces brought from Paris, must have cost a king's ransom.

More, the old mansion, regardless of cost, had been rehabilitated to suit my mother's every whim, mostly of an oriental flavour: hanging silks and tapestries decorated the once cold walls; full-sized figures of Grecian history stood on guard against entry by the under-privileged; tortoise-shell and ivory made opulent the heady sense of riches beyond measure.

In the middle of the wide hall there stood, as if in greeting to aristocrats of education, the refined figure of Sappho resplendent in pink Italian marble.

"She," explained my father, "is here through the insistence of your mother, who sees in her the epitome of her own Afghan birth and intelligence," and I thought I discerned a small cynicism in his tone. He continued, "Plato himself called this marvellous woman, who lived six hundred years before Christ, the 'Tenth Muse,' such was the beauty and intellectual quality of her poems, none of which I have read, for little of her works survives. Are you interested?"

"Tell me more."

"Sappho lived on the island of Lesbos and led a circle of women intellectuals who put the fear of God into the men: she was married, but to whom we do not know; we know only that she had a daughter whose name was

Cleis, almost an image of Sappho herself; both were of great humility."

"How do you know so much of her?" I asked, and he shrugged.

"Like Hywel, your grandfather, I yearned for knowledge, but lost it in the heat of iron-making. But at odd times I would seek the company of rough intellectuals, those who raved at their congregations and led the great Revivals, seeking God. These, though many decry them, Tom, were brilliant in philosophy."

"Where does Mama come into this?"

He smiled. "Where do I, you may ask? Not all can have the wisdom of Solomon or the intellect of Socrates, so allow your mother this small privilege. Women of gentle ancestry have long yearned for a mind like Sappho's, but this is given to only a few: in its stead he granted them the gift of intuition; your mother has many attributes and I want you to respect them."

It was astonishing to me that one of such manhood and independence could allow himself excuses for my mother's behaviour: women of no education gave their drunken husbands more consideration than she.

After this conversation, we left the statue of Sappho, and I followed Dada into his study.

"I am getting into trade," said he, "and because I cannot let you out of my sight now – the death of the Cae White lad confirms the danger – I am taking you with me. You have probably wondered at my ability to keep your mother in the manner she expects," he went on, and he sat down at his big green baize desk and waved me into a chair beside him.

"The Dost made me rich as his Armaments Engineer in Kabul. I was handed an honorarium of 1¼ thousand *lakh* of rupees, which then was about ten thousand pounds. This I invested and we live on the interest; it keeps your mother in luxury." Saying this, he went to the little wall safe behind scarlet curtains and opened its door. Taking out a tiny leather bag he opened its mouth and spilled its contents on to the desk before me.

Diamonds: fifteen, twenty . . . sparkling and flashing in the lamplight. Picking one up he held it before me, saying, "Between five and ten thousand pounds apiece – the quality, the diamond merchants tell me, is astonishing.

"Money to the Dost means nothing," he went on. "In the full regalia of the Afghan Court, bedecked with these from head to foot on ceremonial days, he cannot raise himself from his throne without assistance. So he gave me a handful of them to see me into better days – on one condition – that I left Afghanistan and never saw your mother again." He sighed. "He did not know, of course, that she was with child by me; even then carrying you in her womb, or I would not have left his Court alive. But Karendeesh, as you know, interceded for her and brought the pair of you to Cae White."

Later, Dada said, "And so, Tom, as I said, we are going into trade.

"Last month I bought a directorship in The Cambrian Iron Company, which since the Crimean War has carried out a policy of expansion, and now operates the biggest rail mill in Britain with four furnaces under blast, thirty puddling furnaces, and ten steam-powered rolling mills; in all employing about fifteen hundred workers.

"I have bought a quarter share of its capital and, with the permission of its Board, appointed myself its Assistant Superintending Engineer. Such, Tom, is the ability of three large diamonds! But where do you come into this?"

Rising, he wandered the study, pipe in hand.

"True, I wish you to be educated in the classics, and for this you will have a tutor, but I also want to apprentice you to a trade so that later you can take your place in a firm of your choosing.

"As a beginning, however, you will enter Cambrian Iron as an apprentice and work under the old gentlemen of the trades; they who can tell by the colour of the fire when to make good iron, in itself a miracle of ingenuity. How does that sound?"

"It is excellent, sir," I answered and, raising his deep-set eyes to mine in the lamplight, he put out a hand and gripped my shoulder, saying:

"You do not know it, but you are the image of my father, who gave his life to the making of iron," and he winked. "The iron will put the muscle on you, so that one day my son will become a titan of manhood, as was he: men moved out of his path, women looked over their shoulders. In his mould, Tom, you will live his life again, a noble legacy. To be a true Mortymer makes Afghan royalty into very small fry . . ."

Saying this, he wandered through the french doors of the study into the moonlit garden where white and blue clematis clustered around the mansion walls, and the air was heavy with the scent of the musk my mother had planted to remind her of home.

Beyond the garden and its rolled lawns under the moon, the lane that led through the woods to the lodge on the main road was stark white in the ethereal light; the lodge which the Welsh called Corn Hwch meaning "The Horn of the Sow"; which was quite ridiculous, said the people of the village, for a sow does not possess a horn.

It was in that ghostly light that I saw my father anew, reminding me, as it did, that even he could age; that the square set of his features could dissolve into the looser fatness of older age; one moment the sinews of youth, next the tell-tale years of travail. The Afghan war in all its horror had left its stamp.

Thus do I remember him, standing in the moonlight.

Coo-pidges were sobbing from the woods, sighing, I supposed, for the lost love of Ann and Wil Hopcyn, the ancients of Cefn-Ydfa.

Where are the souls of such lovers now?

Where, indeed, is my father's?

And who did Satan kiss first on the mouth?

Jen Wildflower, or me? But more of this later.

"Come, Tom, it's cold for July," said Dada, and I followed him back into the study.

77

Chapter 11

My proposed apprenticeship with The Cambrian Iron Company was short-lived because almost immediately after buying his position as Assistant Superintending Engineer, Dada quarrelled with its director on a point of policy, was outvoted, sold his stock at a profit and joined the Board of the Llynfi Coal and Iron Company Ltd.

With capital of a quarter of a million pounds, this was a better bet, anyway, said my father, for despite the intervening industrial depression after the Indian Mutiny, the Crimea debâcle and our other colonial wars, there were still four blast and fifty puddling furnaces in operation serving the military; but more importantly, the engineer Mr David Grey was presently the company's chief technical advisor and the two men took to each other like ducks to water.

Mr Grey, a decade or so earlier, had also supervised the sinking of Dyffryn Madog pit, the Gin Pits in 1858 and No. 9 Level five years later: I mention this because it was down one of the Gin Pits that I began my apprenticeship in coal.

More important was Mr Grey's intention to open a tinplate works, and this was Dada's true interest; the future, he asserted, lay in tin.

My father, through his technical experience with the Dost's allies, the Russians, possessed the secrets of what was then talked about in confidential whispers, a process in tin-making called "Rustless Russian".

Armed with this secret process, Grey and my father opened the great Llwydarth Tinplate Works near Cwmfelin, south of Maesteg, which was the beginning of a personal fortune in the Mortymer name that turned talk of the Dost's rewards into loose change.

But I am getting beyond myself in terms of personal history, so let me return to the day I began work at the Gin Pit in the autumn.

My father never did anything by halves: there was only one way to begin a career, he announced, and that was at the bottom, as I did.

"My first day at work," said he, "was at the age of eight, which was late to begin a career in my time, for some Blaenafon children had five years of ore chipping under their belts – male and female, mind – before the age of ten, so consider yourself lucky at the age of fifteen plus."

"I think it is absolutely disgusting!" said Mother. "A princess of the House of Barakzai, and my son is to work underground among members of the vulgar-tongued classes!"

"If he lived in your benighted country, he would be in the mills at the age of six," came his reply. And then followed such a palaver of weeping and wailing that it brought Old Bid up from the kitchen with Bastard, and there was a lot of patting and mopping up that put years on me; for if there is anything I despise it is this women business, with one telling the other what a sod this one is and that one is. I preferred my father, for he pointed at the door and looked like lifting a boot.

"Get going," he commanded, "or you'll never hear the end of it."

"It won't do ye no harm, Tommy me lad," said Dai. "Get down there an' give 'em hell: I shovelled black diamonds in my time, and it anna done me no harm, has it? Look at me!"

Aye, I thought, look at him: head bumps, put there by fists and coal; a face flattened in a fall underground, and the tell-tale tattoos, coal's signature, all over his stunted body.

"Jesus, Mary and Joseph," said Old Bid." A young toff like you working like a navvy – I don't know what the world is comin' to."

Neither did I, to tell the truth of it, for my idea, up until then, as the son of a prospective mining engineer, was to have an easier time than most.

With no illusions left, I collected my first tommy box, ignoring my mother's beseeching and Old Bid's tears, and, whistling to have my teeth out, left Tuk in Dai's care and set out for coal.

Knocking sixteen, with hands as soft as a woman's, I was about to become an apprentice collier.

I didn't know what was coming to me.

Chapter 12

Dai Dando, from the time I was able to take a boxing stance, had instructed me intimately in the secrets of the Noble Art, and by the look of the motley array of pugnacious comrades clustered around the cage entrance at the top of Gin Pits, I was going to need them.

Here indeed was a very fine selection of the rough variety, aged six to fifteen, male and female; and I don't think they possessed a working brain between them.

Dai this and Dai that, with Evans and Jones proliferating among them, and mostly emanating from the new houses recently built by Mr Grey – Olivia Terrace, Brick Row and Gwendoline Terrace.

"How are you?" This from an urchin with a nose for opening doors, and his name was Ieuan Pindle; shoving up my shoulder blades as the cage door slammed open, he gave me one in the ribs so I knew he was there. First he tried me in Welsh, but got no reply.

"New fella, eh?"

"Ay ay," I replied.

"You'll have your knees up yer arse 'afore you're finished, mind."

"You and who else, boyo?" For the great thing is to start the way you intend to go on, and I gave him an elbow in the stomach.

"He be a gippo lad, Pindle, leave him alone," said a girl.

Had she washed that morning she might have been pretty in her ragged sack dress with no arms in it, and her coal-grimed pinafore, but with her hair scragged back and her teeth missing in front she looked like a witch.

"What's ye name?" she asked.

"I be Tom," I answered, having stopped being a gentle-man.

"Ain't you got another name, then?" This from a ragged, unkempt boneyard of a lad, his hair wild around hungry eyes in his skeletal cheeks.

"My mam don't say."

Pushed from behind I reached the cage door as it clanged open like the toll of doom: a horse-gin winder, this one, with a rickety old mare going round in circles, winding a cable on to a drum: later, my father changed her for a steam-engine.

I pitied animals in this world; every time she stopped for a spell they gave her one on the shanks.

Heading the rush, I was spilled into the lifter and the cage door slammed behind us. Down, down now, in a flashing of lights, ten of us crammed together, the women gasping to the drop, and my boots hitting my stomach.

The historians say that there were no women getting coal down the Gins in the sixties; no bother, I was with them. They did light jobs. Patty Jones for one, the girl behind me, aged ten; Little Ellie Goff, the daughter of Wil, who lost a leg down a Midland pit and come down to Wales for clean air, the idiot; she was another. They said she was weak in the chest.

"That right you're a gippo?" asked the lad called Pindle.

"I ain't," I replied as the lifter reached the bottom. "But, what if I was?"

"If you was, then Big Dick will bloody 'ave you, for he don't like Romanys."

"Who's he when he's home?" I talked his language.

"You'll soon find out."

"Ach, he anna so bad when you get to know 'im," said the girl with no teeth in front, and she held out her tallow-saucer for the overman to light it, and her eyes were beautiful in the guttering light.

"Who are you?" demanded a voice; double bass, this one, and his great size, naked from the belt, dominated all about me.

I did not immediately reply.

"Tom Mortymer?" he asked.

This had to be the overman.

"Yes."

Gripping my shoulder he turned me to face his candle. "The son of the new boss topside?"

I nodded.

"Jesus Christ," said he, "don't we get 'em! While you're down 'ere you're like the rest of 'em, that's what ye pa says, understand?"

For answer I looked him over; another few years and six inches and I'd have this one, I thought; bloody cheek, nobody had asked him for anything.

"Ye'll work at the face wi' young Davie Grey, the boss's son, and he don't stand any nonsense."

Nor me, I thought, but didn't say so.

"Davie!" the overman hollered down the stalls into the blackness, and a voice answered faintly.

"Wait here," said Overman, and left me.

"We got another toff – look lively and see him off!" he bellowed.

Another made shape in the shivering candle-light.

"What you on, boyo?" A young face was thrust into mine.

"I'm with Davie Grey," I explained.

"That's me. Get moving." The voice was cultured.

Cultured? Down this bloody place?

Let me be clear on a point: from what my father has told me about working conditions in his time in Blaenafon, the ones I found in the Maesteg area in my time were of no comparison.

For a start, in Dada's town nobody seemed to give a fig for children who laboured in industry, under the ground or above it, under the age of ten. They died, as did their parents, drowned in cinder coolie-pits or balance ponds or were incinerated in the fires of furnaces or brick kilns: of cholera they died, said Dada, some with their heels clamped to their heads in their final withering, like dried sticks: many did not own a grave to record their passing.

The criminals of greed in those days were the Crawshays of Merthyr Tydfil, the Baileys of Nantyglo and a dozen or so similar grasping employers like them who had fashioned the Chartist Rebellion in the hearts of radicals like Mayor John Frost, the Newport draper, William Lovett and Henry Vincent, he who later took the Cloth.

With the attack upon Newport in November 1839 these forged a bond for those who came after them; and, what is more, tempered the attitudes of the new industrialists like David Grey who saw the dignity of man in his lowliest labourer.

People stand so much and no more; this they said in my time, but never in my father's: his life was a fire whose flame was quenched by sacrifice, and we were now reaping their reward.

"It isn't so bad down here after you get used to it," said the lad before me, and turned to face me, and his eyes were gentle in the candle's light. But he was tough too, and didn't stand nonsense: I wouldn't have tried him for size. He said, "So you're Tom Mortymer? I'm Davie Jones. Down among the dead men, people say!"

"We're not dead yet, Davie," said I, and took the shovel he tossed to me. "Is this our stall?"

"Work beside me," he instructed, "not behind me," and positioned himself. "Stick your pick in my bum and you'll regret it, as the old colliers say.

"I've been down this hole for as long as I can remember, for the companionship, mainly, though women don't understand about that. The pit ain't just friendship, it's comradeship. Listen, boyo . . ."

On that day, under Davie's guidance, I became an apprentice collier.

"This is the size of it," said he, and turned his coal-grimed face to mine. "You and I are serving articles, and we've got tough fathers: but mine never asked me to do a job he couldn't do himself, and his sons have got to come up the same way, he says."

"Mine, too. Tough as old boots."

Grasping the shackles of a tram, he swung it on its turn-table, saying, "The Big Dick back there's a pig's aunt but, gipsy or duke, he treats us all the same, and he's right. Put your back into it and he'll pass you by; treat it like a Sunday outing and you'll collect one in the arse."

This was the collier speaking: later I heard the gentleman.

"You heard I was coming down?" I asked.

"Day before yesterday. Now get your back into it," and he flung his weight against the tram, and with me pushing beside him, edged it slowly up the gradient, its iron-shod wheels crunching on the line.

"I saw women back there. Here, down a pit?"

He gasped, "Time was we had four-year-olds pushing the brattice cloth at the ventilators, but my father stopped that years ago; now we've got their big sisters, but soon they're going topside, too, then we'll get their brothers."

"No woman should work underground. Those days are gone."

"You'll be lucky!"

We were sweating now and gasping for breath as the gradient steepened towards the coal collection-point. As we approached the bottom of the pit shaft the guttering light of our candles slowly faltered into the new brightness of the sun reflected down from fifty feet above, and I saw the face of Davie more clearly.

"Stop for a breather," he said.

I had expected, by his dominance and the threats of Big Dick, that this would be a real toughie; instead, there was a poetic beauty about his features which the coal-dust could not hide; the aquiline profile of the true aristocrat; his eyes, large and brown, possessed an almost feminine beauty. Mind you, I have met such men before, my father once said: their good looks belie their manhood; they are throwbacks from the Renaissance, when men dressed like dandies, gave the appearance of fops, then fought to the death with rapiers: so do not judge too quickly the man of gentle countenance, he added, or you could collect a tartar.

"You mentioned your father," I asked. "Is he something to do with the people running this place?"

"Aye – Mr David Grey." He appeared to have said nothing unusual.

"But your name is Jones you said earlier."

"Adopted – officially, any day now – then I'll become David Grey." He laughed. "Complicated, eh?"

"Your real father's dead?"

"Yes. At ten I was working down Tondu Pit with my uncle; the roof came down and took Pa's legs to the thigh."

"I'm sorry."

"Got to take it as it comes; blood on coal." He grinned at me, his teeth suddenly appearing in his blackened face. "How about you?"

"Don't ask about me, mate, I've got a princess for a mother."

"I heard about that! Bad luck."

"What about yours?" I asked, and Davie replied:

"Never knew her, she died at my birth. But she was Squire's Reach gentry – one of the Llewellyns. She wasn't a princess, but folks reckon she was a lady, though I was out of wedlock. You'll hear so, anyway . . ."

"Ain't we got a lot in common!"

"A pair of unwanteds when you weigh us up."

"I'll settle for that, Davie," I answered. "But I tell ye what, son – the first bugger who calls me a bastard lands on his back!"

"And I'll settle for that," said Davie.

Now everything happened at once.

Four sub-humans, twice my size and as black as Barbary apes, sprang upon the tram we had brought and shoved it into the shaft: and no sooner had they done this than a scarecrow in rags flung himself on top of the coal, and kneeling on it pointed upward to the light, bawling:

"Up, men, up with it into the light of God, for the dew of Heaven is falling on the cornstalks of Llangynwyd! Leap for joy, people of the Llynfi Valley, leap for joy!" and with this he danced on top of the coal, his skinny arms and legs akimbo.

"Jesus," I gasped between his yells. "Who's he?"

"Ach, it's only Joe Piety the Revival fanatic," said an ape nearby.

Somebody beside me rang a bell and the cage began to lift, taking the tram and its occupant upward in the shaft, and as it slowly disappeared above us the fanatic's voice rang out:

"The time will come, mark me, when only the forgiven with wool on their shoulders will stand in the light of the Lord. The drinkers of Satan's nectar shall be one with the adulterers and fornicators roasting in the fires of Hell."

"Good God," I whispered to Davie, "a Revivalist?" For I'd begun to remember my phantom dreams of Dozie who, with her nightie up and calling Heavenward, had fled before my lecherous nightmares.

"Something left behind by Dafydd Morgan's Revival a couple of years ago," came the reply, "and now a fully fledged member of the Bridgend Asylum. He arrives down here on a Monday to perform his penance in what he calls Hell; and after absolution returns topside, which he calls Heaven, but he's got his locations confused; the real purity is down here among the comrades . . ."

I stared back at him in the flickering light.

"How old are you?" I asked.

"Knocking eighteen."

I have heard less sense from pulpits. Now Davie pushed past me.

"The day has only just begun, Tom," said he. "Best get started."

After ten hours of picking and shovelling at the Number Three face down Gin Pit, my fingers were blistered, my back nearly breaking and my spirits lower than I could remember.

"This is a place for men," I gasped, leaning on my pick.

Davie nodded, wiping away sweat with his rag.

Black as the ace of spades now, the pair of us, with only our eyes to show we were human.

"That's my old man's idea, he says – turn the boys into men the quickest way possible. But your pa must be even tougher than mine, for I've got years on you."

"They come tougher still from Blaenafon!"

Davie sat down in the darkness; all I could see of him was his teeth.

"You stop and think, Tom," he said, "we've got it easy. Not twenty years ago, down any one of the thirty or so pits and levels in this valley. Duffryn Madog, for instance – five hundred feet deep, or North Pit, deeper than a thousand, kids under ten years old, girls as well as lads, pulled trams and tubs like bloody animals." It was the first time he had sworn. "And they tell me that Coffins Colliery and Maesteg were the worst of the lot."

Clearing his throat he spat on the gob. "Millions of tons of coal they've raked out of this valley and hundreds of men and women have lost their lives under the paternalism of the masters!"

He waved an arm around him. "Take this damned place. They say there's no gas down here, but can't you smell it? One day the galleries will detonate and the whole rotten bundle of greed – us included – will go skywards. It's only a question of time.

"We're still working with candles, yet Davey Lamps have been on the market for years; it's a question of cost, they say. I tell you this, we're an accident waiting to happen, and when I've done this apprenticeship I'm going to let people know about it!"

"Your old man, you mean. Mine already knows it."

"My old man chiefly," he snapped. "I thank him for adopting me, but there's a lot still going on that he either doesn't know about, or doesn't want to hear."

I held my blistered hands up to the flame of the candle.

"I'm with you on that," I replied. "This is only my first day, but I'm giving my pa a piece of my mind when I get home tonight."

"Take it slowly, young 'un," he answered. "Folks who give others pieces of their mind are usually those who can least afford it. You only catch monkeys by taking things slow."

On looking back through my papers, I see that I wrote in my diary:

20th March, 1871. Cefn-Ydfa. Maesteg. Near Bridgend.
After many months down Gin and Duffryn pits with Davie, my apprenticeship to coal is now finished and we are now firm friends.

I am soon to join Mr Edwards, the Overman at the furnaces, taking the iron trades one by one, from barrow-steadier on top-loading to apprentice-puddler in the tapping areas. Davie has already done this and I am going to miss him, for he is going into the office for white-collar work.

But note this . . .

Our house, according to the locals, is haunted! And this I can well believe. Because, last night, on the stroke of midnight, which announced my seventeenth birthday, I heard sobbing coming from downstairs, and, thinking it was my mother, I lit my bedside candle and went down to investigate. Now, if I write here what then happened without checking it, anyone reading it will think I'm a screw loose, so I decided first to talk to Old Bid about it, for she's a great one when it comes to the supernatural: ghosties and hobgoblins are second nature to her.

I cornered Old Bid when on her way back from evening service at Llangynwyd after she had made her peace with the Vicar, the Reverend Pendril Llewelyn, who had begun the living there just after the Chartist Rebellion, said Dai, and looked like staying on for ever.

In fact, it was later rumoured that on his fiftieth year as vicar, the archbishop wrote gently to him with the suggestion that he should consider retirement, only to receive back a cursory note, "Had I known the living here to be a temporary appointment, my lord Bishop, I would never have accepted it in the first place."

Such was the delightful character of the man whose memory is respected in the parish today; so I knew Old Bid was in excellent hands and her soul in a raiment of glory.

Which was necessary, I thought, since recent strange noises in the old mansion may eventually have to be referred to this particular vicar, for exorcising.

"What sort of noises?" Old Bid demanded, after I'd got her in my bedroom. Voluminous in a white nightie was she.

"Sobbing and crying," I replied.

She pushed me sideways. "Ach, Maister, that's nothin'. 'Tis only the ring-doves; sometimes they comes courtin' up at Cefn-Ydfa!"

"No, no, there was more to it than doves or coo-pidges!"

"Jesus, Mary and Joseph!" She crossed herself.

I went on in a stumble of words, "And so, because it was keeping me awake, I went down to the drawing-room and listened there, and heard the noise coming from the cellar . . ."

"Ach, no!" said Biddy, her eyes like saucers.

Bound to the exaltation of the spirit was this one, with her mood varying from disbelief to horror with mercurial speed, and her eyes now threatened to drop out.

"From the cellar, did ye say? Strip the Devil naked! She's back!"

"Who is?"

"Have ye not heard of Ann Thomas, the Maid who wanders around pining for Wil Hopcyn, her chap?"

"Of course, but my father says it's rubbish."

"It ain't, for she comes and goes. What happened then?" She was flushed and urgent.

"I unlocked the cellar door, pushed it open and held the candle high. You know the bacon hook where we hang the hams? She was standing under it in the corner . . ."

"Jesus alive and reigning!"

"And when she saw the light of the candle, she turned to it. Dressed in white she was, with long hair down her back, and seeing me, she pulled her hair down over her face and burst into tears."

At which Old Bid got off the bed and, reaching up fat arms to the ceiling, cried:

"Heaven be praised, it's the sign! She's back, and the Revival is returning! Oh, David Morgan, leave the Big Seat and come among us, and the new Revival will hover over our valley like a crow in the vaults of Heaven. She's back, she's back!" And across the bedroom she went at speed, flung open the lattice window and shouted over the yard, "It's a sign! Kick out the wicked, every hoof and horn! The Lord will turn briars into vineyards and Satan will go to the wall!"

"Biddy, Biddy!" I shouted and got her just before she fainted clean off, slipping to the floor in a tangle of nightie and bosom, and I was kneeling above her slapping the backs of her hands when my father came through the door with a hammer in his hand.

"What's happening?" he demanded.

"Old Bid," said I. "She says the Revival's coming back. She was attacked that way once before, remember?" at which my mother came in with a glass of water and we propped Biddy up and massaged her back to her senses. Opening her eyes she stared momentarily, then, seeing us about her, flung out her arms and cried, "Now that the Maid has returned, so will the great Revival! A mighty Pentecostal wind is sweeping over the world!" and she went out again like a light.

"I've had enough of this," said Dada, as Dai Dando appeared at the door. "Get her downstairs, for God's sake." Which he did, in a fireman's lift over his shoulder.

"Mind you," said my mother as we dispersed, "this has been coming on for some time now. Haven't you heard someone sobbing and moaning in the night?"

"I thought it was you," I said.

Dada did not reply to this, save for the meaningful look he gave me.

Later, in the numbness between sleep and wakefulness, I opened my eyes to see him standing beside my bed.

"You awake, Tom?"

"Yes, sir." I sat up.

91

"A moment or two of your time while the ghosts are still activating," and he sat on the side of my bed. "Imagination can play strange tricks upon us, you realise? Tonight your mother talked of moaning and sobbing: you have heard it, too, and it may surprise you to learn that I have also."

"You?"

He nodded. "And have said nothing about it, and neither should you. Your mother is not of our beliefs, but possesses all the Afghan superstitions, and these are many: she has enough of her own banshees to satisfy a high priest without us adding our Celtic legends. And so, let it go. Tonight, I gather, you've had a signal experience – the effect such . . . such phantasmagoria has upon people. Let us keep it between us as far as we are able."

At the door, he said, "Local people say that this house is haunted. You are now old enough to make up your mind upon it – to believe it or not."

"But you do not believe it?"

He emptied his hands at me. "Oh, but I do, Tom – most certainly."

After he had gone I listened to the old place creaking, talking to itself as old houses do when they think people are asleep; and heard again, unmistakably, the sounds of sobbing coming from the cellar. But of one thing I was sure: the one who said he had actually seen her would finish up in Swansea lunatic asylum, and I didn't intend being caught on that one.

What with one thing and another, Dafydd Morgan, his '59 religious Revival and the Maid of Cefn-Ydfa, Maesteg had something to answer for in our valley.

But one fact is substantially true: from the moment I left Great House her wraith, to my knowledge, was never seen again.

Chapter 13

So far, said Dada, your life has been one of wine and roses; you wait until you hit the trade of tinplate, then you will know what real work is.

Meanwhile, my father was cutting out a responsible position for himself in the estimation of Mr David Grey, a man rapidly becoming one of the leading industrialists in the Llynfi Valley; and who, with names like Colonel North and John Brogden, was following the pioneering genius and traditions of Sir John Bowring.

Indeed, so famous was that name that late in the last century Maesteg was called Bowrington after its benefactor, who, with his brother, Charles, was largely responsible for raising the valley to its present state of industrial eminence.

Bowring, Bedford, Allen and Sir Robert Price – these, with other pioneers, were the magic names; about to be added to the list, of course, was Mortymer and Son, lately of the Eastern Valley, where the men were men, they said in Blaenafon, and the women were delighted.

There were exceptions in Maesteg though, and one was my mother.

With dreams of high office and a life of royal patronage in Afghanistan lessening with every passing month, it appeared that she forsook the nuptial bed for any passing stranger, and Old Bid's dandelion wine for vintage port.

Mid-morning might find her with her hair down over her scarlet dressing-gown, her speech slurred and three sheets in the wind; yet nothing of this indignity distracted the eye from her beauty, or delayed the advances of her countless suitors; these varied from adolescent lads of spotty faces who would droop along the lane in vain hopes of a sighting, to stalwart young majors in the Light Infantry, home on furlough from our colonial wars.

But more, there now existed within Cefn-Ydfa itself a more convenient competitor for my mother's romantic affections; one present on the hoof, so to speak, and this was Bum Bumstead, the bastard.

I determined to keep a wary eye upon him.

Amazingly, and this is often the case in such affairs, my father's trust in Mother's fidelity was absolute. I could name examples of his obvious stupidity, when he appeared ridiculously ignorant of the adultery under his nose.

The Jason Llewellyn business for one, of course, had given rise to violent action, when someone had filled up an aristocratic eye. But the man had to be vacant in the top storey, I thought, if he failed to detect the lecherous glances coming from the shadows when my mother was at her half-cut, jubilant best; usually when her friends were present, the company good and their empty chatter flowing.

Then it was that Bastard would emerge from his shell of professional remove to allow himself a fluttering glance in Mother's direction; or the touch of his knee against her thigh while presenting the wine; or a brush of his hand upon her arm in passing: the while dignifying the lechery with patronising conduct.

From my place at table I saw it all; and fearfully, because I knew my father. Once the betrayal broke upon his unsuspecting head, he would up and at them, getting them figuratively with the same fist.

The princess and the butler; it was worse than a pier-head card show.

I had read of a Chinese gentleman who possessed a young wife he adored; one who began with the local mandarin and finished up with rickshaw boys. It resulted in a death of a thousand cuts.

Empires, they say, have been won and lost within a woman's thighs; from where I stood at that time of betrayal, they didn't appear to me to be a highly prized possession.

*   *   *

Events came to a head on a day I had been dreading; one which heralded my father's departure from Cefn-Ydfa on a business trip for a week or so: it having been arranged, in view of their new business partnership, for he and Mr Grey to tour tinplate works in the Midlands.

Clearly, Bastard would seize this opportunity to come into his own, so to speak.

I determined to prevent it.

To date our paths had not fatally crossed; he treated me with the faint disapproval older men reserve for pernicious young ones; I treated him as if he did not exist, either in this world or out of it.

Dada's proposed absence coincided with a new phase in my apprenticeship training; entry into that holy of holies, the tinplate works, and since Davie had preceded me there, we were at last reunited.

"You all right?"

"Fine and dandy!"

He then tossed me a pair of leather gloves.

"Ternplate it's called. Best start at the beginning . . . ?"

More interesting, however, than the intricacies of tin and ternplate manufacture, were the celebrations attending my father's departure next morning into the realms of Mr Grey's Big Business. In my diary I recorded:

5th October, 1871. Cefn-Ydfa House, Near Maesteg, Bridgend.

My mother is throwing her heart into organising the party to celebrate my father's departure to the Midlands, she being particularly efficient at anything to do with pomp and circumstance.

A professional caterer was brought in from Bridgend to provide the food, and she had special wines sent from London for a banquet which Maesteg would talk about for a generation.

Bastard was in his element, of course, ordering the servants to stand in line, there to examine their fingernails;

lace aprons and caps were rushing here and there long
before any of the guests arrived, and even Dai put on
his Sunday best to receive the broughams and traps of
the incoming gentry.

My father appeared removed from all this, for I saw
him behind the window of his study, thoughtfully smoking
his pipe in contemplation: one never knew what he was
thinking; if he approved of all this palaver, or not.

The Deputy Lord Lieutenant of the County arrived in
splendid paraphernalia, accompanying Colonel North and
his wife and Mr and Mrs Brogden, and a host of special
people came by the invitation of Mr Grey, whose wife was
absent, being ill. The fine suits of the gentlemen, many in
military uniforms, contrived with the coloured dresses of
their womenfolk to make this an occasion fit for a new
captain of industry.

Memories flooded back to me afterwards as I read this year's
diary. Dada was sitting at the head of the great mahogany
table, of which the starched white cloth was a sight in itself
(for our new scrubbing maid, Molly Cule, aged ten, washed
very well).

Mother sat on my father's right and I was on his left, and
the amount of chatter between the off-the-shoulder ladies
and back-slapping, elegant gentlemen must have raised a few
eyebrows in the farmhouse rooms next door, where sat the
last of the Maddocks in moody discontent. Being agricultural
folk, I don't think they approved of the new get-rich-quick
modern people who had come to live as their neighbours.
Over all, with his finger on the pulse of everything going
on, Bastard, my pet aversion, moved with imperious grace.
"Born to serve, sir," he used to say to my father, "born to
serve, although by all accounts, sir, it is not in the Romany
blood."

A Romany? Bastard? I didn't know that before.

"Will you be away long, sir?" he asked my father, bowing.
Dada, distant, sipped his wine. "No more than a week."
"Excellent, if I may say; I hope you do good business."

"Thank you. Meanwhile I depend upon you to keep the place in good order until I return."

This amid a clatter of talk, tinkling glasses and masticating jaws. Personally, sitting in the background of my boyhood, I used to obtain pleasure in watching people at table, for in the business of filling up the belly they are at their most benevolent; and while Lady This and Lord That are powdered and genteel in the drawing-room (and behave fastidiously when chopping up the pheasant), they are very different characters, I find, when off their guard; the dimpling wife of a major competing with a six foot grenadier when it comes to a healthy belch.

I watched them all over the rim of my glass and, behind the mask of high society, its façade of silk and alluring perfumes, I saw the humans with their stays and cummerbunds stripped off: saw them naked in their affectations, their bottoms clamped to the silk-lined chairs, their eyes glued to "what-comes-next" in the business of gluttony. For this is the world of the primeval grunt; no delicacy exists here; only the belly and social artificiality. In the coming and going of servants on slippered feet I saw them not as fellow beings but as prime movers in the law of a jungle of which I would soon be a part.

Eating only enough to remain unnoticed, I watched.

More particularly, I watched Bum Bumstead, who was at that moment serving my mother with fawning servility.

Little Molecule (so named later by Dada) and Dozie Annie were standing behind my chair, the former in the colly-wobbles; vaguely I wondered if she had eaten that day, while we had a table loaded with plenty . . . she being a workhouse orphan training to become a serving-maid, which was why my father had taken her on.

Later, with the speeches delivered and all the compliments given, the guests, chastened by wine and formal embraces, followed one another by carriage and liveried footmen down the lane that led to the lodge: under a flaring sky they went, for the blast furnaces of the Garth were going like marrowbones and cleavers, firemarking the clouds with variegated light of lovely rainbow colours.

I got a piece of pork pie into Molecule's pocket as I left the table, in case . . . and she smiled brilliantly at me with her chapped lips; her hair was scragged back, a queer little human.

Next time I saw her she was up in front of Old Bid for stealing a pound of best-back bacon. "No, you will *not* take it up officially," said Dada. "For God's sake, Biddy, she'll go to transportation!"

"She be a lifter, mind!"

"Biddy, Biddy! Aren't we all?"

He can say that again.

Where is she now, I wonder, that poor Molecule?

My father had no sooner left the house with Mr Grey for Bridgend station than Bastard got up to his tricks.

Concealed in the garden, I saw his image on the window of Dada's study, getting into the malt whisky, which did not concern me much. But, since this was the first time Dada was away overnight, I lay in bed and listened to the big grandfather clock strike the hours down in the hall, and watched the crack under my bedroom door for lamplight.

The floor of the landing lightened just after midnight.

The butler, with a lighted lamp held high, was coming up the stairs.

I knew where he was going.

On stockinged feet I ran out on to the landing and down the back stairs to Dozie's room. It opened to my touch and I held my candle-stick high: Dozie asleep, out to the wide, with her sleeping-cap over her ears, and her snores would have graced Dai Dando.

"Annie . . ." I shook her gently and her eyes opened wide, then her jaw dropped for the shriek, but I clamped a hand over her mouth.

"Heisht, you!"

For answer she sat up and gave me the old, "Well I never did, sir," look.

I whispered again. "Bumstead is prowling the house, and he's drinking my father's whisky. Listen to me. Go down the back stairs to the coach-house, wake Dai Dando and tell him to wait for me down in the hall, by the stairs, understand?"

She sat there fighting for intelligence. "Dai Dando . . ." I repeated. "Tell him to wait in the hall! Quickly! *Go!*"

After Dozie had gone I tiptoed to the banisters, looked down the stairs and saw Bastard on the second floor: momentarily, he paused outside my mother's room; holding the lamp high, he stared around him, staggering, clearly tipsy; and at that moment my mother's bedroom door came slowly open, framing her diminutive figure against a background of fire-shot windows, the glare of Troedyrhiw Garth.

I made a fist of my hand and put it against my face.

The butler entered and she closed the door silently behind him.

Racing down to my father's study I got his shot-gun and returned to the landing.

Outside my mother's bedroom, I listened, fighting to control the pumping of my heart; anger and sickness were rising in my throat, restricting breath. The gun was unloaded, I had checked this while coming up the stairs; had it been loaded I think I would have kicked open the door and fired blindly within; such was my sudden fury.

I listened, ears straining: there was no sound but a gentle cooing of wood-pidges, and the distant hammering of the Garth; an engine shunted, outraging the sudden stillness of the house; then I heard voices coming from within the bedroom; faintly at first, then louder, in whispered consultation. Raising the gun I struck its butt against the door, splintering a panel.

"Open this door!"

My voice echoed down into the hall, and I heard my words in repetition.

Silence. The world appeared to have stopped to listen.

Furious now, I shouted shrilly, "Mama! Open the door!" and I clubbed at it again. "Come on, open it!"

99

No answer. Then a footstep scraped the tiled floor of the hall.

Leaning over the banisters I saw a light gleam, and then the face of a man stricken with disbelief; Dai with his lantern held high, staring upward. And as I turned to face the bedroom door again, it slowly opened and my mother stood there.

Behind her Bastard moved against the red flare of the window.

"At this time of night? What do you want?" she demanded.

I presented the gun at her.

"Put that damned thing away. Are you mad?"

"Tell him to come out!" I commanded.

It was a voice trembling with emotion; I couldn't believe that it was mine. My mother said, slowly approaching, so that I backed away on the landing, "Now stop this, Tom – this is another nightmare. There is nobody in here. Tonight your father went . . ."

"Send him out, or I'll go in there and blow his head off!"

"Give me the gun! Come on now, Tommy, let me have the gun . . ." and her hand went out for it.

My courage was failing me; all of my life she had commanded and I had obeyed. And as I faltered, I became aware that somebody was behind me: Dai Dando.

He said quietly, "Send him out, Missus. The lad's right. He's speaking for his father," and pushing me away he went into the room despite my mother's frantic protests and the blows she beat upon his face and arms. "Come out, ye sod!" he shouted. "Come out or I'll be under the bed an' bloody fetch ye!"

The butler came, shame-faced; and as he reached us Dai put one on his chops that must have rattled his relatives from here to Maesteg.

With Bumstead being prodded before us, we took him down the stairs to the hall and out of it into the yard, and his bags and trews went flying after him.

"I'm speakin' for me Maister!" bawled Dai. "The young 'un or the old 'un, I dunna care. But don't you show your

100

face around here no more – understand – never no more!"
and he landed a boot in the Bumstead arse that helped him
five yards along the road to Bridgend.

But it was the greatest mistake of my life: I had reason, later,
to bitterly regret it, the outcome staying with Mortymers
down the generations.

This became more apparent when my father arrived back
from the Midlands; that same evening he called me into his
study after conferring with Dai Dando.

My mother was at her worst that night, a shrieking virago.
But now in the clock-ticking silence of his study, Dada
said, filling his pipe: "It appears that we have had a little
trouble . . . ?"

Always he managed to understate everything, and I did
not reply.

He said, "According to your mother and the servants, you
slept through it all . . ."

I took the hint and asked, "What actually happened? I
heard a cufuffle and people shouting, but decided I was best
out of it."

He was clearly relieved, and I pitied him. Moving uncom-
fortably, he said, "Well, it appears that your mother awoke
to find an intruder in her bedroom, and believe it or not, it
was Mr Bumstead; clearly it was her jewellery he was after
– and Dai Dando, hearing her cries, came to her assistance,
thank God!"

I said quickly, "The only thing I saw was Bumstead leaving
at speed. It . . . it's coming to something when the burglars
are actually living in the house!"

It sufficed him. Sweat was upon his forehead and he wiped
it into his hair.

"So what happens now?" I asked, and he rose, wandering about.

"Well, the butler has gone, and that should have been the
end of it. Some of your mother's trinkets were discovered
in his room but she got those back. Unfortunately, however, she has reported it all to the Bridgend constabulary;

Bumstead has accordingly been arrested and charged with attempted theft."

"What will happen to him?"

"If he's found guilty, prison; if the magistrate is in a bad mood, transportation."

"Transportation!" I was appalled.

"Five years – more if he's unlucky."

"You'll speak for him?"

"How can I? I wasn't here."

He lit the pipe, exhaling smoke. "Thank God you weren't in any way involved, Tom. According to Dai he went very quietly. Your mother confirms this. Why she didn't leave it at that, God only knows! Meanwhile, I'm trying to get her to retract her charges, but you know what she is."

"An Afghan princess!"

I was surprised that this did not anger him; instead, he gave me a grin, saying, "Well, doesn't it serve him right, the fool? But there'll be the usual gossip, of course, and with this deal with Mr Grey coming off, I could do without the scandal . . . young as you are, you surely must realise it; a servant discovered in the mistress's bedroom with her husband away . . . You understand the sort of thing . . . ?"

"Of course."

"Therefore, I want to say this to you before the innuendos start; not only is your mother a princess, she is also a lady, and a law unto herself; her virtue is unquestioned, more especially since she is a wife and mother."

I sat in silence; I could not meet his eyes.

"If . . . if the time ever comes when the innocence of your wife is questioned, her purity must be upheld, whatever the cost to you. Marriage, Tom, is trust, and upon that trust is built all happiness . . . do you know what I am trying to say?"

"Yes, sir."

"That man entered her room unbidden; it was an invasion of her privacy and unforgivable. The theft itself doesn't come into it. Had I been in our coachman's position, I would have killed him."

There was no sound but the ticking of the clock, and I felt closer to my father than at any time in my life.

"Meanwhile, keep out of it; leave it to me."

Chapter 14

With the evacuation of Bastard from Cefn-Ydfa on the end of Dai's boot, everything started happening at once.

Within forty-eight hours I witnessed the Maid herself with such clarity that it became a seed-change of my belief in the paranormal. Ghosts exist, believe me.

Out of nowhere in the half light, she made her appearance.

Waking after a hard day in the experimental tinning shed with Davie as my instructor, and suffering what was known in the trade as pickled hands, I had just plunged them into cooling water in my bedroom when I saw with a shock that she was standing so close that I could have reached out and touched her. Nor was she distressed, as I had witnessed before, but calm and seemingly resolute: meeting my astonished gaze with a gentle smile.

"Good God!" I ejaculated, and with dripping hands sank down on to my bed: there to sit in mute amazement while she drifted around my room as in pursuit of her morning toilet; pausing to flash a glance at herself in the mirror beside the window, with a pat or two at her hair, as women do; now over in the corner by my wardrobe, to run her hands over my clothes within as if in search of a garment.

Completely, utterly substantial in form and movement, she then went to my bedroom door, opened it, and passed through it out of my sight.

In the absence of anyone in the place with belief in such happenings, I chanced to think of Mrs Maddocks, the tenant of the next-door farmhouse, and found her after breakfast sitting outside of her door in morning sunlight.

Approaching the age of sixty, with her husband, Morgan, considerably older, Mrs Catherine Maddocks was mature enough not only to have witnessed haunting activities, but likely to have had conversation with local ghosts. Reflecting on this, the lady turned her face to the sun, replying to my query in a genteel voice.

"Oh no, I've never had an actual discussion, young man, but I have observed the Maid on many occasions."

Sitting cross-legged at her feet, I asked her, "It's said that before her marriage to Anthony Maddocks, she actually lived here in your farmhouse?"

"That is so. Legend has it that her mother imprisoned her in one of our bedrooms when she refused to marry our relative, but this was not so. For that disobedience she was confined in the cellar of Great House."

"Cefn-Ydfa?"

"We call it by the old name, Morgan and I."

I said, "I have heard bits of the tale, but never the whole. Do you know it?"

Her old face smiled with the tolerance one shows to the young.

"Know it? I've supped it for breakfast, dinner and tea these past fifty years," and she settled more comfortably in her chair, lowering her needlework.

"It is said that our generation put a gloss on the behaviour of Anthony Maddocks. Not so. The truth is that he was a philanderer and speculator, using his charms to advance his fortune. As for the Maid, she was in love with Wil Hopcyn, who wrote the famous old Welsh love song, '*Bugeilio'r Gwenith Gwyn*', and who as a sort of odd-job man did repairs to Great House; the couple met and fell in love.

"However, her ambitious mother wanted Ann to marry Maddocks, who as a marriage settlement was to receive most of the Cefn-Ydfa estate, then of considerable value; a local solicitor at the time, he lived nearby at Cwm-yr-isga." She waved an arm in its general direction.

She continued, "The marriage is recorded in the parish register of May 1725, and in expectation of this, Anthony Maddocks built Cefn-Ydfa for his new bride. But Ann continued to pine for Wil Hopcyn, and, we're told, while working in Bristol Wil dreamed that Maddocks had suddenly died and that Ann was free to marry him. Hurrying back to Llangynwyd, he discovered that far from being free, she had suffered a broken heart: she died in Wil's arms while Maddocks was out hunting."

"That is the whole story?"

"Yes, except that while Wil remained single until his death in 1741, Anthony Maddocks married another heiress within a few months of Ann's death, and lived to serve privileged people. He died a rich man."

"Missus," said her husband, joining us, "I could do with a sovereign every time we've told that yarn!" He sat down and cuddled himself on his chair.

"*Jawch*," he added jovially, "that Ann's a bugger o' a woman for seein' what's goin' on! If anything's a-comin' and goin', she's up at the front window before the streets is aired."

His wife added complacently, "Yes, that is true enough. A few days ago when you had guests at the mansion, we saw her clearly, as if greeting them one by one . . . !"

I looked from one to the other.

What elemental chemistry existed at Cefn-Ydfa that so bound the opposites? I wondered. Here was the ebullient Morgan with his yokel chattering; there Catherine, his wife, dignified, genteel.

Come to think of it, I pondered, here was Ann, the wealthy heiress, and the penniless poet, Wil Hopcyn; to say nothing of my father, the Welsh ironworker, and his Afghan princess.

Indeed, going a step further, there was the Romany sweetheart of my childhood, and I myself, to whom a foreign king was laying siege.

My philosophising ceased when Mrs Maddocks suddenly called, "Oh, Morgan, look what is coming!"

"An' she's up in the window again, girl – *look*!" and he pointed up at my bedroom window.

* * *

If indeed the ghost of Ann Thomas was there – and I never saw her on that occasion – it was to greet a very unusual guest to Cefn-Ydfa, and he was no apparition.

I could not believe my eyes.

Karendeesh, of all people; coming up the drive.

But before I leave one phenomenon to discuss another, let me stay on the subject of the Maid, especially since my mother had now become involved. This occurred about the time of Bum Bumstead's trial for burglary at the Carmarthen Assizes, and therefore a difficult time for everybody, including Bumstead.

The strange thing about the paranormal appearances was that they varied from person to person.

Father, for instance, had apparently so far seen nothing abnormal, though, as a very Celtic Welshman, he implicitly believed in corpse candles and goblins, while visitations by the *tylwyth teg*, the Welsh Fairies, were meat and drink to him.

The same applied to Dai Dando, which was acceptable because he was thick between the ears.

Dozie, it appeared, had seen the Maid once – sitting at my mother's dressing-table and powdering her face with Mama's utensils as Dozie called them, and this had sent her, skirts up and flying halfway down to Maesteg. Old Bid had reacted as earlier reported.

Nothing of which explained the experiences of little Molecule, aged ten, who accepted a ghost on the premises with adolescent simplicity.

"Master," said Molecule to me one day, "permission to speak?" – which was the way she was taught to address her superiors when in the Workhouse.

We had met, the child and I, on the landing outside my mother's bedroom.

"Hey up, girl!" I said. "What are you up to?" – my usual greeting to her.

"Polishing the floor o' my lady's bedroom," said she, "and just found her rouge and powder spattered all over."

107

"Perhaps your Mistress spilled it?"

"No, it's her, Master. Fast as I mops it up she chucks it around again."

Her little face was piquant in the half light; the Workhouse had left its mark.

"My mother, you mean?"

I peered at her, and terror sprang to her eyes, and I saw momentarily the child she might have been as I soothed her; then her fear vanished and her eyes grew big beneath her mop cap.

"Oh, Gawd, no, sir, I doesn't mean so! The ghost it were. So I told her, didn't I! I says to her, 'You got no business touchin' my lady's paints and powders, no ye don't! I lays 'em out lovely, you mess 'em up, and then I gets the stick.' "

"You told her that?" Involuntarily, I shivered.

"Dang me, sir, I keeps on tellin' her, but it makes no difference, and last night she puts it on, going hoity-toity like, an' sayin' back, 'Anyway, who are you, Molly Cule? You've only been here a week or so, while I have lived here a year o' Sundays. You get about your business,' an' then she kissed me . . . and she put a finger to her cheek."

I said, "Are you telling me the truth, Molecule?"

"Oh aye! Cross my heart." She paused. "She did kiss me, mind, but her face were that cold I reckon she'd been out all night."

Collecting myself, I said, "Try to get her to be more tidy, if you can . . ."

It was insufficient and ineffective, but the best I could do: from then on the face of the child, pure and truthful, haunted my dreams.

To date, thank God, my mother didn't know of the haunting of Cefn-Ydfa; there's bound to be a palaver when once she do, said Dai.

Remembering my mother, I said on the landing, "Best not to mention this to your mistress, eh?"

"About spilling the powder?"

"Best not, Molecule. Promise?"

"Like you say, Master," she said, curtseying, and left me.

108

Chapter 15

The unannounced arrival of the Chief Vizier of the Court of Barakzai needed official recording in my diary. Therefore:

7th, October, 1871. Cefn-Ydfa House, Maesteg, Near Bridgend.
Quite unexpectedly, there arrived today one named Karendeesh, of whom I have heard talk in the house. He came not only as Chief Vizier of the Court of Barakzai to which, as a royal princess of Afghanistan, my mother belongs, but as the official representative of King Shir 'Ali Khan, the third son of the late Dost Mohammed, who, until June 1863, reigned in Kabul. . .

He came with the pomp and regalia usually reserved for a visiting Eastern potentate and not, as my mother disdainfully referred to him, as an upstart of the lower orders who, in her time in Kabul, was once a common *chuprassey*: the lowly messenger, it appeared, had now become a king-maker.

In the silken green, black and gold robes of his high office came Karendeesh, lounging on cushions in the back of a white landau drawn by four white horses, and so utterly astonished was I by the vision clip-clopping up to our entrance that I expected it to turn into a pumpkin and four white mice.

Sporting a silver headdress crowned with ostrich feathers, the visitor alighted from the carriage with the languid grace born of his station, and on the arm of one of his postillions was about to walk through the entrance to the hall when I confronted him.

In perfect English, he said, "I am Karendeesh, representative of the King of Afghanistan, come by the arrangement of your Lord Lieutenant. I wish to be received by the master of this house, Mr Mortymer, whom Allah preserve," and he bowed.

"My father is not at home, sir," I replied. "Neither is my mother. I am their son."

He had just realised this; in astonishment he now dropped to one knee in the middle of the hall and touched his breast and forehead in servility. Behind him his manservant, a huge man in flunkey uniform, went full length, one arm beneath him, the other outstretched.

Dozie, suddenly appearing with a broom, turned and fled.

Karendeesh rose, snapping his fingers at the man behind him, who crawled away. I said, "Kindly follow me," and led him into the drawing-room; there, he turned and faced me.

"Sire, I bring greetings from my King and the Court of Barakzai; also felicitations from the viziers of Afghanistan to the princess whom all honour; may she and her son live a long and illustrious life at the behest of Allah."

"My parents will not be long," I said, and indicated a chair. "I doubt if they have been informed of your visit, otherwise they would be here," and I thought, this one is up to no good, his good looks and impeccable manners belied this.

"It is of small importance," said he. "Your princess-mother is beloved of our people; your father is an old and trusted friend; it is in such company that a vizier knows tolerance, for I come to be in service and pray that I will be tolerated. You have heard of me?"

"Of course."

His self-assurance was patronising; the high official and the boy . . .

He said, wandering towards the life-size statue of Sappho, "Doubtless you are aware of my King's resolve to return you to your rightful role – a prince pretender to his throne; one day to reign along the lands of the Oxus to as far east as the Indian states, and one day, perhaps, beyond?"

I nodded.

"Then believe me when I say that your heart will surge with joy at the prospect of such kingship!" and he waved a hand airily around the room, which doubtless, compared with his munificence, was but a hovel. "Wealth and privilege will be yours for the asking, your every whim obeyed, and your life made free of sorcerers and incantation, such as exists here. Free, young Sire, from bedevilment and mysticism: divination is our only weakness, which is at Allah's behest for us to rule the world and make it free of the black art called Christianity."

He bent towards me, his dark eyes smiling. "Have you the faintest idea what I am talking about?"

I did not answer this, and he said, standing before Sappho's statue, "And who might this be?"

Quoting my father and speaking in the Karendeesh tongue, I replied, "She is Sappho, one of the poets: she lived in Greece six centuries before the coming of Christ."

He made a face. "Sappho . . . Sappho . . . ? I have never heard of her."

"Perhaps one needs to be a student of Greek mythology."

It turned him, instantly delighted. "Excellent! I had begun to wonder when you would cease to be a Celt, and adopt the proud role for which you were born!"

I did not reply, and he said, "This . . . this Greek . . . A lady poet?"

"As I have said, one of the world's great poets."

"Do you not overstate? Forgive me . . . I did not even know that female poets existed, even less that they should be celebrated."

"My father will tell you more of her."

He was not satisfied. "But a woman, Suresh! Oh, come!" and he turned away. "Is it in the province of male propriety to grant such a status? Does that not also grant them intellectual parity, which is impossible? Women can only claim comparison with the beasts of the field – to give birth to us, true, they are excellent at that – but poets . . . !"

I said abruptly, "This is Wales, not Afghanistan, and my name is not Suresh!"

111

It had no effect upon him; his inborn arrogance betrayed his boredom at being received by so callow a youth, and I suddenly hated him and everything he stood for. Now he was glancing at his watch, which he replaced within his robes, saying:

"Without doubt we have much to discuss. Do you think your mother will be much longer? It is my hope that she, too, will accompany me back to my country . . ."

"They are coming now," I answered, for I had seen, with growing relief, Dai Dando handing my mother down from the trap, and seconds later the postillion stood aside with a bow as my parents entered the hall.

Instantly, Karendeesh was upon a knee before her, the hem of her skirt raised to his lips, and I heard her cry:

"Truly, we apologise! You came early and our train was late; the Lord Lieutenant sends you his compliments and felicitations to your King. Greetings, Karendeesh, greetings to your country!"

As for my father, he did not even return the man's formal bow, but stood there frowning upon my mother's transparently overdone reception of one she had claimed she hated.

As for me, if he thought he would end up by escorting me back to Afghanistan, he had another think coming.

Chapter 16

Within an hour, the three of us seated in our drawing-room, a discussion about my future began; this was chiefly between my mother and Karendeesh: I, as the potential victim, sat motionless; my mother, always at her vivacious best when impressing, accompanied her soprano chattering with gestures from expressive hands. A trembling Dozie brought tea on our finest silver tray and bone china, then backed off, clumsily salaaming as she went; my father, with the ability to blanket anything artificial with silence, said nothing, but frowned at this effeminate man with obvious displeasure. The opening gambits were preceded by affable remarks.

"My dear princess," said the guest, "it was impossible for me to appraise you of my coming via your Lord Lieutenant until I arrived at Margam; such are the affairs of State."

Dada sipped his tea, watching him.

"How did you come?" asked Mother.

Karendeesh crossed his silk-clad legs, and I was fascinated by the toe-arched silver sandal that dangled from his naked foot, and visions of Arabian nights assaulted my melancholy, when voluptuous Uzbek girls, the toys of hook-nosed rapists, tinkle-danced for brain-thudders in harem palaces, all bosom and bottom to the clang-crashing of cymbals and wailing lutes, a delightful release from the stiff formality.

Perhaps the Court of Kabul, where such individuals were apparently plentiful, was not such a bad place after all?

Karendeesh replied:

"How did I come, you ask? I sailed into Aberafon. Your Lord Lieutenant brought me to his magnificent castle at Margam where I rested before coming here in his ceremonial coach."

"You are having a better reception now than you would have received in my time," said Dada.

"Ah yes, but in your time our countries were at war; now, thanks be to Allah, peace reigns; peace and plenty are all we Afghans pray for, but to the reason for my visit . . ."

We looked at one another in the ensuing silence; my mother said archly, "You have come to return my son and I to our rightful people?" and Dada interjected:

"Rightful? Your place may be with the Afghans, Durrani, but my son's birthright is here."

"Which is open to challenge," observed Karendeesh. "Please, let us not be too imperative before the facts are argued . . ."

"The facts are clear, Vizier. I am Welsh and so is my son."

Karendeesh laughed. "But born in Afghanistan of an Afghan princess? Come, Mortymer, your position would have no legal basis if taken to law! Which will happen unless this argument is pursued with equanimity and fairness!"

"Oh yes? Then let me tell you that possession is nine points of such a law, and whatever legality you may have in mind, this will prevail." Dada rose and wandered about, then said to my mother, "You may go to Kabul or any other place that takes your fancy, woman, but my boy stays here."

"And what chance would you have if my King opposed you?" she countered. "Do you really believe you would find a lawyer to take your case in the face of an action by the Court of Barakzai?" She laughed aloud. "No Queen's Counsel, surely; defeat would make him a laughing stock for even daring to oppose Afghanistan!"

Karendeesh now leaned forward, thumping his small fist into his palm. "Dost Mahommed, he who hated the English for their meddling in Afghan affairs and bringing bloodshed to my country – even under his reign you would have stood no chance in the international courts. But now he is dead, and under my new monarch, the noble Shir 'Ali Khan, the country is riven with internecine war. Do you honestly believe I would travel half the world for a new king unless the matter was an imperative?

114

"Yes, Shir 'Ali rules, but his two elder brothers daily threaten him with hostility that could lead to a blood bath worse than anything perpetrated by your colonial attacks – bitter civil war, Mortymer, nothing less; civil war that could set fire not only to Kabul and its environs, but spread like a flame from Kandahar to the northern Khanates, and from there into India, the gem of Victoria's crown."

"My God, Karendeesh, you've got the gift of the gab!" said Dada.

"The gift of defending my country against the wrangling of her enemies! I had this gift when you laid us waste, and it is with me still."

"So you would have me believe, my friend! But nepotism is at the root of it, is it not? Personal ambitions, Karendeesh – they have driven you since a boy! And it is the same with your Court – a hornet's nest of intrigue, connivance and killing – and don't contradict me because I've been there, remember?"

While all this was going on, I was thinking of how ineffective grown-up people were when the temper was in and the wit out; their words evaporate with neither sense nor meaning, each trying to score a point within the viperous hatreds: strangely, it was my mother who put an end to the wrangling:

"Crystallise this, Karendeesh; what do you want of us?"

The man took a deep breath and his eyes moved slowly over us. "To return to Afghanistan with Suresh, your son, where he will be enthroned in the capital with you, his mother, as Regent."

My father did not immediately reply, then said, "You honestly believe that the murderous nest of vipers you call a government would allow my son, born of mixed blood, to rule your country as a boy-king?" and I saw in the eye of my mind a sky-line of Eastern cupolas, golden roofs flashing in fierce sunlight, and harem dancing girls with teeth of rose-coloured pearls, for of these I had once seen paintings.

Karendeesh, with a sort of conjurer's flourish, said, "My people are weary of kingship squabbles; under the present

115

dynasty they have suffered slaughter by the British to the point of annihilation, and they are sinking under the weight of murderous taxes: more, a child should be forgiven for the sins of his fathers; also, our beloved Dost is no more, and his sons squabble over the royal spoils. They pray for the return of their princess and the fruit of her womb."

It was the old language, and it stilled us. He continued.

"You may say that it is easier to gather water from the moon, but Allah, he who can see simultaneously both ends of a stick, has ordained that this be so, while the words of the mob baying for our blood will be like wind from the anus of a protesting donkey." And Dada replied coldly:

"Ah yes, my friend, you have all the words! Had I not owed you my life, however, I would not have listened this far; meanwhile, remember that my wife is here, so please mind your language."

My mother interjected with her inborn daintiness:

"Husband, I beg you, see the advantages! Think of the Court of Kabul, the processional hymns, elephant trains, the dances of the Hindi Kush – the smells, the noise, the market places – do you not remember?" I heard all this from the depth of a somnolent dream, for, bored, I had nearly dropped off: under a bone-white Afghan moon I was lazing in a sea of fawning courtiers, with my feet up and munching Turkish Delight; while before me, prancing in harem silk, was a dusky beauty in half-on-half-off Arabian pantaloons, her outsize bosom cavorting and cuddling with Eastern delight.

Actually, this confrontation with Karendeesh had come at a particularly bad time for me, for on one hand I was hating the sight of females, while on the other hand the lift of a skirt above a knee was enough to send me berserk.

Knocking around the age of seventeen is difficult, I was finding, with grown-ups saying, "Don't you dare", and older lads talking about bits on the side What with one and the other of them I didn't know which way up I was.

As to what was best for me, the throne of Afghanistan or The Llwydarth Tinplate Works, I didn't care a lot; but when

I got the drift of what my father was saying, it rocketed me back to the drawing-room.

"Clearly," said he to Karendeesh, "you are prepared to commit murder to get your way. Isn't the death of one boy enough to satisfy you killers?"

"The death of what boy?" asked Karendeesh.

"The son of Sir William ap Tristan-Evans, who bought Cae White Farm from us," said Dada, hotly.

"He was murdered, you say?"

"I cannot prove it. I merely repeat what the coroner returned at the time – that he died under suspicious circumstances."

The Afghan smiled, shaking his head in dismay. "How could my people possibly be involved, Mortymer? Half a world away, and with no possible interest in this unfortunate young man?"

"Every interest to your confounded spies because he lived at Cae White and was about the same age – they mistook him for my lad."

Karendeesh sighed. "Mortymer, you are living in a land of dreams. Our secret service simply does not make such infantile mistakes – besides, since we openly want Suresh to rule our country, what would we gain by his death?"

Mama sat silently, watching them; Dada answered:

"Listen for once. I am not that stupid. Of course you did not murder him because you believed he was Suresh; you did it as a warning to me that the same could happen to my son if I disobeyed you."

The man was cool. "Then, if you know that to be so, why didn't you report your suspicions to the authorities?"

"What kind of a fool would I have looked? I have no proof!"

The other played with a silver locket at his throat; it held a single diamond that flashed to his every movement.

"In some ways I pity you, Mortymer. You have everything a man could wish for – a beautiful wife, a fine son, wealth and station . . ." He smiled thinly. "You are also a man of property at the behest of my dead king, the Dost, to whom, for such acquisitions, you ought to be indebted. Yet your mind is warped with suspicions and hatred of the very man who befriended you." He rose from his chair. "And you, Durrani?"

My mother rose, too, saying, "I want to return to my country, but only as Regent to my son, who belongs to the Afghan people."

Karendeesh nodded. "This I will report to the Committee of Viziers, who will repeat it to my king." Turning, he said to my father, "As for you, your obstinacy doesn't commend you, for you owe much to my people. But let me hear it again – what do I report?"

Dada went to the door and opened it for him to pass, saying, "Go back to Kabul. Tell all there that never, as long as I live, will I allow my son to leave these shores to rule in Kabul. He is my son and here he will remain."

The Afghan bowed, his hand touching his breast and forehead, and answered, "This I will tell my people, but we Afghans do not easily admit defeat, as you stupid British should by now have learned. The game is not yet over, Mortymer . . ."

"And I, Karendeesh?" my mother asked anxiously. "What happens to me?"

"You are welcome to return to Kabul with me now, if your husband allows it."

My heart was beating in my throat; sweat was on my face. She was about to leave us: it could not possibly be happening, I thought: not now, not at this moment . . .

Mama went to the door, shouting, "Annie, Biddy, come quickly. I am returning to Afghanistan," and without another word she ran out of the room; with my face low, alone, I listened to her scampering haste.

"Doubtless you have been expecting this," said Karendeesh drily.

"Of course. She only needed the opportunity, did she not?" replied my father, and added, putting his arm around my shoulder:

"It's best this way, Tom. But it is only a question of time before we shall all be together again," and here he glared at the man before him. "One doesn't divide my family so easily!"

"Of course not," said the Afghan. "Soon you will all be reunited – in Afghanistan!"

Chapter 17

When a mother leaves her family, her house dies: she can be a fat bore, a skinny shrew, the Virgin of Cairo or the Whore of Babylon, when she goes she takes its soul with her and the rooms expire.

So it was with my family.

After the coach had gone, taking Durrani and Karendeesh to Margam Castle, their first step on the road to Afghanistan, I left my father in the drawing-room and went upstairs to my mother's bedroom.

The place was exactly as she had left it in her furious haste to return to her own people: there the scattered jewellery, upturned cosmetics; here the discarded shelves of unwanted underclothes, petticoats of silk, bodices of satin. Robes of Afghan national colours had been flung across the velvet counterpane, and the beautiful Nottingham lace tapestries around the bed thrown aside.

Sitting at her dressing-table, I closed my eyes, allowing the perfume of her presence to waft over me, stifling my senses but doing nothing to evaporate my tears.

Yet she had done little but bring disharmony to the house, and her adulterous betrayal of my father, almost to the moment of her departure, had widened the rift between them into a chasm that could never be bridged.

Why, then, I wondered, sitting with the evening sun shafting the room, could I hear the rustle of her skirt and her gentle footsteps on the thick Arabian carpet; and more, the sound of her whispering my secret loss?

Nobody, I recall thinking then, should possess the power

to switch off the very light of one's being and bring darkness to a day as beautiful as this.

That night I wrote in my diary:

To my earlier entry I now add the following.

My mother has left us; she has gone with Karendeesh to return to her people in Afghanistan. Should this diary in future years be read by strangers, let it be understood that in my opinion her behaviour while in my father's house has been intolerable, and I wonder he has put up with it for so long.

My father's Bible tells me to respect our parents, but I do not respect my mother, for she has never behaved as such to me; nor has she proved a good wife in the biblical sense, a woman beyond the price of rubies.

It may seem cruel, but I am glad she is gone, for now despair will be lifted from my father; truthfully, I wouldn't care if I never saw her again.

Having written this sitting up in bed, I then put my hands over my face.

Chapter 18

Important things happened after my mother left Cefn-Ydfa, but not immediately: it was as if the old mansion was taking a long breath before deciding the fate of its occupants, and wolf-howling winds and the cold continued unabated.

The year of 1869 had brought the opening of Mr Grey's Tinplate Works, in which Dada had bought a partnership, and I completed my apprenticeship in the tinning trade in the spring of the following year.

Gone eighteen-years-old now, me, hair on my chest, the sap rising, and an eye for anything in skirts; also, anyone in trews looking for trouble in the village could have it, and quick.

Eh dear, it's good to be growing up with all its pains and fanciful endearments, and my mate Davie, knocking twenty-one now, wasn't behind the door, either, when females were about, as I was soon to discover to my cost. He and I spare time used to meet to knock hell out of each other with the gloves, which delighted Dai Dando, and brought to my father one of his whimsical smiles, for I'd heard he'd been a terror with fists when boasting his way around Blaenafon with them about a hundred years back.

These were the mornings when I'd be up and about in the spring mist with the early frosts riming the hedges, and getting a hammer to the ice in the rainwater tub, for we still washed the way colliers washed, my father and me – outside, not indoors like pansies, and towelling down with the wind whistling round the privates.

Oh, I loved those days in Cefn-Ydfa, when the old currant bun shafted the woods right down to the Lodge, and the trees were flashing with the shine of blackbirds, and everything in Nature in full song.

With Tuk scampering before me I'd wander those fifty acres, and such was the growing strength and manhood's dominance within me that every time the fairs came to Bridgend I was there with a guinea to back myself against the best in Llynfi Valley, just for the hell of it. One day, warned my father, you will arrive home with both eyes filled up and your nose over your face.

"Oh aye, now tell me who?"

He answered, "He'll probably be a very ordinary sort of chap – call him Jones or Evans, but with skill – real skill, not just your Welsh hooking and roundhouse swings – and he'll hand you an outing you'll never forget!"

There had grown between me and my father now a respect and love that was nothing to do with filial piety or dutiful son; and his loneliness in the face of my mother's absence appalled me.

Now I was learning through him what life is like without a woman.

Then, unexpectedly, his hungering came to a head, for he mentioned casually:

"We have a friend camping out down in the Big Pasture again . . ."

"Who?" I asked, mouth full, for we were at table.

But with Dozie all ears he wasn't giving a lot away.

"Pop down there and see," said he, so I did.

Diawch! What charms can emerge in the breast of Man when he sees in secret memories the smoke coming up from a Romany caravan . . . !

Jen Wildflower and her mam back from their Romany wandering, and all set up for a visitor!

But decorum has to be observed, whatever the excitement, for the last time I'd set eyes on Jen she'd got crooked teeth in front and stains on her pinafore. Or was that the other one I'd cornered in a haystack in Ogmore woods last Michaelmas? It was a job to remember: but of one thing be certain, it's a mistake to show you're keen.

With Tuk on the lead, my bowler set firm on the ears, my starched collar cutting my throat, and my new boots killing me, I tapped the caravan door.

Good God!

How to tell of this new Jen Wildflower?

Black was her hair in long plaits down to her waist; scarlet gown reaching to the floor, a white bodice and enough inside it to kill a cleric; a lovely face, pale and proud, that didn't give a damn for anyone, including me; and her eyes, dark and lustrous in her high-boned cheeks, moved slowly over my fumbling apprehension.

"Yes?" Not a sign of recognition; *nothing*.

I said, screwing at my hands, "Tom Mortymer . . . You and me, Jen Wildflower, remember?"

"You and me? I beg your pardon!"

Dear Jesus!

I quaked before her beauty, wondering what miracle of rebirth could possibly have brought it about. Tuk was going mad for her at my feet, remembering, and I pulled him in on the leash, saying miserably, "Oh, Jen, don't tell me you've forgotten . . . ?"

"Oh yes of course, I remember you," came the reply. "Tom Mortymer, the lad up at Cefn-Ydfa, isn't it? Well, I never did, and how you've grown!" And she stood back in the van, weighing me up for weight like a County Cork porker.

Miserably, I said, "Is your mam all right?" and she leaned forward in the deep divide and fluttered me down to my lace-holes.

"She be lovely, remember I used to say that? But then we all change, don't we! I'll tell Mam you called, and saying this she shut the bloody door and left me standing.

I was about to tell her that I had waited years for her, that I'd go mad for her given the chance, but everything was cold within me, and Tuk, as if tuning up on my misery, put up his snout and whined like a dog at my feet.

Turning away, I hove off back to the house, hearing her as I went, singing in the van like an angel; then the singing ceased abruptly and the door of the caravan went back on its hinges.

I turned.

Jen Wildflower again, with her knees bobbing up and down, her plaits flying and her arms wide open as she ran for me. And reaching me, she flung herself against me, knocking my bowler off, and wrapped her arms around me in a bear hug.

"Oh, Tom, oh my sweet, my precious!" she said, breathless, and held me at arm's length. "But a girl mustn't show too keen, eh? Got to keep 'em guessing! Oh, Tom Mortymer, how I've missed you!"

And Tuk scampered around us in decreasing circles, going mad with joy as she pressed her mouth on mine.

One up to Jen; but my time will come.

I'll have her, don't worry!

Nevertheless, I realised that she was dangling me on a string, with Davie on the other end of it, for wandering down the lanes hand in hand one dusk of day, she said pertly:

"You ever written poetry, Tom Mortymer?"

"Bedamn, no! I leave that to poets."

"Davie does."

"I bet!"

She made a pretty little face at the dying sun. "No, no, but he does! A week last Sunday he sent me a bit he'd composed. Would you like to hear it?"

"Go on," I said miserably.

"Mind you, Davie looks like a poet, you realise? You ever seen a painting of Lord Byron?"

"He's dead."

"I know he's dead, I'm not that daft," and she made a sweet, wistful sound with her heart. "Spit and image – him and my Davie – you know, really romantic; *aristocratic*, that's the word."

"I'd rather have a rough old chap like me – he'd keep you warm in bed."

"Now, that's what I mean, see? I'd rather be courted by a

refined chap than some of the nobbly old hooligans knocking round here."

"Meaning me?"

"Oh, Tom, don't be ridiculous!" She was peeved. "It . . . it's just that since I've been at Highfield, I've met a few like Davie; essayists and poets, you know, beautifully educated people."

We stopped at the stile that led to Big Pasture, and Jen leaned against it, her eyes going dreamy, and when that big moon pulled down his breeches, the whole world was suddenly covered with silver light, and an owl, as if in greeting to it, shrieked his terrible song, and the forest about us echoed and reverberated. Involuntarily, I shivered, for it could have been an omen.

"Some mother has just lost her baby," said Jen.

"What?"

She was suddenly unaware of me, and in her indecision I held her against me.

"When a Jinny Oolert shrieks once it's because she's tongue-tied with grief, for someone's baby has died."

She was going Romany again and I didn't want this: I wanted her to keep standing close to me so that the softness of her was against me; nor did I want any more talk about Davie and his bloody old poems.

"You want me to read you one?"

Oh, *God* . . . !

And she fished out a crumpled piece of paper from down the front of her and even its presence in that secret place brought me to the old dry-bone shivering, and I reckon she must have heard my knees knocking.

Holding the paper up to the moon, she read:

> "'I will make you brooches and toys for your delight
> Of bird-song at morning and star-shine at night.
> I will make a palace fit for you and me
> Of green days in forests and blue days at sea.''

"Now, isn't that beautiful, Tom?"
I could not reply.

She continued:

> "'I will make my kitchen, and you shall keep your room,
> Where white flows the river and bright blows the broom,
> And you shall wash your linen and keep your body white
> In rainfall at morning and dewfall at night.'"

I closed my eyes, and think I knew then that she was lost to me; only one with a soul like Davie's could awaken her Romany blood and send it racing; even her voice had changed in the poetry, and now changed again, back to Highfield School, when she spoke again, as if confirming my unspoken fears:

"Only a chap with a beautiful nature could write poetry like that, eh?"

"That's right," I answered, "*if* he wrote it!"

"But he *did*!" She pushed me.

"Bugger that for a tale. I've heard that poem before. Did Davie say he wrote it?"

"Well no, but . . ."

"Then don't make out that he did!"

Momentarily it appeared that she had not heard me, for she said at the moon, "The fellas I was brought up with in the vans were that cold and snappy wi' a girl, Tom; not that you're like that, but they were fighters, like you. A gipsy girl may look tough outside, but inside she's warm like cuddle-down floss in the nest, and hunting for kisses, an' no fumblin' hands, you get me?" Suddenly she was Romany Jen Wildflower again.

"I'd never fumble you, Jen," I said.

"Ay ay, I do know, but . . ." and her eyes searched mine in the moonlight. "Well, ye . . . you don't really understand, do you?"

"I only know that I love you, Jen Wildflower."

"That Davie don't fumble, either. I . . . I don't reckon he ever fumbled anyone." She stared past me into the dark. "Ah well, this won't change the baby's belly-band; I'd better be off before Mam gets wind of me gone."

Perhaps I liked her better as a Highfield girl, her words

perfectly modulated, but I doubt it: in my heart I knew I preferred her as a Romany, and that poem old Davie sent her was perfectly suited to her gipsy temperament.

One moment I had lost my Jen to this educated chap who had all the words; next I lost my little Molecule, for she died that year.

She died quickly, like the flash of a swallow's wing, and so did Tuk, in her arms.

Come hunting time, the beery old killers on horseback were carousing with their hounds, breaking down the hedgerows and generally telling folks who owned the world, and Dai Dando was guarding our woods to keep them away, for my father would not tolerate them.

But Dai was at market that Thursday and I was in the Llwydarth pickling shed with Davie, sparking up a big order just come through from the North . . . when Molecule decided to take Tuk through the woods to visit the Wildflowers in their caravan.

But the Tondu Hunt was out, the biggest pack in the valley, and its hounds scented Tuk from a mile off, turned and came racing along the foothills of Mynydd Baedan, and cut her off on the edge of Big Pasture.

Hearing the hounds and the screeching of the horn, the child picked up Tuk and ran for the caravan, where Jen and her mother had come out to pull her to safety. But the hounds got Tuk by the tail before Jen could reach them, and the little one screamed and went in circles, holding Tuk high in her arms; so they went for her, pulling her down and swarming all over her in snarls and yelping, and tore the pair of them to pieces before the Master of the Hunt arrived.

"Death by misadventure," said the coroner. "This is hunting country; the child should have been accompanied."

My father took five hundred pounds off the Hunt Master to keep it out of the courts, but who to award it to since Molecule had no relatives?

I am not sure what happened to that money, but heard that they had given it to Swansea Workhouse, to alleviate the lot of the poor, for that is where Molecule came from.

Chapter 19

Death, it appeared, was having a good time of it in our valley, and Dai Dando was one of the first to suffer its cynical attitude.

For months now Dai had been awaiting the departure from this mortal coil of a beloved uncle and had been constant in his inquiries, sometimes hourly, as to how his relative was faring, the tight old sod, said Dai; in due course, the will having been read, he received a letter, saying, "Dear Dai Dando, you, as is well known in the family, have always been my favourite nephew, and so consistent have been your kind inquiries after my health, that I am leaving you five thousand pounds in my will: you will find the cheque in the breast pocket of the Sunday suit they are burying me in."

My father wouldn't believe it, until he read it for himself; the deceased, said he, often have the best sense of humour.

Little of such humour accompanied Molecule upon her journey to Llangynwyd cemetery; every Sunday morning regularly I went down the fields to the Big Pasture, and from there walked with Jen and her mother to put flowers on the grave.

Arriving there on this particular Sunday I was surprised to find my father, spotlessly attired in his morning suit, as if awaiting us. Off came his top hat, and down went Jen and Mrs Wildflower in their dying swan curtseys, for they were Romanys and knew how to behave.

"Well, Mrs Wildflower, this is a pleasant surprise," said Dada, handing her up, and I knew it was a set-up job since, for the past few weeks, he had been showing an interest in

Jen's whereabouts and how is her good mother and all that sort of thing.

"Pleased I am to meet you again, for sure," said Mrs Wildflower while Jen and I moved away, but still within earshot in case we missed anything.

They stood silently for a bit, these two, mainly examining their boots.

"Yes, indeed," said Dada. "And what a lovely spring morning, too! Would that our little Molecule had lived to enjoy it!"

"Give them a hand," whispered Jen to me, "they'll dry up again lest we do," and sure enough, they did. I asked in the silence:

"Father, did you know that Jenny's been away to school?"

This appeared to beat him for some reason, then Mrs Wildflower interjected, "Of course he do know, don't ye, sir? It was your pa's who's a'paying for it." And Jen said:

"I'm truly grateful, Mr Mortymer – I was just about to say so."

"It is the least a man can do for his friends," came the reply, double bass, and he bowed. "And may I say, Jenny, that you have grown into a most beautiful young lady?"

A lot had been going on of which I was unaware, it seemed.

Dada asked, "You like Highfield?"

The sun shone down upon us, and it was splendid; congregation people, blinking like moles, surged about us now in smells of hot cloth and Church of England cassocks; spring birds shouted in a growing chorus.

As my Jen was that spring morning beside Molecule's grave, with the sun upon her, so will I always remember her. She is gone away from me now, but her memory lingers on . . . the perfume, the sounds of her.

Jen, *Jen* . . . !

Now her mother said in her singing Welsh idiom:

"She do speak like gentry now an' all, thanks to you, sir. Grateful is as grateful does – always in your service, Mr Mortymer – my man would 'ave been that proud!"

131

Dada fidgeted, always a sign of unease, and looked apprehensively about him as one fearing a listener.

"Mrs Wildflower, I . . . I was wondering . . . indeed, I pray you would not think me forward . . . were I to invite you to afternoon tea . . . ?"

Silence; even the wind held its breath; one would have thought he was asking to go to bed with her.

"Why, Mr Mortymer, Jen and me, we . . ." she began.

"No . . . not the children." Swiftly this arrived, for nobody was more affirmative than Father, once he had made up his mind. "Just you and I? At Cefn-Ydfa? With . . . with Jen away at the school, we . . . we would have much to discuss." He then mopped his face with a large white handkerchief.

And this was the one, I'd heard on the grapevine, who had flattened the best in Blaenafon!

Make no mistake, Jen's mother commanded more than a glance, turning heads in Chapel as she did, for there was a fine, wild beauty about her, the antithesis of my mother's diminutive loveliness.

But there her talent ended, for whilst my mother had been beautifully educated in the classics, it was debatable if Mrs Wildflower could read or write; not that this would have deterred my father, if he set his cap at her; he himself was entirely self-educated, and spoke to me of the necessity that I should be "in trade". His was a technical world of little finesse . . .

But I need not have worried, for Fate, unwanted as usual, was about to take a cruel hand in their affairs.

We made the most of Jen's half-term from Highfield School, which was far away down in Devon. During the day I worked with Davie in my father's tin-sheds, learning the trade, for tin-making is one of the most complicated of all.

At week-ends we would meet, Jen and I, secretly for some unexplained reason; partly because her mother didn't seem keen on having me around, with kind smiles and excuses, such as, "Your pa wants you to make your way, that proud of you he is," or, "You got to realise, young Tom, that

132

there's a world of difference between you and my Jen, she being a Romany and you a prince of the realm," or some such nonsense.

There is a peace that comes to a man on Sundays, with the bells ringing in the valley calling folks to Chapel and birds singing demented; and I can think of nothing better than to lie secretly with the one you love in some quiet place, and put your ear to the earth and listen to its musing. For, as I said before, the soil itself is only the spirit of tongues long dead, from Norman conqueror to Roman bondmaid; all reaching out dead arms for lovers.

Beyond the dazzle of the sun I would see the smooth brown of Jen's profile, and the way her lashes spread wide upon her cheeks, when she pretended to be asleep beside me.

A queer old piece she used to be years back with her carroty hair and dirt under her fingernails, but I'd have to hit a few out to keep her now, if the lads got wind that she was around, for the men are women-killers in Maesteg.

Oh yes, she was another woman these days, the cygnet grown into a swan, said Old Bid. "You're a lucky old boy, Tom Mortymer," she used to crow at me. "You had a mam they called 'The Pearl of the Age', and now you've landed another."

She can say that again, I thought: for the only pearl that ever came into my life (my mother having disappeared off the face of the earth, it seemed – not a word from her) is the one lying beside me now in Big Pasture; or sitting with a straw in her mouth like her gipsy ancestors; and when the breeze sips up from the Llynfi Valley and touches my lips, she smells as sweet as a nut come Christmas . . . as if she has been out picking mint-herbs and pinned them on to her petticoats. But I don't take no liberties with this one, not even if she asks me, for I'm in love with Jen Wildflower and she with me.

Only this morning, on the day before she returned to Highfield School, I quoted poetry to her; having Wil Hopcyn in mind (and to put one up on old Davie):

" 'If you to me were given, my life with joy and light
    Would glow, as gloweth heaven, with myriad stars
    bedight . . .' "

And she replied, wrinkling up her nose at me:

" *'Mae'i gran fel gloyw berlyn, a'r rhosyn yn haf:*
    On trow'd hi i garu arall, er mw yn fy nghadw'n
    glaf.' "

"*Jawch*, Jen, speak English!"

"What? When quoting Wil Hopcyn? Don't be daft! And
stop doing that, or I'll tell my mam!"

A dog fox barked in the valley below us and his vixen
replied, and I remembered my poor little Tuk, also Molecule
who was in her grave, and I hated the landed so-called gentry
and everything they stood for. The very thought of them set
me quiet and contained within myself.

"What's wrong?" asked Jen, but I didn't reply.

It was wrong to talk of it amid such loveliness, and the
summer sang about us.

The sweet contagion of romantic love is an accepted infec-
tion, and Cefn-Ydfa wasn't behind the door when this was
handed out. Once I had caught the spots, they spread all over
the place.

Village talk had it that Dozie Annie was now sparking
a lad who worked down a local pit; the growing attraction
between my father and Jen's mother, I've already covered;
Ann Thomas, the ghost, was still mooning around the rooms,
looking for Wil Hopcyn, and according to rumour emanating
from the local taverns (there were twenty-four public houses
and the same number of ale-houses in the valley, most of
which a happy Dai Dando seemed to frequent), he and Old
Bid had been seen hand in hand, walking in public.

I think it very pretty when ancient folk like them fall in
love in the evening of their lives.

I knew, of course, that Dai had aspirations in Old Bid's

134

direction – chiefly her plum duff and suchlike – and when it came to her steak and kidney he weighed the old girl in diamonds; but I didn't think his interest went any further; marriage, for instance, being totally out of the question, announced Dada, for what Biddy knew about conjugal rights could be discounted.

Here, of course, came the rub, for while Old Bid's idea of romance was restricted to star-gazing, Dai, when it came to the ladies, was a case-hardened professional.

Came the time, nevertheless, after he had popped the question and been shyly accepted, when Old Bid was presented to the Vicar of Llangwynyd church for holy matrimony.

"Dear me, there ain't half goin' to be a row," said Dozie Annie, and for once she was right.

My father was something more than just the Master of Cefn-Ydfa: he was the father-confessor of the household; so loved was he by the servants that anything ranging from local vendettas to high temperatures were instantly referred to him for the Judgement of Solomon.

Therefore, when Dai and Biddy stood before him in his study, hand in hand, stating their intention, my father decided that things would be done properly or not at all, and a white wedding was organised, for which he would pay.

So, after his paternal blessing upon them was delivered, Dada sent for a dressmaker and tailor to come and fit out the bride and groom, and fine looked Dai in his wedding suit, its seams stretched to the width of his shoulders and his black stock arched beneath the square cut of his chin, with dabs of female powder to hide the boxing cuts over his eyes.

Biddy, meanwhile, was up on a stool with half the females in Maesteg pushing and prodding her and take it in a bit here, for God's sake, and let it out there; but pretty she looked, take it from me, for though clothes might not turn a goose into a swan, they go a long way; and this bride, said Dada, is going to look splendid if I am going to give her away.

I had a soft spot for Llangwynyd church; this new affection had grown into love from the time my mother returned to Afghanistan.

All the time Mama was in our house she was hauling me off into the Moslem faith, while Dada was trying to trap me into the chapels. This put me off religion for a bit, and I contented myself with just believing in Jesus, for he was a man and a half, I reckon.

Then, hearing that Wil Hopcyn and the Maid were buried in Llangwynyd, I chanced a walk around the graves and read the inscriptions of the beautiful people long gone, who had left their mark on the parish.

From there it was only a step to creep in and sit in a back pew and listen to the sermons; and while this didn't turn me into a monk overnight, it shed a new perspective in my mind, which took me away from the cruelties of religious fervour into admiration for those like William Williams, great with the word, and the great concourse of the dead who had put their fists in the flame of Belief and gritted their teeth to the withering tendons; and others of the pagan market-places who shouted God's name even while the knives searched them.

Personally, I believe that too much is made of organised religion, such as you go into that church and I'll see you later after I've worshipped in mine, for if we all do the best we can and help our neighbours, we'll probably end up in the same place.

I've noticed, for instance, that many of the churches and chapels are nearly empty come Sunday when things are good in the valley; but you only need a hint of the cholera and you can't get into the pews. This, to me, is no kind of faith.

But back to Dai, Biddy and holy matrimony.

For a start the ale-houses took note of it, and on the happy morning a couple of hundred of Dai's beer-bellies, from Old House at Llangwynyd to the Garth Inn in Bridgend Road and from the Bear Inn (where the landlady performed on the harp) to the Fox and Hounds, where George Rees summoned the doctors to the Oakwood Colliery explosion.

136

From such as these hostelries Dai's comrades took passage; either to the church itself for the wedding, or massed outside Cefn-Ydfa where my father gently persuaded them to disperse. For this was a respectable ceremony and candidates three sheets in the wind were undesirable company – even the thick-eared community, he gently told them – so kindly remove yourselves or I will be handing out noses to match the ears.

I have never seen anyone handle the roughs in the way my father could, and soon, with the wedding knot happily tied, we awaited with bated breath the arrival at the mansion of the happy couple.

They came in style in a specially decorated trap, with Mr and Mrs Elias Cohen, the Jew people down at the Lodge, hanging out of the windows waving flags; they came with the little mare in coloured bunting clip-clopping up the drive; followed by a score of customers from the Maesteg Inn waving and cheering, most with scarcely a leg between them.

The day was sunny and hot: the trees around the house were turning up their leaves to each fresh rush of the sun as Dai's entourage carried out casks of ale and cider and small beer for the women, and the band hired from the White Hart (where they used to meet to practise) was already seated in the front garden and well down into its collars, playing "The Bridegroom Cometh".

He came, sure enough, but not in the way we had hoped; in the company of roisterers Dai arrived from the Rose and Crown with his back teeth submerged and songs bawdy enough to make Satan's hair curl. Naturally, this put paid to Old Bid's ambitions to sign him up for the Maesteg Temperance Society, and there was much weeping and wailing and don't worry, duck, he'll settle down eventually, from the valley matrons. But my father's anger was terrible to see. He got one boot behind the roisterers and another behind Dai, bawling:

"Into the coachhouse and sober up, you limb of Beelzebub!" or some such statement, and there was Old Bid soaking with her tears, and Dozie and our new parlourmaid patting her; all of which put paid to the celebrations; Biddy being the sole occupant of the marriage bed by midnight and Dai snoring horizontal in the coachhouse.

I think it a terrible thing that chaps go on the rampage on the day of the wedding, for as Jen told me later, a wedding-day is very special to an expectant bride. And so it was in Cefn-Yfda on this occasion, and I went to bed, I remember, with everything in Great House as silent as the tomb, save for Old Bid's sobbing in the "special bedroom" Dada had put aside for them, and ring doves tuning in with their perpetual orchestra.

But all this came to a stop when the night was riven by a piercing scream, and I leaped out of my bed in time to see Old Bid going at speed across the landing on the first floor with Dai Dando after her in a flurry of nightshirts. Throwing on my dressing-gown I arrived outside the bridal chamber in haste and there collided with my father.

"What's happening?" he demanded.

"Whatever it is, it doesn't sound savoury," I replied, and we listened outside the door.

"Our Biddy," Dada announced at length, "appears reluctant . . ."

And so she was, for when we got inside, she was on one side of the bed and Dai was on the other, and she was shrieking for a pig-sticking, brandishing her fists, and every time Dai tried to corner her she was over the bed and out of the other side.

"Mr Dando!" my father said commandingly, "Stop this at once and return to the coachhouse!" but Dai had got his dander up; the ale was in him and the wit was out. With a huge fist held high, he shouted:

"Drunk or not, Maister, she's the wife of my bosom and I'm here to tie the nuptial knot; so lay off, the pair of ye!"

"Mr Dando," said my father, holding up his candle, "this is hooligan behaviour and I will not stand for it," and he pointed to the door. "Out of here this minute – back to the coachhouse, I say!"

Dai drew from Old Bid like a tiger from prey.

"Oh aye? Then you try to bloody shift me!" and Biddy cried in the astonished silence that followed:

"The fella's a madman and whooping, Maister, and me a virgin woman. He ask for my hand, and I gave it, but only if he slept in the coachhouse!" and she panted at us.

"You did what?" demanded my father, now in command of the situation.

"I promised that in me cups!" bawled Dai.

"Save me!" wailed Old Bid, and Dada put his hand up, saying severely:

"Let me get this right, the pair of you. Did you, Biddy, take this man in marriage in the belief that he would make no demands upon you?"

"Ay ay, it don't include any hanky-panky, and not while he's drunk, for sure."

My father pulled me aside. "This, as you can see, is going to be difficult," then said:

"Biddy, listen to me. Dai may be a little tipsy, but he is within his rights, for he is your husband . . ."

"I anna goin' for immorality, mind," said she vehemently. "I don't hold with it."

"You are married to him, Biddy. It is not a question of immorality. Dai has a perfect right to share your bed, it is the accepted thing in marriage."

"Not by me it ain't!"

"I'm not leavin' here empty-handed," announced Dai. "Ye can bring in a regiment o' guards, if ye like; I ain't sleepin' in the coachhouse."

My father thought hard about this.

"Besides, me mates from the Rose and Crown is waitin' to see the bedroom window go up, and if I don't ring the bell tonight, I'll never hear the end of it."

My father stirred from his reverie of deep thought, saying, "Listen, the pair of you. You, Dai, want to sleep in this bed tonight, and you, Biddy, refuse to allow it. How about individual beds?"

"That do suit me, Maister," cried Old Bid, joyful.

"But it don't suit me," growled Dai.

"Supposing we put a bolster down the middle of this one?" I suggested.

There was a long pause while they considered this.

"Suits me," said Dai.

Biddy, pushing stray hair back from her face, looked at the window where the moon, tipsy with his full meal of summer, was rolling over the world, and said reluctantly:

"So long as he don't come over the top, the spalpeen."

So I went like the wind to the spare bedroom and came back with a bolster and, with the penitents standing each side of the bed, my father put it down the middle.

"Me first," said Dai, and got in one side. "Now then, me lovely!"

"I ain't gettin' in while folks is looking," said Biddy adamantly, and we stood outside the bedroom door and listened to the old bed protesting as she eased herself into it.

It was the Judgement of Solomon, as I said earlier.

I saw Old Bid at breakfast next morning, with Dai still out to the wide in the special bedroom.

" 'Mornin', young Maister!" said she, and gave me a broad Irish smile.

And as far as I know she's been smiling ever since.

Chapter 20

With Dai and Old Bid showing us the way, romance was in the air for everybody in Cefn-Ydfa, including me.

Eighteen years old is the age for a man! Until then life is fiddling with him, rising this anger here and that passion there without much shape or meaning. But at eighteen I say he's got the hang of it, with energy rising in his bones, his muscles vibrant and building up a wish to have a go at something in particular, the tougher the better when it come to the men and a desire to assist the women when it come to the creative process.

Very sorry I am for females if they had to putting up with the same temptations as me; having to accommodate the conventional moral codes And in the middle of winter I longed for a new summer to come sweeping over the mountains, bringing with it the usual clutch of beauties in their coloured flounces and parasols, giving out their ancient come-hither glances and fluttering their eyes.

Down Commercial Street in town they came chattering like magpies, usually in pairs, giving it out here, whispering it there, scandalising everybody, including Davie Grey and me, from William the Fourth to the Bishop of Bangor, their gesticulating hands like flowers before their maid-enly faces, peeking from behind them with a quick wink-come-hither.

But summer and coloured dresses had abandoned the valley now, and first came winter, celebrating my entry into The Llwydarth Tinplate Works as a full-blown professional, for my apprenticeship under Davie was finished.

Aye, winter! In the year of 1873 its black clouds came

storming in from the Atlantic wastes like flocks of famished birds, bringing gales howling like Irish banshees.

Then the winds of the ocean settled upon us, covering the hills with a glaring whiteness, and the land was hammered into ice by the fists of December: the little brooks that boasted over the crags on their way to the river froze solid, and the human wastage of the Industrial Revolution huddled around the furnaces for warmth: the worn-out ones were found dead in the brickyards and shattered ironworks of an earlier era of exploitation; a child was found dead at its mother's breast in the vagrants' lodging house, but at least the cold put paid to the Asiatic cholera.

Then came spring and the clouds of thunder fled, leaving behind the verdant hills in all their youthful decoration. Crocuses and dandies vied with daffodils, primroses and buttercups to paint up Wales in all her gorgeous clothes: from a sprightly little maiden to a woman in all her bloom, the country shone, and the woods of Cefn-Ydfa blazed with bluebells that April, I remember . . . the wind sighing gently around the dead oak where the Maid left her messages for Wil Hopcyn, the sycamore leaves upon which she had written with her own blood . . .

But more blood than this was spilled in the Llynfi Valley that spring: a collier with a smashed leg, pulled out from under a pit, would have it amputated in the presence of his family on his own kitchen table; the nearest hospital being at Cardiff, miles away, while the nearest asylum was at Bridgend. Teeth were being extracted without an anaesthetic; women of gentility used laudanum in childbirth to "take off the worst of the pains": those of the "lower orders" had to put up with it.

What with one thing and another, Davie and I were becoming sick of the mounting injustices. The cruelties of the past we had accepted as standard; our fathers accepted it, why shouldn't we? But now, thrust into a lack of social services, the revolting system of Truck long outlawed by Parliament (but happily continued by "benevolent" employers), the social injustices were under question by a rising generation who considered the situation iniquitous.

For the moment, however, we were both dominated by the business of "getting out the orders" for the tinplate company headed by Mr Grey and my father; one rapidly becoming the most important tinplate works in Wales.

A word about the making of tin while on the subject.

Tin making was first established in Wales in 1720 by Mr Hanbury of Pontypool after he had visited Germany in 1665 and observed their methods of manufacture. This led to the production of his beautiful Japanware and its decoration. The manufacture of the famous Japanware was not confined to Pontypool, although historians claim that it was. I myself have seen trays exhibited at a Bridgend National Eisteddfod which bore the name, "Maesteg Japanning by Ginster", then the foreman at our Maesteg works.

By 1825 sixteen tinplate works were hammering away in Wales, the power of steam taking over from hand-working; but fair to say that Mr Grey and my father owned one of the first to put into operation the successful "Russian Process". "Rustless Russian" speaks for itself, the finished product being a brightly polished plate free from the possibility of rust.

Our works, when I joined as a qualified tin-worker in 1872, then aged eighteen, comprised a black plate mill with cold rollers and three small tinning sets worked by fifty tradesmen; this grew into a vast industrial complex which lasted for the next ten years, covering a decade of social disgrace which has conveniently been omitted by our establishment-biased historians.

The manufacture of tin is comparatively simple, but its physical effects upon the working population made it unacceptable in human terms; the social conditions in the Llynfi Valley in my time being deplorable.

Davie Grey and I became even firmer friends that year,

with pints together down at the Rose and Crown where the new landlady, Cushy Cuddlecome from the Eastern Valley, held court.

An outsize in females was Cushy, the best bolster in the valley, and with her came her two minders, Hambone and Swillickin' Jock, both of the broken-nosed brigade, but neither of whom fistically impressed me; if you can't duck and dive the right crosses and left hooks, you're only really an ornament when it comes to minding a lady.

"Not that this new Cushy is much of a lady," said Davie.

My friend Davie requires greater description, being unusual.

The years had changed him from the carefree lad that once I knew, bringing him through an unhealthy adolescence into a slim young chap of aesthetic appearance.

There was now about Davie a Byronic quality, with his unruly black hair and gentle demeanour; it was as if the pit and tin labouring of our apprentice days had moulded him into a different shape, compared to me.

I had thrived in the furnace glare of the bar iron. Stripped to the waist, I enjoyed the bellowing threats of the rollers, drinking quarts with the workmen (for which I was always in trouble with Mr Grey) and generally playing up the women stacking the boxes.

The sweat of the furnaces in all its muscular activity had turned me into a heavyweight, six feet up and wide in the shoulders; yet the same had somehow diminished Davie, physically and psychologically.

It could have been that his earlier years in the Workhouse had taken their toll, for his mother had died a pauper's death in there, and he was raised by a wet nurse before Mr Grey and his wife adopted him. Women were kept in milk for this official purpose, and his nurse could well have been tubercular.

Thin and pale was Davie's face in the days after we had shovelled and sweated buckets together; his eyes being large and dark and filled with shadow . . . the trade mark of the born consumptive.

"Take ye turn, mister," said Hambone, one of Cushy's minders, and pushed Davie away from the bar in the taproom of the tavern.

"You take your hands off him!" said I and swung the minder to face me, a fist raised.

"Oho!" he exclaimed, double bass, "got young livelies in this valley now, 'ave we? We got dandy-fire customers on a thirst in by 'ere, an' you're strangers; take your turn, son." And he turned as Cushy, the landlady, put down a pair of quart pewters and moved behind the bar to face me.

"Now ye've got her blood up, boyo," said Peg Cuddle, her assistant, to roars of approval. "And when Cushy's got 'er blood up she 'as 'em for breakfast."

"What's wrong here?" said the woman before me.

Her eyes, bright blue, shone like opals in her rouged and powdered face; a face that had died in service to customers, for Cushy had a name, and not only in the county; talk had it that people who complained about Cushy's hotpot got it over the head, and she'd spent last Easter in the Bridewell for doing a naked charity act as Lady Godiva.

Smiling now, she said, "Watch it, son, or my Hambone'll 'ave ye."

"Oh aye? If he shoves my mate around I'll 'ave your bloody Hambone."

It pleased her: the blue eyes shone.

"What's ye name?"

"Tom Mortymer."

"Educated, ain't ye?" And I answered her in collier's talk.

"No odds to that, missus – two pints he asked for – are ye serving us or not?"

"Cefn-Ydfa – those Mortymers?" she asked, hands on hips.

"It makes no difference!"

"Oh yes, it do, son! It's the difference between a county gent and a pig's ear like my Hambone," and reaching out she caught the front of me in a huge fist and pulled me towards her. "Listen, when you drinks in by 'ere you takes your turn,

145

or I'll come your side o' the bar and strip orf – then God help ye! Our Peg!"

The other barmaid put a hand up, and Cushy bawled, "Draw two pints for the young gennulmen on the 'ouse, for happens I know his pa," and she wagged a fat finger in my face. "An' next time ye come by 'ere, ye spalpeens, ye'll take your turn or I'll be over there and see to the pair of ye, understand?"

"Yes, missus," we said, penitent.

Outside, in the summer night, Davie said, "Your father knows her? It's beyond belief!"

"Don't even mention it!"

Talking of fathers, ours were reasonable; they gave the rising generation the option of speaking its mind without fear or favour.

"You don't agree with the Truck system?" asked Mr Grey.

He was portly and bald-headed, a man made calm by the inner vision of the true entrepreneur. He had come to build up Maesteg from Morriston, and now lived happily with his family in the Russian Villa, so named as a tribute to the Russian Process.

"We do not, sir," I replied, "and neither does Parliament, for a change."

"And what does my son think?" He smiled at Davie.

"I agree with Tom, sir," said he. "A labourer is worth his hire and should spend his wages where he thinks fit."

"Why not at our shops, then?" He appeared nonplussed, and Dada, joining the conversation, replied:

"Largely because the prices in our Tommy Shops are dearer than those in town. Apart from which, the ills are evident, for it ties the worker to us body and soul; the less thrifty among them get into debt and can't leave our employ even if they wish."

"This has been a long time coming out, Iestyn!"

"Perhaps. As a new director I thought my intervention too early."

Mr Grey replied, "The men themselves would not accept a

146

change – they look upon town prices as the new 'shopocracy', I've heard. What makes you believe that they would accept closure of the Tommys?"

"Give them the opportunity," said Dada. "Put it to the vote."

He nodded. "I'll consider it . . ."

Davie said, "With respect, Father, that isn't enough. You gave us a free hand to criticise, and we're doing so. Truck must go. It's outdated."

"All right. Go around the houses, visit the workmen's homes; get a consensus of opinion and put it to me again."

That conversation occurred in the autumn: Davie and I conducted our house-to-house inquiries in December.

Quiet and still was our town that winter; the starlight was cold enough for mittens above the hills of the valley, the river was misted and frozen, with the coots slipping on their backside well into March.

Brilliant were the full moons, and the Milky Way that bright you could chop up its stars and put them, glittering, over Swansea.

The clank-clanking of the valley tramways played its sleeper-music on the still air: air so cold you could have stuck a pin into it and watch it glint in the moonlight. And some nights, when the wind got its dander up it would howl like werewolves down the valley, tugging at shawls and mufflers where the oldies of earlier generations were coughing up the dust.

The wind is beautiful when it sips up from the river in summer, and the valley is all done up like a young girl in bright petticoats; but when he is in a fury, as he was that winter, he is frightening, especially on the night when Davie and I mooched up and down the little black-stained cottages, tapping on windows, knocking on doors.

Come nearer . . . peep . . . *listen* . . .

Aye, listen hard, for the Maesteg Iron Works over the way is going at it like a lunatic.

For this is the other side of the Maesteg coin, the one the bosses have tucked away out of sight . . .

Come on tiptoe down Commercial Street for a start; for I tell you this, if animals went to Heaven I'd be on my knees to their god.

Stop outside the window of Mrs O'Leary's house; an Irishwoman from County Cork is Mrs O'Leary, and her chap a roller-labourer in our Works; in the family way again is she, looking pretty with her sack dress tied up in front; now bending to blaze the grate where she's got Welsh *cawl* on the boil for his dinner; sweating with the bending is she, but healthy for an Irish, for they're usually skin and bone.

Come closer. Here's a chink in her curtains.

With Davie on one side of you and me on the other, bend and peep.

See the mantel with the picture of King William, the winter flowers in the jam-jar, the poodle sniffs of her china dogs? And the place, be fair, is like a new pin.

Some plaintive Irish air she is humming as she works, mainly out of tune, can you hear?

You can't? Then hear this . . .

Tramping boots arriving; coming down Commercial Street; nearer, nearer . . . Didn't you hear the accident hooter blowing an hour ago?

Boots, boots, echoing in the sudden silence.

Mrs O'Leary comes to the window; back goes the curtain, and she peers down the street. A stretcher comin'? Who, for Mary's sake, who has caught it? Can't be my fella, for he's finished his shift . . .

The stretcher stops outside her door (she's Number Twelve, later Mrs Wildflower lived three doors up). Mind, I always said that Bowrington Street (it was called that in her time) was lucky.

Bang, bang on the door, and our Works foreman tips his cap.

"Sorry I am to tell ye, missus . . . your hubby's had an accident."

"Oh, sweet Jesus," says Mrs O'Leary. "Bring 'im in."

"The surgeon will be here directly," says the foreman.

"Oh, my love, my precious," says Mrs O'Leary, down on her knees beside the stretcher.

"He's bleedin' a bit, but we've brought a bucket o' sawdust. Can we get him on the bed? The surgeon will be here to trim 'im up directly . . . it's his legs, see?"

"God Almighty!" says Mrs O'Leary. "But, he ain't got any legs!"

Come on, come further.

Come down to Number Six near Smokey Cot weighbridge. Lots of garbage in the street here, like dead cats and dogs, and where things in chamber pots come flying out of the windows. All right for Bowrington, see; since it was on a slope they floated the sewage downhill to the river, "though the tram-line running through the middle of the street made it very unsightly," said Mrs Rhys Evans.

"Jesus, Mrs Evans," I wanted to say. "And the *stink*!"

"No gas and no water supply in them days," said she, "and no railway, even. You don't know you're born, you lot: water from the well, if it rained; if it didn't, none; and only one well to three rows of houses, even then. Mind, I been in my Number Six for as long as I can remember – came down from Stoke Newington, we did, me and my fella. And he started first in the Llynfi Iron Works t'other side o' the river.

"A good husband he were – fine set-up fella – let me tell you; six pints on a Saturday night, none for the rest o' the week. North Country chap, see; big leather belt and a stomach in it like a barrel of ale, but never once did he leather the childer or me: weren't in 'im, ye understand? Though I seen him once brush up his whiskers and lay out à six foot Welsh collier – no bother.

"Mind you, I gets lonely in Number Six, except on Sundays when I goes up to the cemetery wi' my cat in her basket. Half sighted? I'm nearly blind – 'ave been these past ten years, didn't I say? But I can find me way up to see my Rhys in the cemetery: Sundays regular, never miss.

"Beg pardon? Rhys Evans is a Welsh name, ye say? Ay ay,

of course it is: sparked and married twice, you see? First a Geordie ironworker, then a Welsh collier – bedded and buried 'em both, I did. Good men, the pair of 'em, though it were Rhys who kept me short; ten bob a week he gave me to run the 'ouse, the bugger. But I had me own back when he went off to Jerusalem, 'cause I put 'im in with my Big Alf, and he were six foot six – sort that lot out, I says to him, one on top o' the other.

"But it were a mistake, when I come to think of it, because I bet the pair of 'em had me over when the nights was warm shiny, the ould sods.

"Eh, what's that? Children? Of course I 'ad children, for I was all woman, my men said – ay ay, six I had – all boys: two killed down Ogmore, two cut and married, and the two others off to Americay – Carnegie's Pittsburgh, they do say – and married proper, mind, all decent, but I don't hear from 'em now. Reckon they've forgot their old mam. I suppose it's part of being a mother.

"Ay ay, me too, I'm off as well. Got to get me old man's supper. Married again, ye say? Of course! Got to have someone to take care of, innit?"

She didn't see us do it, of course, but we smiled, Davie and me, as she made her way past us to see her Rhys in the cemetery. And then suddenly she turned back to us, shouting, "Hey, you asked me if I wanted Truck in my time, didn't you?"

"That was the general idea," I called back.

"Wouldn't be without it – did ye get that? Me an' mine would 'ave been six foot under 'afore now, if it hadn't been for the old Tommy!"

Dave and I called at a dozen or so houses during the next two weeks, and the last we visited was that of Mr Tom Williams who lived at Four, Neath Road, not far away from Big Pond (called Pond Mawr in those days).

Here we had to wait at the Crossing while teams of shire horses pulled over trams of finished iron on its way to Porthcawl Docks.

Powerful and sinewy were those horses, their coats brushed up and shining in the winter sun. Animals doing better than humans in the industry these days, observed Davie.

Old Whiter-than-White Dai Shenkins, the mad Revivalist collier, was standing on the corner of Neath Road and shaking his blue-veined hands upward.

Gaunt as a pile of haunches and shinbones was Dai, his bones wasted by the vivacity of his faith, and as we passed he croaked parsimoniously, "Thus shall thy souls burn with a majestic fire, thou sons of Belia! But Satan is going to the wall, remember, and the Lord will strike a match for the tinder of your bodies, you young ones!"

"Ach, dry up, Dai," I said, pushing past him.

"You bum-faced sinners and fornicators! It was an east wind that ship-wrecked Paul, remember, and Heaven is blowing it now. Repent, repent before it is too late!"

We tried to get away, but he followed us to Tom Williams's door and hammered upon it with a gnarled fist, bawling, "Open up, Tom, open up! But beware, for the followers of Baal are demanding entry!" and Davie said, pushing him off:

"Ay ay, and Old Nick's down in the cellar trying on the old girl's drawers, so get after him, Dai," and suddenly Tom's door flew open and we were inside.

It was so quiet in the tiny hall that I heard a mouse scuttling.

"Lovely" Tom Williams, the invalid collier, lived with Bronny, his daughter, and this was about all we knew about him, except that he had been abed with a broken back these past three years; and the women neighbours told us that in his prime he was the most handsome man in the vale.

But the press had got him while working the face down a pit owned by Lemon and Company, to whom David Grey was articled once. And it was Mr Grey, we were told, who had him taken to the two-up-two-down in Neath Road, and housed him there after his accident on a pension of three shillings a week, rent paid.

Very grateful for this was Tom Williams; "for I'm only working class", said he; "right and fair it is that Mr Grey should live surrounded with servants, for he be a gentleman, and that's the way life goes, innit?

"Mind, ye canna do a lot on three bob a week, though I got the slates, ain't I? A fella can count himself lucky when he's got the roof, I always say."

Now, standing besides Tom's bed, I asked, "Is it true that you're cared for by your daughter?"

"Ay ay, sir, and she be a good 'un, I'm telling you. She's out shopping just now, but she'll be back to get me supper before she goes on night shift at the face," and he wound up his big Pit watch lying on the bedside table, its glass still cracked from when they had hauled him out from under the press.

I said intolerantly, "She works underground? That's against the law."

"Aye, mun, down old Oakwood Number 1, on tram-hauling, though it do come hard on her stomach these days, she says."

"For how much, Mr Williams?" asked Davie.

"How much what?"

"How much does she earn?"

"On good days twelve shillings a week, but it's a wet pit, so sometimes nothin'. She dunna work Sundays, mind."

There was about him a fragility that denied his forty years and he had recently been shaved, for normally he was bearded, the neighbours said.

Davie asked, "So, if Bron earns twelve bob and your pension is three shillings, you're not really doing so bad?"

"Doin' fine and dandy, sir. If the prices in the Tommy Shop weren't that high," replied Tom, and I said:

"We were coming to that. In fact, that's why we're here. To find out what you think about Truck."

"Don't ask me, mun, ask God," and he looked beyond us to the window where the higgledy-piggledy streets were framed downhill on the glass. "It's a scandal, really speakin', mun. If we want cash instead of tokens we pay fifteen per cent for it in the pound, and the rates in the shops in town

152

are five per cent lower than the Tommy: maybe Mr Grey's a gennumun, an' all that, beggin' your pardon for sayin' it, sir, but three year ago I gave 'im me back, and now he wants me lifeblood.

"My girl works all the hours that God sends, Mr Mortymer, and she'll walk five miles to save a penny – down to Maesteg an' the shops, I mean – but that ain't fair, right? Some nights we don't sleep 'cause she's so done up."

He made a face of dull acceptance. "Mind, I got to be fair, the neighbours help a lot. But I'm dead from the waist down, see, and though my girl can manage me bottle, I gotta have the Jew girl, Eli Joseph's missus, in for the bedpan, you know, and the turning . . ."

"I'm very sorry," said Davie.

"Aye. But sorry anna good enough, is it?"

I bent above the bed. "You shouldn't be lying here at all, Tom Williams, you ought to be in hospital . . ."

"Ay ay, an' pigs might fly, eh? Listen, you two – don't you come by 'ere seekin' after my business – and then go off and forget what bloody day it is, for it's you that's responsible, innit? You and ye feythers . . ."

"We are trying to help, Mr Williams."

"Oh aye? By arrivin' in me 'ouse in dandy suits and well fed? You go back home to ye folks and tell 'em what a sod it is livin' in this valley. But it ain't always goin' to be this way, for there's others comin' after chaps like me – with sticks and guns – I'm tellin' ye. And they'll pull the whole thing down around your bloody ears like they tried in the '39 Rebellion, and they won't mess it up next time, take it from Tom Williams."

He lay there, his hair white on the pillow, and I understood his anger. Davie said, before I could stop him:

"We . . . we will talk to our people, Mr Williams. Meanwhile, may I leave this money here . . ." and he put a ten bob note on the table beside the bed, and the man thrust out a hand and swept it on to the floor, shouting:

"Out, *out*! The bloody pair of ye, for I'm sick to death of alms for the poor. I only take money from neighbours same as me. *Out!*" And he struggled up in the bed.

Strangely, although I heard and saw all this within the gloomy bedroom, my mind had broken free and I saw a gold-domed city of coloured roofs shining in the sun; it was a phenomenon of the brain, a sudden and ecstatic release from the impoverishment all around.

Reaching out, he pulled on a rope and I heard the front door go back on its hinges. "That's open for the neighbours, not the likes of you!" And he lay back gasping with the effort.

We were on our way out, me and Davie, when his daughter came through the open door.

In a ragged sack dress she came, with her tram-towing belt trailing the floor behind her; her long hair was scragged back with string and there was about her a weariness.

"Are you Tom Williams's daughter?" I asked softly, but Tom had heard, and roared from the bed:

"Leave her alone! Didn't I tell the pair of you to sod off outta here?"

"How old are you?" I asked her.

"Twelve come Sunday," said she, and smiled, adding, "You're Mr Mortymer, the new manager's son, ain't you? I seen you in Chapel once," and she jerked her head towards the bedroom. "Don't worry about my da, he do get it up his apron somethin' awful these days, but there ain't no harm in him . . ." and she lowered her basket.

When we reached the door she said, "Don't bother, Mr Grey – we're all right – but thanks for the ten bob.

"Mind, Miss Cuddlecome and her sister, Peg, do collect for us often, for the lads are good down the Rose and Crown. And Mrs Eli Joseph next door but six comes in for turning, and others help wi' the washing. I can manage." Yes, I thought, it was ever the same – nobody is more generous than those who have nothing.

Uncertainly, we stood before her, and she said, "It . . . it's easy, really speakin'. After me eight hour shift I takes over, see – with his bottle an' all that, you understand – but neighbours do 'im during the day, like I said." And she smiled brilliantly, her face radiant, then shouted past us to the bedroom. "Don't you worry, me lovely, I'm home now, mun, and I've a penny herring for ye supper!"

Davie returned my look, and I knew what he was thinking: twelve years old, and she was underground towing trams of coal with a belt around her middle: and this while the tame historians tell us that no female worked underground in the Llynfi Valley after 1850!

One lie being as good as another when it came to Wales in the mid-nineteenth century.

The people of the Llynfi Valley were, for me, the people of the earth, so a word about them after visiting their homes.

While it is true that endemic diseases in our valley were never as terrible as in Merthyr Tydfil, where, in 1849, 1500 died, the level of them was nonetheless a tragedy: one caused by employers, who, confiscating water for their works, failed to replace the source with a decent domestic supply.

Similarly, although ranks of houses were flung up by them for incoming labour, they gave no thought to drainage: all was tuned to the god of Mammon, and the belief that where there was dirt there would be money.

It was the people themselves who learned, through the killings of Merthyr and Dowlais (under the acquisitive Crawshays and Guests), that the putrescence flooding their lives brought cholera, typhus, smallpox, measles and other such contagions.

The beautiful Llynfi River, once a bright watercourse in a sylvan valley, became, with the onset of Industry, a sewer of coal and iron slurry, and a burial ground of unwanted dogs and cats.

Serving the land through its tributaries, it sent fingers of death into the community: St Vitus's dance, diphtheria, whooping cough and ringworm became the accepted norm for growing children. Indeed, until the advent of Dr Kay's Sanitary Report, the basic cause of such outbreaks was not properly understood.

As illnesses increased, so did the families, one street in

155

town being known as Incubator Row. Families of ten and even twenty children were socially acceptable at a time when malnutrition and the exploitation of the young was the accepted norm.

On our visits to the people of the valley, Davie and I learned much of the plight of the working man. We noted the spurious overcrowding, where people sometimes slept six to a room and four to a bed; and we pitied the average housewife in her duties of feeding and cleaning for a proliferation of lodgers in her efforts to make ends meet.

Life in and around Maesteg, Davie and I concluded, was a hell on earth.

In our pathetic ignorance of the difficulties to be overcome, we decided to do something about it.

Before the coming of the Industrial Revolution, which almost simultaneously embraced and captured the Top Towns of Gwent and areas of Glamorganshire, the people of the Llynfi Valley lived a life of domestic simplicity and agrarian routine.

In their farmsteads and smallholdings they eked out a precarious living amid a halcyon serenity that was envied by the harassed masses of the industrial cities.

No proper town drainage system existed in Maesteg when my family arrived there in the middle of the nineteenth century. Waste disposal was simple: one threw the contents of chamber pots out of a window or carried it to a local brook where it dissembled into the natural water supply; and since the killing of animals was by pole axe and otherwise uncontrolled, the area around such centres was unofficially named the Shambles, as in most towns.

With the Llynfi now polluted, inhabitants were restricted to valley wells, and these proliferated; some of which were supposed to possess healing properties. To these wells the workers walked miles for daily water.

Maesteg possessed no hospital then; even the Isolation Hospital was not built until 1903. Crime in the Llynfi

Valley was plentiful, but no comparison could be made with Merthyr. As the home of dreaded transgressors like Dai Cantir and Shoni Sbugor Fawr, "the Emperor of China" Merthyr held a historical criminal element then in its prime.

The streets in mid-nineteenth-century towns were unlit, and haunted by footpads in search of the unwary. No pit-head baths existed; a family shared a tin bath in the kitchen in front of a red-toothed grate. Bath stone or sand was spread on the kitchen floor for ease of sweeping up accumulated dirt, even as late as 1910 many houses in the valley lacked bathrooms. The method of washing clothes was by the "dolly" and scrubbing board. Women baked their own bread, and the family, if rich enough, kept a sacrificial pig. Small beer and home-made drinks were consumed in great quantities.

Maesteg people were unaware, apparently, that their lives were precarious – that they were sitting on fortunes of mineral deposits – the basic needs that had rung the death knell of the equally innocent Blaenafon in Gwent. Nor had they endured the revolutionary demands of the Carmarthenshire Welsh who, short of geological limestone (without which their farms could not survive), had fallen prey to the greed of speculators. The Rebecca Riots (the burning of the iniquitous toll gates) had not touched the Llynfi Valley.

I have heard it said within family circles that if a finger was slammed in a gate in Maesteg in the early 1800s, it was "known all over the county". Not so. Such was the state of the farming poor that every day was a struggle; the onslaught of land taxes, "landlordism" and the weight of Church tithes so reducing the income of small farmers that they stood constantly on the brink of penury.

It is recorded that the poet Ap Vechan protested unsuccessfully to his Church Commissioners that his dying father had had his bed removed from under him for payment of Church tithes; and while no such iniquities have been recorded in Maesteg, they doubtless existed.

The influence of neighbourhood religion played a leading

part in the lives of parishioners, and produced an enviable standard of Christian behaviour in the agrarian communities. Further, the names of religious leaders stand today; and while the Quakers have not recorded their presence officially in the Llynfi Valley area, there is word-of-mouth statements that "they entered with their soup kitchens to relieve the distressed poor during the height of industrial activity".

The Mormons of Aberkanfig extended their influence during the middle of the last century.

Tom Pugh, the president of the Cwmafan Mormons, left his legal wife and took the wives of others with him to America, violence being shown there to any male Mormon if he failed to conform with the rules (ten wives was the norm, apparently), victims being summarily shot by Brigham Young's fanatics.

Equally fanatical, however, were some religious factions in the Llynfi in my time, the tortures of eternal damnation being threatened from pulpits of every denomination. From later Apostolic and Pentecostal churches (with the advent of the later Evans Roberts religious revival) the same message rang out: repetitive reminders of the fate reserved for those who would one day stand before St Peter. The children of the valley shivered under the threats and blandishments of travelling preachers who regaled their congregations with flowery, and often beautiful, phrases; lifting their hearers above the dusty rafters into realms of unimaginable glory; or casting them down into caverns of fire.

That the community reacted passionately against the immigrants who came from the 1830s onwards has been recorded. On one side of a Maesteg street the reserved, mainly Welsh, community would be jeered all the way to church or chapel by vagrants living rough. Shocked by the multiplicity of the ale-houses and inns, the domestic Welsh would be accosted by drunken, itinerant newcomers, sauntering and arrogant in their demands for accommodation: the more desperate begging their way from door to door for food, surrounded, as always, by half-starved children.

Lodging houses opened and flourished as the homeless swarmed in from the ports of Swansea, Cardiff and Newport. Eating their way south like an army of locusts came the Irish, fleeing from the famines of a country ravaged by English rule. The speculators, always the first when misery is abroad, cornered them and, housed them in temporary shelter and waterless cottages; homes which, even in my time in the valley, were beginning to decay until eventually swept away by the tide of progress.

The streets of the towns were full of beggars: wealth and privilege going hand in hand with hunger and desolation, the domestic Welsh forced out of decency to open their doors to the homeless. A working man's wife was fortunate if she cooked for less than two lodgers. The night-shift system in iron, coal and tinplate works ensured that the mattresses of such cottages never grew cold: as one got out of a bed, another got into it.

Minor rioting occurred, for most workers were customers of the Tommy Shop (Truck) by compulsion.

Having to wait nine weeks for his pay, a man in debt to his local shop, where he drew paper tokens in lieu of money (fifteen per cent for cash), could find himself overdrawn, for the shops sold alcohol as well as groceries.

In my time four such company shops existed, owned by various employers: ours being at the top of Brick Row and run by our Llwydarth Tinplate Works.

On pay nights hordes of shawled, anxious women would wait outside the Works to get their hands on the house-keeping money before their menfolk got to the ale-houses, and under the influence of the likes of Cushy Cuddlecome. Some men actually sold their groceries to larger families at a cut price to obtain more ready cash for their ale.

One could tell these drunks, said Old Bid, by their women who queued outside the Truck Shop, shivering in the winter cold.

It was recorded in Merthyr in my father's time that an ironworker who still owed money after cashing his Truck tokens drowned himself in a local pond rather than go home empty-handed: the pond, noted for suicides, had the notorious name of "Standing Room Only".

Maesteg, let me say, was no better or worse off than most of Gwent's Top Towns when it came to such misery. And the cause of this was basically Truck, in which Mr Grey, my father's partner, played a leading role.

In retrospect, men like David Grey and my father were looked upon as benefactors, because they provided employment; "and I suppose there's something in that," said Davie. "Oh aye?" I replied. "I don't agree. To my mind they should be indicted as heartless people whose graphs are tuned to the gods of profit."

If the mortality rate in Maesteg never reached the extent of that suffered by the people of Merthyr and Dowlais, that was because our town had learned through their mistakes . . . that endemic diseases manufactured coffins, and that this was caused by putrescence, poverty and the condition of the workforce; these problems were endemic despite the frantic efforts of the people to keep themselves clean.

Walk down our streets and see the little lace curtains, the china dogs who poodle-sniffed the wind: see the snow-white doorsteps where the wives scrubbed their little circles of purity into an uncaring world: see the washed faces of the children, even if their clothes were ragged and patched, the Welsh in their Sunday best going off to church or chapel, and don't talk to me about slipping standards. The only standards that slipped in my town were the standards of decency on the part of employers.

It is said that every generation produces its heroes, but mine were heroines – the average housewife in Maesteg and the surrounding towns of the valley who fought to keep herself and her family within bounds of respectability in the face of an exploitation the like of which had never been seen before in Wales; and one which I pray my country will never see again.

"What about this house?" said Davie. "Last one before going to tea?" And he paused, bending to stroke the face of a passing child; she, aged six, stared up at him. "And where are you off to, pray?" And she replied:

"I'm off home to see if there's any tea, Mr Grey," and dimpled a smile at the pair of us.

"*Jawch*," whispered Davie after she had gone. "We can't win!"

Chapter 21

I see that I wrote in my diary that spring:

2nd April, 1874. Cefn-Ydfa House, Maesteg, Nr. Bridgend.
Davie and I have been given a free hand to criticise; this
we have done avidly, from impoverished wages to Truck
exploitation, but with little effect; everybody we approach
appears so tired; senility being the last refuge of the old.

It is all sanctimonious hypocrisy, and I am ashamed that
my father is a party to it. Where have gone the ideals
he cherished in his fight with the Chartist Rebellion in
Gwent? Some of his comrades are still in prison for
their part in it, but he is free to perpetuate the social
injustices.

Davie is equally critical of his own father, saying that
years of employing others has turned the pair of them into
money-bags, and he quoted,"A financier is to a financier
what a tiger is to a tiger; both have claws, and prey upon
the weak."

I met Dada in the hall when I got back to the house, and
he asked, "What's wrong with you? You've a face as long
as tomorrow!"

"Forget it," I snapped, and went to pass but he gripped
my arm and swung me to face him. "Oh no, Tom, it's not
as easy as that. What's wrong?"

"What's right, you mean!"

His eyes assessed my mood. "Am I in this?"

"Up to the neck."

"Then let it be said without dancing pumps and moods!"

I took a deep breath. "Davie and I have been round the

162

houses. God, I didn't realise! We sit here in luxury and the people who earn it are practically dying under our noses."

"Oh dear me, we are having a rush of conscience, aren't we!"

"Don't trifle with me, I mean it!"

"And so do I! How many years have you been in this place? Since, in your language, you were knee-high to a grasshopper, eh? In all that time you've heard the accident bells dozens of times, but not seen the mutilations, because I kept you free of them. Now you've seen it you have the bloody audacity to lecture me on the rights and wrongs!"

I waited until he cooled. "It's wrong, Pa. I . . . I didn't really know of it until now, but it's *wrong* . . . !"

"Don't you think I know that? Jesus! Standards that have been accepted for years – even by compassionate men like David Grey – can't be changed overnight by people like us coming in on a few diamonds and an overdraft!"

"You were sharp enough up in Gwent, weren't you?" I faced his eyes. "Why was it so necessary to change things there, but not here? You've got the same mutilations – the nearest hospital is miles away in Cardiff – the same cholera and stinking conditions of housing – the same child labour."

"It takes time, Tom," he said wearily.

"Aye, when you do nothing about it!"

He said, struggling for composure, "In '39 we followed John Frost into rebellion, and where did it land us? A few on gibbets, in prison or aboard the transportation hulks like me. A lot of good people gave their lives, for what?"

I said bitterly, "So what do we do about it now? Sit on our backsides?"

Strangely, this appeared to quieten his anger, for he said sadly, "Wales, all the time she is neighbour to England, is a poem written in blood; comradeship is based on fear, not love of one's contemporaries. Unionism is the true answer, but even unity is subject to private and public exploitation. True socialism is our only hope."

"Great words, but they get us no further. Either we accept the state of things here or we set out our stall and fight. All my life you've taught me to think for myself; now you can't blame me for doing it!"

He smiled at me. "So when's the blood-bath?"

"That isn't worthy of you!"

"Maybe not, but that's the size of it! Or do you propose to teach these bloody hooligans to become public benefactors overnight? I've said this before, and I'll say it again, it takes money, and money they will not give. You can insult their wives and rape their daughters. Only by paying them can you change them . . . profit!

"So, what's the alternative?" he continued. "Go into rebellion against a state that is practised in the business of putting down rebellions? They'd bring back the stake before shifting the King's arse two inches off his throne. For the Throne and Church are there to keep us in thrall, the aristocracy in its stolen lands, the bishops in palaces, royalty in finery and its stockbrokers safe in the cities."

He paused, breathing heavily.

"And so it has been in this country since the start of Time, and in this particular town since the Industrial Revolution!"

For the first time I realised that my father was becoming old. Until now it seemed impossible that his shoulders could stoop, his throat sag above the fine cut of his stock, his eyes take on weariness.

Turning away heavily, he added, "Don't pester me with your youth, Tom. I've tried to raise you decently and find joy in knowing that the effort was not entirely wasted." And here he held up his hands, showing upon his wrists the scars of the manacles.

Softly, he added, "I had hoped not to lean on this, but knew that one day I might come to it. The years were not gentle, the oppression too long; I've watched men die for the hopes that stir you now, and vainly, believe me.

"For God's sake, accept what Fate offers you and try, as I do from day to day, to change things for the better, but *slowly*, in the name of God. Or you will land as I did, unaccepted by society."

*   *   *

I left him and walked out into the night, thinking that life was a farce; a vile theatre over whose stage the actors of our conscience stride, leaving behind the husk of good intentions.

As Davie said later, "Us? We're only a pair of young dogs learning new tricks; like my old man says, we're wasting our time – it has all happened before."

On the way to town I met Dai Dando; three sheets in the wind was he and contemplating the moon, but I wasn't in the mood for his inebriated talk and walked on, leaving him to it. God help him when he gets home to Biddy, I thought.

Talking of Dai Dando brings me back to the Maid, the restless ghost of another generation.

The knowledge that Dai was a personal friend of Cushy Cuddlecome at the Rose and Crown didn't put much reliance upon his claim to have had dealings with Ann Thomas; for most Saturdays, like tonight, he would escape from Old Bid and plait his knees on the way home with quarts aboard.

On one of these nights in passing Corn Hwch, the round-house lodge at the bottom of our lane, he claimed he was confronted by Ann's ghost, weeping its eyes out.

Naturally, Dai was a little disturbed, especially when the ghost put its hand on his arm and asked him if he'd seen Wil Hopcyn lately; it caused Dai to take off at a gallop back to Old Bid, who usually broke things over his head when he came home inebriated.

Therefore, I didn't put much faith in his story until next day when I met Mr and Mrs Joby ap Rhys, the caretakers of our local Bethania whose belief in hell-fire was part of their accepted faith.

They, it appeared, had been similarly accosted by the Maid with the same question at the same place, and had also taken to their heels.

Even this evidence didn't really convince me, until I casually mentioned it to my father at next morning's breakfast table.

"Undoubtedly true," said he, munching toast, while Dozie Annie's lace cap literally stood on end beside me. "Last week, returning from a meeting of Cymanfa Morgannwg on foot, she accosted me also."

"Good God, what did she say?"

Dada munched on, saying, "She asked me if I'd seen anything of Wil Hopcyn lately, and I replied that to my knowledge there were at least three Wil Hopcyns living in the valley, and which one did she mean? The reply was immediate:

" 'The one who lives near Llangynwyd Church, and who is working in Bristol.'

" 'I see. And where do you reside, may I ask?' I said and spoke in Welsh, the old language, for greater clarity.

" 'In the mansion of Cefn-Ydfa I live,' came the reply. 'It is necessary that he returns quickly from Bristol, sir, for I am about to die, and my soul calls to him.' "

I stared at my father, aware that Dozie had staggered away to the safety of the kitchen, and asked, "You had no drink?"

"It was Cwmanfa."

"Did you touch her?"

"I did not, but she touched me."

"Anything else?"

"Only that she spoke the old Welsh, the ancient intonation; and her hand on mine, I remember, was cold; as cold as ice that hand, which was to be expected for a woman long dead."

It was incredible.

"You accept her existence?"

"Totally. I have always done so. The existence of the spirit is not some phantasmagoria of the deranged mind, but reality. I did not need her apparition to convince me of Ann Thomas's existence in the house, for she has been with me since entering the place.

"I can give you another such instance – this time an occurrence in Blaenafon in the Eastern Valley – near the house in Shepherds' Square where I was born – are you interested?"

"Who isn't?"

"During a local disturbance, when the military was brought in to quell the rioting, there lived in Barrack Row a Welshman of Blaenau Festiniog, an old retired soldier wounded at Quatre Bras in June 1815 – this date I remember because the old dragoon told it to my father outside his cottage in Blaenafon where he lived alone; always he could be seen in the town walking with the aid of a broom, for he had lost a leg in the battle."

Dozie Annie, now returned to duty, listened with equal intent, practically with her chops on my shoulder.

My father continued. "Now, it happened that a detachment of dragoons who had fought the French for possession of the farmhouses at La Haye Sainte was of the same regiment, ordered into our town to keep the peace."

Dozie and I listened.

"And this mounted detachment – the regiment with which our soldier had fought – came riding past the Rifleman's Arms – fine black horses, mind you, arrogant with their military pride. And the old dragoon came out of his cottage to greet them.

"In the full uniform of his regiment – they who were flung at the French Imperial Guard under Marshal Ney – he stood outside his cottage door, awaiting them. But then came the rioting Welsh with sticks and Irish confetti, trying to stampede the horses, but disdainfully the soldiers rode on, and at their head was a fine sight: a captain of the dragoons with a crested helmet and full breastplate armour.

"I was young at the time but saw it all; the soldiers, the old dragoon standing on his threshold, the mob of ragged, starving Welsh, and by God, I was hungry, too, for the place had been on strike for months . . ." Dada paused and there was no sound but the ticking of our old grandfather clock in the hall.

"Go on," I whispered.

He drew himself up. "The ringleaders of our lot were bawling insults at the dragoons, such as, 'Get back home, you English bastards!' and 'Go and sort out the poor sods back in England, you sons of whores!' and other such niceties, and as they rioted I stood in a sheltered place and watched.

"I saw the old soldier come into the middle of the road. The dragoons rode on, their bridles jingling. The captain drew his sabre and rode at the ready, but the old soldier stood his ground, unmoving on his broom. Then, at the moment when I expected him to be cut down . . . the captain raised his sabre in a military salute, and the old man shouted:

" 'Hold ye fire, lads! For it's the people ag'in the people, and these ain't ironmasters! They're the likes of us just doin't the job! For I seen 'em at Hougoumont wi' my grenadiers – forty-five thousand dead in three days, aye, I see'd 'em fight for Britain, and they was bloody marvellous! So let 'em pass, fellas, let 'em pass!'

"The mob went so quiet that I heard the wind sighing in the heather, and there was no movement in the street: only the flash of the captain's sabre as he sheathed it, and the old soldier's hand as he stood rigidly, raising it in the salute. It was the end of the rioting which had been going on for days."

"What 'appened to the old soldier, sir? Beggin' your pardon, sir . . ." whispered Dozie, her eyes on stalks.

"I was one of the first to find him," said Dada. "Stiff as an old crow, he was, in his bed; he'd been dead for a week; we went in – me and others – and brought him out of his cottage and laid him at the captain's feet."

"But he were standin' in the middle of the road, saluting," protested Dozie, askance.

"That's just what I'm saying – you sort it out."

"Oh, my Gawd!" said she, and left us at speed.

"Which brings me to a point, now she has gone," said Dada. "Soon I will be leaving Cefn-Yfda. Are you listening? – for this is important." Rising, he took his coffee cup and wandered around the room, speaking as if to himself:

"It is needful, Tom, for a man to have a woman in the house, and this is a privilege denied to me for many years. You have no doubt noticed that Jenny's mother and I have been walking out of late?"

I had noticed, and more than walking out, too; lights had been going on and off in the house, and silent assignations made on the landings, all of which I ignored; not my business what the old man got up to.

"I asked you if you'd noticed . . ."

"Of course."

"Since your mother came to Maesteg, she was lost to me; the one woman I loved truly, Welsh Mari Dirion, lies in her grave at Aberdare. Meanwhile Clara Wildflower is a good and quiet woman, and of my class; at heart, you see, I am still an ironworker, and give short fuses to boardroom directorships and financial connivings . . ."

"I am glad."

"You approve?"

"Of course!" I gripped his hand.

"But she is a Romany, with all her customs and superstitions, and marriage in a chapel is not for her – little more, perhaps, than jumping over a broom before witnesses," and we laughed quietly together. "Therefore we have agreed to dispense with formality and sail off together for a month or so, to get the lie of the land, so to speak."

"I am delighted."

"This Afghanistan affair and Karendeesh; it appears – although I have heard nothing of her – that your mother's presence in Kabul suffices their nation, and I hope they will leave you alone to continue your life here. Young Jenny is safely at school in the west, and will be still there upon our return in a couple of months. Dai, Biddy and the girls will keep the house and feed and water you until then."

"Where will you and Clara be going?"

"Nothing arranged to date – generally a tour of Europe. When we return I am setting up a tinplate company of my own, for I'm sick of playing second fiddle to non-technicians who are more interested in stockbrokers' profits than the real business of tin-making, so much of which lies in technical research. The secrets of can manufacture should not be entirely dependent upon now outdated Russian processes, and I have new ideas."

"That's what Davie and I say – count us in!"

"I am talking about you in partnership, not Davie: Mr Grey is a good man, and I am not coming between father and son."

I left for work then, not knowing that I had just had my last conversation with my father.

Chapter 22

Jen's half terms had come and gone with cold regularity, but with no homecoming. When I raised with Dada the loneliness she must have been enduring, he had referred me to her mother: she must be the judge of it, said he.

More strangely, Jenny never replied to my letters inquiring about her absence from Cefn-Yfda, and in the end I gave up trying to communicate with her. After all, I told myself, our affection for one another scarcely extended beyond the role of good friends, and when one is twenty and bursting with vitality, the bird in the hand is more important than one on the perch of a public school in Devon.

Nevertheless, the attitude of Jen's mother angered me, and I determined to find a reason for it.

My father's increasing interest in Clara Wildflower expressed itself by closing and locking her caravan and moving her into Number Twelve Gwenllian Terrace (later changed to Gwendoline Terrace), recently built (together with Brick Row and Olivia Terrace) for occupation by employees of the Llwydarth company. I recall a small altercation over this – David Grey persisting that these houses, two-up-and-two-down, were for his employees only; thus small rifts were appearing between the two directors.

My father's practice of stripping off his suit and, naked to the waist in the annealing shed, playing the role of labourer might have endeared him to the workforce, but not to his fellow directors; this widened the rift further.

Certainly, it was time for the Mortymers to withdraw from a partnership which had sensitive issues, and when news came of the romance between Dada and a Romany living in a caravan, the pot of discontent came suddenly to the boil.

"You're aware that they no longer approve of us?" I asked him.

Dada was in his best mood that day, spotlessly attired in a morning coat, with a buttonhole in his lapel big enough to bury him.

He waited for Dai to bring the mare and trap up to the house entrance.

"Up to them," said he aggressively. "If they don't approve of Clara, to hell with the lot of them."

"Davie reckons they might soon ask you to resign."

The morning was bright with sun-shafts through the woods of Cefn-Ydfa, with the old currant bun doing its best to kick spring into full-blooded summer, but with just enough of a late April breeze to cool old Dai's dew-drop.

On the tack was Dai, sullen and down in the mouth, Old Bid having recently taken a firm line in respect of the Rose and Crown and his ambitions in Peg Cuddle's direction, which surprised me: indeed, it surprised me greatly, for it strikes me that a lady of Old Bid's proportions ought to be enough for any chap, even an ex-pugilist as tough as Dai Dando.

Kitchen talk had it that Biddy sometimes enforced her argument with a copper-stick, and I knew the truth of it when Dai, bowing low to my father as he boarded the trap, let his collier's cap fall off; there on his bald pate was a lump as big as a duck's egg, and sparking.

"Where to, Maister?" he asked, closing the trap door.

"To town," said Dada. "For I am about to arrange a continental holiday for two with no expense spared, Dai. And do not tell me that romance is dead in late middle age, for I know otherwise – look well upon me," and he struck a pose. Never had I seen him behave in such a manner.

"Spring is in the air, Dai, and this old fool's fancy lightly turns to thoughts of love!" And he kissed the air with pinched fingers like a French Lothario.

172

"Bloody hell, Maister," said Dai, more sullen than ever. "Mind ye don't end up wi' a boiling joint, like me."

Waving Dada off, and reinforced by his mood of youthful gaiety, I then bathed, put on my Sunday suit and set forth on foot for Number Twelve Gwenllian Terrace and Jen's mother; being keen to get to the bottom of her determination to lock up her daughter when it came to the young randy living in Cefn-Ydfa.

A strange woman this; make no bones about it. Steeped in Romany lore and custom, hers was a character difficult to engage in intimate conversation.

Bang, bang on her door and I am there, cap in hand, my quiff well brushed up, shaved close and powdered.

" 'Morning, Mrs Wildflower!"

She was wearing a faded, multi-coloured sort of shift that reached from her throat to her bare feet, and I remembered my mother in all her gorgeous silks and satins and the upturned slippers of scarlet brocade: she the princess, this the witch; give this one a broom, I thought, and she'd have been up and around the chimneys. It was impossible at that moment to understand my father's delight in her.

"Remember me?" I asked, for she appeared doubtful.

Suddenly her eyes, becoming alive, danced in her high-boned cheeks, and her face widened into a welcoming smile; unaccountably she became beautiful.

"Why, yes! Of course! 'Tis the young master!"

"Not 'young master' – Tom, remember?"

"Ay ay, sir, dunna you wait there none, come inside!" and she opened the door wider and pulled me in, for I too had noticed curtains moving over windows and who's that fancy fella a'knockin' on Widow Wildflower's door, for God's sake?

The Welsh aren't nosey, but like to know what's going on.

In with me quick before she changed her mind.

Man's female requirements I fail to understand.

173

Take Dai Dando, for instance; engulfed in Old Bid's attractions, he had temporarily forsaken them for Peg Cuddle's, and though both were beef to the heels, it was Biddy who possessed the Irish charm.

In my mother lay all the magnetism of the Orient, yet this Romany had changed Dada overnight into a fumbling adolescent.

Yet, the longer I sat before this woman's dark, impenetrable smile, the better I understood her spell over my father, for her eyes were hypnotic.

I began gently by saying, "I have written many times to Jenny but have had not one reply; it is not like her to ignore my letters, and I am wondering why."

The reply was immediate, "She don't reply, Tom Mortymer, because I say her nay. She be Romany; our childer don't argue."

"Do you dislike me?"

"Ach no, sir. You're the spit an' wisdoms o' your feyther, an' I think the world o' him." She warmed to me.

"Then why interfere?"

Her eyes became dreamily distant.

"You and my Jen ain't in the same world, really speakin', Tom. The owl in the night he hoots and screams, but you and she hear it different; words come on the wind, but you don't read 'em, while my Jen knows 'em like the poetry of the woods, like when the trees chatter together about the last beautiful summer. For you it is only the wind, but for our Jen it's forest-talk. When the vixen shouts in the night, Tom Mortymer, you call it for a fox, but for Romanies it's a cry from God about the cruelty of men. You understand me?"

"No, missus."

"The same as men and women; the Big Man in the sky, He picks them up and throws 'em apart, then kisses their faces and stitches 'em back together, same as your pa and me. You know about witches?"

"Not a lot."

"Our Jen do, for she met one once, and she told her as how one fell in love with a wizard, each promising the other

174

to change 'em into somethin' beautiful; but who betrayed the other, the witch or the wizard?"

"Don't know, Mrs Wildflower."

"Our Jen do, for she found a witch's cloak beneath an oak and her petticoat tangled in its branches . . ."

I said, "Once she told me about magic nutmeg, but otherwise didn't talk a lot about witches and wizards."

The woman shook her head sadly. "But you have to, see? – you got to know the Romany lore – like, throwing frog-spawn about for luck in loving, and cutting each wrist for the mingling of blood." She smiled. "When's your Christmas, Tom Mortymer?"

"Twenty-fifth of December."

"Ours ain't, son – we do the Gorgio custom – January the sixth, and ye can keep your tough old turkey, for we got roast suckling pig if you're poor, and a great fat sow if you're rich; and our Boxing Day comes on January the seventh.

"Do ye know about scissors and shears on Wednesdays and Fridays? Ye don't, son? So, I'll tell ye, for you'd shock our Jen rigid if you used 'em then – ye could cut the girl down in the prime of her life, and she wouldn'a go much on that. Do ye think peacocks are beautiful . . . ?"

"Well . . ."

"Of course ye do, like most disbelievers, but Jen knows that it was the only one of Nature's flocks that agreed to guide Old Nick to Paradise, where he could do most damage. And I could go on and on and on, Tom Mortymer, givin' ye a thousand reasons why kisses from your mouth could lead her soul into Hell.

"I'm tellin' you now and once and for all, my girl anna for you."

My voice rose in protest. "Yes, but what about my father and you. Do you love him?"

Her dark eyes softened. "With the blood of my heart!"

"And he loves you, he says, and plans to marry you and bring you to Cefn-Ydfa. Don't do as I do, but do as I say, eh? I've heard that one before!"

She sat before me smiling, but not with her eyes, and said:

"Listen, for you ain't a kid no more, you're grown, and know of such things. When your father takes me to his bed he lies wi' a stony womb, and no fruit will come from it. But if you take our Jen and divide her body in marriage, you'll loosen her seed and she'll bring forth childer, and that will be the curse of it. Cursed, cursed will be your house, not by me, but by Romany law." She paused, breathing heavily. "And three times cursed will be the childer."

We stared at each other. I had no words for her.

Later, Clara made tea, fed me oatmeal cakes and honey from the woods around Gwenllian, and the neighbours paused in their gossiping outside her window and looked past the snow-white curtains and had us over, as neighbours do; and look what that Romany piece is up to – she's got the son of the gaffer in there ye know! But I did not care.

I didn't care, for the thought was in me that by talk and sweetness I could win her over, so that one day my Romany girl might come to me: then we would lie together in the Big Pasture and listen to the bells ringing in the valley. So I said, to placate her motherly mood:

"Tell me about yourself, Clara – may I call you that?"

Her eyes became wistful. "I was born by a brook somewhere up north and danced before I was four years old around Romany fires.

"And when I become a woman at thirteen, my pa, who was a peg-tinker, read my thumb, for the telling of the thumb-palm proves the existence of God. Babies know this, which is why they close it in their fingers to keep it safe," and she held out a hand to me. "Little thumbs tell of poetry and intellect; big thumbs do speak of strength of body and power."

She paused, smiling at nothing. "So, when I were sixteen I knew inside me that I was made for a man and went in search of one, and found 'im, but he weren't a Romany: he were a big strappin' lad workin' down Ogmore Colliery, and me pa heard about his Irish shenanigans – the lad liked his pint and came from County Cork – and Pa beat the ass's reins off me till I was black and blue.

"But me thumb was determined, see, so still I courted this lad strong, and me pa warned me – like I be warnin' you – that if I married outta the tribe I'd be cursed for everlasting, which I was. It were a heavy curse on me soul, Tom Mortymer, for after me fella came home from the war in the Crimea, his back was broke in a coal-fall down Ogmore pit; an' they brought 'im home on a litter, and put him on the bed and left me to it."

She took my cup, poured me more tea, and continued:

"Couldn't go back to the tribe for Pa wouldn't 'ave us; couldn't afford the rent, so the landlord kicked us out in the middle of January. And there I was roamin' the snowy lanes and pullin' me fella behind me on a trolley his mates 'ad knocked up for us. Then I come to child, didn't I?"

She raised her dark eyes to mine, saying softly, "Ay ay, and you're like the rest of 'em. How come this Romany girl is full an' her man's wi' a broken back? they asked. So I told 'em what I tell you now – don't ask me, ask God."

Suddenly she began to cry and the tears flooded and splashed down her shift and she made a fist of one hand and pressed it against her mouth. I wanted to hold her, but thought it wrong to impose upon her grief; so I just sat there until she dried up, sniffing and wiping, as women do.

"And then?" I asked quietly.

"Then the tribe built us our caravan, and in it I raised our Jen, and one day your feyther met us on the road and give us a pike he'd caught – pike for gipsy folk, said he, they'll tell ye what to do wi' salmon – then told us I could bring the van on to his land, and here I be, comin' and goin' ever since."

"When . . . when did your husband die?" I asked.

"Soon after that bitch Betsy Ramrod got him liquifyin' his gullet down in her Black Boar tavern, for when the ale was in him his little fires were quenched; his weren't much of a life, was it?" She smiled nostalgically. "But, mind you, when he were on his two legs an' fighting fit, no woman ever had such a man . . . !"

On the doorstep she said, "Meanwhile, you keep away from our Jen, for she's of the tribe we'll one day go back to. And as for you, Tom Mortymer – I don't know about you.

You're a tinplate worker now, next you'll be dressed up for a Turkish harem, or somethin', and going off to Afghanistan or some such place. So you anna lyin' in marriage with my Romany girl, though you be your father's son!"

I mooched off back to Cefn-Ydfa, wondering if Jen was lost to me.

But she wasn't, for I don't give up as easily as that.

It's only a question of time.

Romany magic, nutmeg, fortune-telling thumbs and gipsy's warnings, eh?

She's my woman, take it from me.

Chapter 23

I have no proof of the accusation I make here, but I am
certain that my father and Clara, his prospective wife, would
be alive today had I realised the hidden threat in the message
we next received from Afghanistan.

This letter from Karendeesh arrived at Cefn-Ydfa three
days after they had left by train from Bridgend en route for
Southampton, there to begin a tour of the continent.

With my father's authority to open all mail, I read the
letter after noting that, though emanating from Kabul, the
envelope had been franked as posted in Swansea; proof that
my father's movements were being locally observed.

The Palace of Barakzai
Kabul, Afghanistan.

Beloved Friend,
Greetings to you! Affectionate greetings from the city of
Kabul, where reigns His Royal Highness King Shir 'Ali
Khan who rules his subjects with felicity and compassion.
This message comes to you not from the King, however,
but from his Chief Vizier, one who represents ministers
of the Council of our Royal Dynasty. Under their seal I
am commanded to address you as follows:

Since the international discord of 1843 and the occupation by our beloved Dost Mohammed of the throne of
Kabul for two decades, peace has brought tranquillity to
our two nations: diplomatic relations are happily restored
between Afghanistan and Britain; our amir has now cast
his shoe from Kandahar to the northern Khanates; our
country lives in international contentment.

But, with the death of our beloved Dost (and may his

soul dwell in the tents of Allah), internecine war has plagued the Durrani dynasty: Shir 'Ali ruled in 1863, and was deposed three years later by elder brothers; he regained the throne in 1868, and now again rules in Kabul. But internal strife still rages, and remembering British defection historically (and in some measure we hold Britain responsible), the King has therefore refused audience to your deputations and seeks assistance from a Russian mission. It is necessary that you be appraised of this urgent situation before civil war encompasses our people, and many suffer for lack of wisdom in one.

Our Princess Durrani, granddaughter of our lamented Dost, waits in Kabul to be Regent to her son, the noble Suresh: in joy and expectation our ministers await his arrival to claim the throne of Kabul: even our beloved King Shir 'Ali accepts the need of a royal line undefiled by contest and political expectation.

That our young monarch be returned to us for obedience to Allah and the House of Barakzai is the earnest prayer of your loyal friend and servant,

April 8th 1875.   Karendeesh. Chief Vizier.

The letter was trembling in my hand; at that moment the girl Angharad, our new scullery maid, entered; she was about sixteen, freckled and possessed of a disturbing ability to appear when she was least wanted; I waved her away, for now was such a time.

I felt frustrated, unequal to the responsibility suddenly thrust upon me, and had a flash vision of Dada in one of his laughing moods, gaily talking with Clara of some inconsequential happening while I held the weight of a country upon my shoulders. It was monstrous self-pity, but the mood persisted, and when Dozie Annie put her head around the door, lace cap awry as usual, I was curt.

"Yes?"

"Angie do say as how ye waved her off, sir . . ."

I sighed. "For God's sake! Her name is Angharad. It is a beautiful name, don't shorten it."

"The packman is still waitin', mind."

"What packman?"

"The one on the terrace, sir, see?" and she pointed at the study window.

A packman traveller was sitting on his battered suitcase at the edge of the terrace lawn; they were a proliferating nuisance in Wales these days, their English poor, their goods valueless; and seemed to regulate their appearances when you could least afford the time.

I said, "Tell him to make himself scarce, it's a busy morning."

"Told 'im to go, sir, but he don't."

"Then get Dai after him. Christ!" I added, turning to the creak of a board in the hall. Then the packman appeared in the study doorway.

"Good morning, sir." He bowed gracefully.

"Good morning! Will you tell me who invited you into my house?"

"Very many marvellous Indian goods to offer you, sir," and he bowed again, profusely.

In his silk coat and narrow trews he would have been insignificant, had it not been for the beauty of his voice; this came not from his throat, it seemed, but his soul.

"Things from India do not appeal to me," I answered. "I've had enough of that place to last me a lifetime."

"But truly beautiful, sir – perfumes and incense! The East will return to you. Afghanistan, for instance?"

It stilled me.

"I'll ring if I need you, Annie," I said, and the stranger, waiting until she had gone, opened a suitcase and spread its contents upon the carpet before me. I said, "Stop this bloody nonsense and tell me why you are here!"

For reply he nodded at the open letter on the table beside me, then said, "It appears, sir, that you have received our correspondence?"

"This letter is for my father," I said, putting it away. "Unfortunately, it has missed him; three days ago he left for a continental holiday."

181

"With his wife to be?" He smiled, his white teeth appearing in his dark, aquiline face; his movements as he rose from the floor had the agility of a cobra.

"You knew of her?"

He nodded, sitting down without invitation, saying, "Of course. From the cradle to the grave, we know all about the Mortymers, sir! That letter you received, it was intentionally late because it is for you, though addressed to your father."

"Who are you, for God's sake?" but this he ignored, saying:

"It is for your eyes because you are infinitely more concerned with its contents; it is you our country wants, not your father."

I sat down facing him. "To return to Afghanistan of course!" I was cynical.

"To the country of your birth, sir. And here I must apologise to you. For the benefit of the servants you must treat me reasonably. Later, for the benefit of the Afghan people, I will lie with one hand beneath your shoe, as befits a chuprassey in the presence of his king."

"This is Wales, so stop this nonsense. Tell me why you're here, or get out. What's your name, for a start?"

"My full name would be unpronounceable in your tongue; in the Agency I am known as Ransit."

"Agency?"

"We are a highly professional and organised body, Mr Mortymer."

"No doubt."

The Afghan secret service . . .

I got up and walked around him, already bored with his attempts to impress me.

Such as he, I had heard, were ten a penny in the alleys of the Afghan cities, where you could get a throat cut for the price of a rupee, or arrange the demise of a relative with one of their brain-thudders; they roamed at will, maiming or murdering on a whim. And more, said my father, they had to be watched abroad, for behind the smiles and banal politeness lay finely tuned brains ready to betray or execute the orders of their masters; and the man before me was doubtless one of these agents: when a boy's face shines, look behind his ears, I thought.

"What do you want of me?" I asked, to gain time.

"To return with me to Kabul. Now, immediately."

"For what reason?"

"Is it not made quite clear in the letter?"

"And if I refuse?"

"Then the issue is no longer simple; who knows what complications could flow from such disobedience? The command – it is from our Ministers of State this time, and they can be pitiless. The time for talking is over, sir, and nothing can prevent it. Your father, he is well?"

"He was when he left here." I met the man's eyes; his perpetual smile was wider, and he moved now with the air of one who considered the discussion over and was not to be inconvenienced by delay. He said:

"Let us hope that he remains so. Your young friend, the son of the man who bought your home in Carmarthenshire, was not so fortunate. His death was a mistake and I apologise in the name of the Vizier Karendeesh, who incidentally sends you his personal regards – ah yes, also the love and felicitations of your beautiful mother. You will now make ready to leave?"

"To come with you immediately is not possible, Mr Ransit," I replied. "With my father abroad I am now handling his affairs. Tell the Viziers that I have read their letter; tell Karendeesh that I am aware of my responsibility in this matter. I will take my place in the Court of Barakzai when my father returns safely home."

"And that will be . . . ?" Rummaging in a pocket he brought out a diary and consulted dates. "Let me see . . . he is due back at Southampton about eight weeks from now – their holiday in Denmark and Holland ends on the 24th, and they intend to rest for a week in Paris before their tour to Spain, which ends in Granada on June the 30th: this allows them, as planned, a full week to travel by coach to Oporto in Portugal." He snapped the diary shut. "Yes, it is a leisurely timetable, but they could easily meet their dates back to Wales on the 7th of July, unless I am mistaken."

Picking up his suitcase he went to the hall door, adding: "Meanwhile, you will reply to our letter assuring the Court that it is your intention to return to Kabul the moment you are able?"

"And if I do not?" I was suddenly infuriated by his self-assurance.

Opening the door, he said, "To say the least of it, Mr Mortymer, the outcome would not be to your liking," and he bowed again. "Good day to you. May Allah deliver you out of the hands of your enemies, and grant you tranquillity."

I stood watching while he hauled his suitcase down the drive to Maesteg station, and I was sickened by the danger to my father.

Kabul was now acting with political determination, for there was about this man the chaotic stamp of death.

Chapter 24

Now I waited pent with apprehension for a letter from Dada; working emptily in the firm's office; automatically checking weighbridge vouchers and orders for our new ternplate, which were arriving now from all parts of the world. Despite Davie's attempts to temper my worries with carefully chosen phrases, I knew, unaccountably, that my father was already lost to me.

The days dragged by into a week and from weeks into a month, and then a postcard arrived from Berne in Switzerland; it was to the point and so typical of Dada:

"This is the life! Strawberries and cream beside a lake. We roam the mountain foothills by day; by night we dine in wayside restaurants under the stars. At this rate of delinquency we will never come home!"

It was his last message to me.

I think I guessed the outcome of his fatal honeymoon with Clara; nothing diluted my sense of impending disaster. This crystallised into fact on the afternoon a trap stopped outside the entrance of the house, and Davie got out, accompanied by a journalist employed by the local branch of *The Cambrian* newspaper.

It was the expression upon Davie's face. He said, his eyes filled with tears: "Bad news, Tom. The . . . the worst possible. Your pa and Clara, on the day after they married in Berne, have been drowned in a ferry accident."

It was out. Sweat sprang to his face and he wiped it into his hair.

"For God's sake, man," I said. "How?"

The journalist, as diminutive as an Irish leprechaun, touched his cap, saying apologetically, "Beggin' your pardon, sir, it was a submarine cable telegram direct from Lausanne. Yesterday morning the passenger ferry from Montreux to Geneva sank with all hands; among the eighteen passengers drowned was Mr Iestyn Mortymer and his wife, Clara; the address sent by the Swiss police is Cefn-Ydfa."

I raised my face. "No possible hope of a mistake?"

He did not reply.

"Sorry, Tom," said Davie.

And that is all there was to it. The official confirmation of their deaths by drowning came direct from the Swiss Service within a week.

Old Bid wept and would not be comforted; Dai, with Dozie Annie clinging to him, stared at me with tear-filled eyes.

As for me, I wandered, lost, possessed by the stony emptiness that follows the loss of a beloved.

No need to tell of grief; it needs no elaboration.

My father was lost to me, and that was an end to it.

And by going to Kabul I could have saved them both.

Chapter 25

Summer came again to the Llynfi Valley in all her sumptuous drowse, and the lanes were all over decorated with
piss-a-beds and meadow buttercups.

With the dying of our bluebells in the woods of Cefn-Ydfa,
out came the foxgloves with their stamens looking out
for bumble-bees; sea pinks got lost, came too far south,
then relented and cast their seeds for later blooms of
purplish-blue; and the oxlip bowed her head in case she
saw a drunkard. Wild garlic perfumed the lane down to our
lodge; the sun was made sweet by lords and ladies whom
some call cuckoo-pint.

Dear God, give me Wales when it comes to beauty!

Every summer the Great Painter arrives down these parts
with His paints and brushes, and only when He's done Wales
does He give a thought to other parts, such as Hampshire and
Kent, which they say is the Garden of England. Aye? Well,
we've got a garden that stretches from Bangor to Swansea,
and I cannot think what the place was like before Man got his
dirty hands upon it. And though personally I like the English,
I wish to God they'd stayed in their own back yard instead of
ripping up ours.

Take our valley, for instance: time was in the Beginning
when the Painter first breathed upon it, it was a land of
heart's desire; a sylvan landscape where the air was sweet
and clean, and now look at it.

In our valley alone we've got a flannel mill, four ironworks
and God knows how many pits and drifts, to say nothing of
horse-drawn and engine-shunted tram-roads wriggling like a

187

clutch of snakes over the land; with fire-shot brick chimneys belching sulphurous fumes over a country that once was of incomparable beauty.

And to cope with this lot we've got foreign labour thronging in, from Irish to North Country boogers, Philadelphian Americans and Pittsburgh specialists sent by the likes of Frick and Carnegie; and they were two bright sparks in the industrial firmament if ever – old Clay Frick and Andy; the latter blessing his Maker, and both squeezing the lifeblood out of their workers at fifty cents an hour.

The new societies like the Ivorites, who came to us from Wrexham twenty years ago, were supposed to put paid to the exploitation of the masses; this particular Order having derived its name from a chap called Ifor the Generous, with Unity, Love and Truth as the avowed principles of the movement. But a lot of this must have got lost on the way down south, for the effect on the grasping nature of our employers was minimal.

The Benefit Clubs springing up left and right in our valley appear mainly directed towards sumptuous dinners for members and afternoon tea for their wives; even ten years ago we had over twenty such societies activating in Maesteg, but to what main purpose I never really discovered.

When it came to welfare for the workers my father had ambitions in that direction, and I think he might have improved things given a free hand. Therefore, I had made up my mind that if ever I rose to the dizzy height of a captain of industry, I would base my ethics upon those of the saint, Robert Owen; he who turned his cotton mills into a philanthropic trust, advocated the Factory Acts and established social reform. His death in '58 was a personal sadness to my father, who intended to model the new tin factory he had in mind upon Owenite principles.

Communistic principles? I once heard David Grey ask him. Aye, replied Dada, the principles of Jesus, unless they are betrayed by the likes of us, which is likely.

Yes, I thought – highly likely.

But that was all for the future, and at the time I had other things in mind.

In love, me. In love with Jenny Wildflower, presently at school in Devon; but soon, God willing, to be under the same roof as me in Cefn-Ydfa.

My father was dead, as was Jen's mother. Apart from the servants and Davie, I had nobody else in the world to care about, except Jenny. So I sat down and wrote her a letter, first telling her of her loss, and asking her to come to Cefn-Ydfa; a safer place with Afghans mooching around than a school in Devon.

Came the great day when she arrived . . . But not because of my letter, for she didn't receive it. She wrote to me.

I took the mare and trap down to Bridgend station to meet the two-thirty afternoon train from Swansea: poshed up, bowlered and with soap behind the ears, I pushed a path through the summer holiday crowds looking for a wide-brimmed straw hat, and saw it coming in a flourish of summer skirts and lace what-nots. The next moment she was in my arms.

Where does the girl go when she turns into a woman?

She shamed every female there, and I kissed and kissed her again and her straw hat fell off and her hair came down, and she protested in happy tears, as women do when they meet a lover.

The only difficulty here was that, knowing somebody was at my elbow, I turned to find Davie there as well; polished up and bowlered was he also, looking suntanned and even more expectant than me.

"Jenny!" he shouted, easing me out of it.

"Davie!" cried she. "Oh, how lovely to see you again!" And she got him in a clinch that would have been the envy of Dai Dando.

Very strange happenings with a woman you thought you'd got sewn up to be cut and carried, and to my utter

189

astonishment he hooked his arm through hers, and was off with her while a porter followed with her luggage. I stood watching while, in a flurry of laughter and petticoats, they jumped into a station trap and were away with friendly shouts and waves, leaving me in ruins.

I had earlier suggested to Biddy that she should prepare the guest room for a very special visitor.

"Oh no, young maister," Biddy admonished me with a wagging finger, "that ain't right and possible, is it? Wi' your feyther in a watery grave in foreign parts, it were right for a virgin lady to go off with Davie to his family; what would the neighbours say?"

"To hell with the neighbours – *you* could be her chaperone."

But clearly she had more suspicions than teeth.

"And that don't sound so healthy to me, neither!"

God Almighty!

Six foot two in socks, fourteen stone, all done up for the bridal chamber, and your best friend scarpers off with the bride.

Later, Jenny said, "So what did you expect me to do? I was in that school for years and years; my mother refused to have me home, so I had to spend half-terms with boring teachers. And I wrote to you repeatedly, and never once did you reply."

"I wrote to you for months begging you to answer my letters," I said. "Who was stopping the correspondence?"

This resolved her impatience into a mood of quiet resentment. "You wrote, you say . . . ?"

"Sometimes twice a month, Jen, I swear it."

She looked past me to the distant fields. "Then who . . . ?" Then added, "We had to collect our mail from the headmistress, of course . . ."

"That's it; she intercepted mine."

Jen screwed at her fingers. "But who instructed her to do so?"

"Your mother, without a doubt. On your own admission she didn't approve of us getting together, and she made it perfectly clear to me that I wasn't the one for you with this Afghan thing hanging over me."

I took her into my arms despite her faint resistance, and asked, "So what happens now?"

"What *can* happen? I promised myself to Davie on the day he took me home to his family. Even his father was delighted, and you know what he thinks about Romanies."

"I love you, Jen, and I always have. This can't happen."

She turned out of my arms, and I knew she was lost to me.

The effect of losing her was terrible; at first I wandered around the ale-houses of Maesteg and found odd corners, drinking silently, aloof to everyone and everything about me. I finished up at Cushy's Rose and Crown where, bemused and angry at somebody's intervention, I laid out Swillickin' Jock, one of Cushy's minders, then made off before she got wind of me.

But ale has many ways out of a man, and I vacillated between telling Dai and Old Bid to get about their business to bawdy singing of the military songs Dada had taught me, while systematically emptying bottles.

It was weak and unworthy of them all, especially Jen, but I couldn't help it: nothing relieved the self-inflicted wound of the love I held for her; no bottle could ease the pain.

The weeks wore on into months, and a year passed in a haze of alcoholic vapour.

Book Three

Chapter 26

Let me not beat about the bush. There were consolations.

While they had bothered me little when Jenny was in the offing, now the sparkling eyes and snowy bosoms of the young hotel maids called me, for I was dying for the touch of a woman; and I was sick to death of Dada's crack-skulled lawyers and the greedy antics of tinplate shareholders. Further, it was like the end of my world on the day Jenny married Davie.

Meanwhile, I was fed up to the back teeth with managerial talk about increasing the privileges of our urban poor and improving our starvation wages, for our valley was no better than any other in Wales.

As the spinning jennies in the northern towns filled the bellies of rich ruffians, so tin making in South Wales was lining the coffers of mainly English bankers at the expense of tram-towers like little Bronny Williams – on a ten-hour shift to keep her pa alive.

And always there accompanied me in my journeys around industrial Wales the spectre of the burned out relics of our factory waste; the poor begging for a share of the wealth which the rich like me enjoyed.

Having tried to lose my sense of the loss of Jenny, I turned to the great reformers, the idealists of the past; and found in Robert Owen's *A New View of Society* a document comparable only with the ideals of Tom Mann, the labour leader.

By coincidence I was actually studying Owen's pamphlets

when the mood took me down to the Rose and Crown, Dai's old public, for a quart of what he called skull-attack.

A stink of fresh hops and stale beer hit me as I pushed open the ale-house door, and there was Cushy and Peg Cuddle, hand in hand, doing a fancy fandango to the roars of Irish navvies, with half-cut clients clapping the time. No sooner had they finished, and with Cushy patting her bosom and "Oh Gawd, Peg, I ain't up to it these days," when upon a table jumped a little old loom-worker with a red necktie around his scraggy throat, and sang in a high-pitched nasal twang from Lancashire:

"Poverty, poverty knock, me loom's
a'sayin' it all day and night. Poverty,
poverty knock, knock knock, we'll hand
old Gaffer a fright. Tuner should shackle
me loom, but he'd rather sit on 'is
bum. He's far too busy a'courtin' our
Lizzie, I can't get the bugger to come.
So it's poverty, poverty, knock knock knock,
poverty, poverty knock, knock, knock . . ."

With the labourer beating time, the customers, led by Peg Cuddle, who was now up on the table beside him, roared the "povertys" in a chorus that must have put the breeze up Ann Thomas in the rooms of Cefn-Ydfa, and I was just getting my teeth into my third pint when a fat hand came out and clamped over my mouth, and I stared over my pewter mug into the mascara eyes of Cushy. Through the fug of ale-hops and smoke she asked, "Hold it, mister. Ain't you that gentry fella slummin' it up in Cefn-Ydfa wi' the ghost?"

"Right ghost, wrong fella, missus, for I ain't gentry more'n you." Which was her language, and it pleased her, for her dull blue eyes suddenly shone like jewels in her powdered face.

"That right your mate beat ye to it with the Romany piece?" she asked.

"Wrong again, she ain't a piece."

196

The gusto of the crowded room beat about us and she spoke again, her lips moving soundlessly, then cupped her hands to her mouth and shouted:

"*Jawch*, I do like a bit o' romance, see, but when the movin' parts go wrong, boyo, I be scuppered." And she dabbed at her eyes with a little lace handkerchief. "Very sorry I am, and your pa died an' all, they tell me."

I drank, watching her, speech being impossible, for now a Peto navvy was up on the table; a brightly coloured waistcoat had he and a cherubic face with a bunch of laughs, and he bellowed:

"I don't go for the ladies grand, nor them of high degree.
A winsome wench who's willin' is the only one for me.
So I'll drink and whore where'er I can,
Till life runs out its mortal span,
The end of which is a roadside ditch for a Peto navvy man."

And the room bellowed the chorus gustily:

"Roll her round, lads, pat her tum,
Wiggle your hips and waggle ye bum."

"Bloody disgustin', ain't it?" bawled Cushy. "But they're dyin' like flies over on the viaduct down Swansea way, so ye've gotta make allowances. What are you on these days?"

"I'm making a move from Maesteg. Swansea for me. They say you know the place."

The clients quietened, for the ale was going down:

"Know it? Born and bred there, Butty. What do ye want to know?"

"Tinplate factories. I want one."

"Ten-a-penny – recession, see? Don't you know that?"

"I want a special – bargain price."

"Somebody selling up, ye mean?"

I nodded.

"And what's in it for Cushy?"

"Put me on to the right fella, somebody wasting out, and you can name your price. You know the customers?"

"Do I know the customers!" Cushy laughed, her head back, her great bosom shaking.

"Hey, Peg – did ye hear that? He's askin' if we knows the customers down Swansea way!" And she picked up her quart and drank deep, gasping.

"Mister, we know 'em in all shapes and sizes, from the Crumlin Viaduct up Newport way to Porthcawl Docks: we got 'em tabbed and tickled from Blaenafon in the Eastern Valley to the Cornish tinners off Land's End! We knows 'em marvellous when in their cups and watering regrets to when they be roisterers around their women." And she reached out and grabbed me by the front. "Normal I charge five per cent, me darlin', but if ye want it cut rate – sort of private investigation – you'll 'ave no cheaper deal in the country; but then I'm on ten per cent and up to fifty-five."

"I've got the money, I can pay for it clean," I said.

"Oh Gawd, another bloody pew-polisher! Ah well, we take it as it comes." And she shouted bawdy laughter, and rose in wobbling obesity. "Leave it wi' Cushy for a day or two, and I'll put ye on to a bargain, son – what ye doin' tonight, for I can likely fit ye in?" And she shrieked with joy, holding her stays.

"I can see you after the Bible class at half-past seven."

"*Dammo di!* Don't I collect 'em! Six foot up! Don't get killed on the way out, boyo, I'm aimin' to move to Swansea meself, so may need ye!"

It was similar to being dismissed, for Hambone suddenly appeared at my elbow. I saw him through a glaze of ale, though I was a whisky tippler since my pa had died, not beer, which I suppose was half my trouble, and Hambone said, gigantic:

"This way out, happy gent, and if ye get across my woman you won't know which end up ye are."

Then suddenly a hand shot out and Hambone disappeared,

and in his place arose a broken-nosed vision with a cauliflow-ered ear.

"What the hell are ye doin' in this filthy place?" it asked.

It was Dai Dando, terrible in righteous indignation.

"Hallo, me old son," I said. "Your waterin' hole too, is it?"

"*Diawch*, ain't your mate Davie right? Since your fine feyther died you be goin' to pieces, Maister. Now come on, get your legs under ye. How much 'as he had, missus?" he asked Peg Cuddle on the way out.

"Two pints," I said, stroking his face.

"More like six or seven," said Peg. "Earlier, he laid out Swillickin' Jock again, and now he's after Hambone."

"That's me boy!" said Dai, and hauled me off.

Glorious is the feeling of beginning to get drunk: the spirits are high with a marvellous delight in fellow creatures, from docile wives to a mouse scuttling in the woodwork.

But oh, it's different in the morning when you awake with two heads and your stomach protesting about the night before. You don't want breakfast and you can do without visitors, especially Old Bid, of the "I just don't know what's happening to you lately" kind. Davie, my mate who married my Jen, was also one of these. Outraged virtue was his, when he visited next morning.

"If you don't know, then nobody does," I replied in answer to his question, and fanned my wrath to keep it warm.

"Jen, you mean?" He appeared astonished.

"Of course, you bloody idiot – who else?"

Lying in the bed, my head thumping, I couldn't think with sufficient clarity to encompass the reason for his visit.

It was about fourteen months since he and Jen were married and, now that I had stopped work at the tinplate factory and was taken up with full-time farming of the estate land, I had seen little of the pair of them; which was probably sensible from every aspect.

But today I was aware, despite my indisposition, of the growing pallor of Davie's face. His poetic features had

199

become accentuated; his natural slimness caricatured by clothes which appeared suddenly to hang upon his bones; he had become cadaverous, and I could not understand it.

"Dai Dando sent me a message," he said now, sitting beside the bed. "How d'you feel?"

"Like a hair of the dog that bit me – how about you?"

Davie smiled thinly. "Not . . . not too good these days."

"Have you been to a doctor?"

"These last three months, on and off." And he shrugged. "I'm all right, really, just that everything's such . . . such a bloody effort . . ."

I glanced at him. He so rarely swore. "What's wrong – don't they know?"

I was being matter of fact with him; knew it was wrong, but couldn't help myself.

The shock of their marriage, coming as it did so soon after my father's death, appeared unforgivable; I knew my attitude was wrong, that they had been perfectly in order to carry on their relationship when mine and Jen's had died.

I cursed Clara's memory; certainly, my father had never once protested about the possibility of Jen and I getting together, but in retrospect he now appeared as one who had stood on the fringe, neither discouraging nor approving it. Lost in a reverie, I heard Davie's words as an echo.

"Would . . . would you like me to leave, Tom?"

"Of course not. But there's more to this than a health inquiry. Why not say what you've come to say?"

There was a silence; then, "You're going to find it pretty brutal, mate."

Only when our affinity was strong did he call me this. Then:

"I'm off to Switzerland. My father's booked me a room in a sanatorium in the mountains – quite near to Geneva, where . . . where your father and Clara died . . ." He faltered. "Mountain air, and all that stuff . . . T.B. . . . ."

I closed my eyes. "Oh God, Davie, I'm sorry . . ."

"Don't worry, you didn't know. We . . . we've kept it a family secret up until now . . ."

"How's Jen taking it?"

"You can imagine!"

"She'll be going with you, of course."

"No, she won't – close proximity. It is catching. Even now I . . . I'm not allowed to kiss her." He smiled brilliantly, his eyes bright with unshed tears. Empty of emotion, he shrugged. "Rotten luck . . . just as we were getting to know and understand one another, eh?" Now he looked close to tears, so I said quickly:

"Listen, look on the bright side. You're young. You won't be the first to beat consumption, and you've got the best reason of all to stay alive." But I knew he wasn't listening, and he interjected:

"But that isn't all, Tom. We've a baby coming."

My head was aching and a sickness, nothing to do with my hangover, restricting my reply. I said with an effort:

"So, what's wrong with that? Doesn't that make you even more determined to come back to the pair of them? Congratulations! And tell Jen I'm delighted for her. When – when is the baby due?"

"The quack reckons it'll be six months." And he smiled with sudden radiance, took out a handkerchief and dabbed at his mouth. "That . . . that's what Jenny said – 'That's right,' she said, 'you shove off to the nursing home and leave me to it – leave the old girl to manage as best she can!' " And he laughed softly. "You know Jenny. And everybody's as pleased as can be in the Grey household. But . . ." And he faltered again, staring at me, his eyes suddenly incredibly big in his pale face.

"But what, Davie?"

"Keep . . . keep an eye on the pair of 'em till I get back, eh?"

"Of course."

Now his eyes met mine. "If I don't make it, Tom – I mean, though it's only a chance in a million – but if I kick the bucket, will you care for them as if they were your own?"

"You will come back to them, son."

"Yes, yes, I know that, but if . . ."

I touched his hand, perhaps the first time I had touched him over the years, and answered, "If . . . if they will have me, yes. I . . . I'll hang around to see what happens, and, well, if things don't work out right, you can count on me."

Davie closed his eyes and, rising, went to the door; to stand there momentarily, smiling; and as such will I always remember him.

"Be seeing you, Tom."

No tears; no handshakes or declarations of fond farewell. I never saw him again.

Chapter 27

Jen's old caravan, glowing red in the dusk and polished with sun in the mornings, was still patiently there on the edge of Brook Coppice; waiting for what? Waiting for me, perhaps, for often I would get aboard our mare, the trap horse, and trot her over the Big Pasture in that direction: yet were I asked why, I could have given no answer. Perhaps I was seeking the nearness of Jen, and abhorring the thought that I was waiting for Davie to die . . .

Trembling with expectancy, I'd sometimes ride to within sight of the Grey home, called the Russian Villa, to which Mr Grey and his wife had recently returned from Rock House at Glanllynfi.

Their new home needs a mention, the Villa having been built on the proceeds of the famous secret process – incidentally a misnomer, because it was my father, and he alone, who had brought to Welsh tinplate the rustless surface which the Russians had invented.

But it was no commercial invention that took me to the vicinity of the Russian Villa; it was the hope that I might stumble across Jen while she was out walking; her route having been suggested to me by a wily Dando, whose life was pledged to romanticism. These days Old Bid never knew of his philanderings from minute to minute, and now he was concerned with mine.

It was a necessity that I should soon meet with Jen and talk with her; first because I was concerned about Davie – he had been in Switzerland for eighteen months now and I had received little news about his condition; secondly because, having been given the name of a bankrupt tin manufacturer in the Swansea area, I intended to move west and start up on my own.

At this time I wrote in my diary:

3rd February, 1878. Cefn-Ydfa House, Maesteg.
I am going to the devil here, living on my own. This week I spent in a state of inebriation, having begun to drink at home – the path to the grave if done seriously, says Dai. Old Bid and Dozie Annie will not talk to me, yet I'm the one who pays their wages! Even the ghost of Ann Thomas shuns me; I haven't seen her in months!

Levity is fine in its place, but my life is no joke, and I make the following entry in the nature of a confession.

There are houses in the city areas known as "ill fame" and loneliness and physical need have taken me into them; necessary introduction being the stock-in-trade of Miss Cuddlecome who knows where gentlemen of means can be accommodated by the most genteel of ladies. One of these being the wife of a Parliamentary Member recently advanced to the House of Lords; she picks and chooses from Cushy's constituency, tho' I doubt if her needs are as great as mine.

One doesn't pay her directly, but leaves on the mantel what one thinks she is worth. The night before last I left a sixpence in the hope that I had paid her off: on the contrary, she was delighted; proof, she asserted, that at last her true value is appreciated. They tell me that in her spare time she studies Plato and Homer, being an amateur intellectual.

I shall call upon her again: hers is the one face on the pillow in which I can formulate, aided by the coming of dawn . . . the beloved shape of a face lost to me – Jen Wildflower. . . Only in this philanderer can I build the *doppelganger* of one whose touch I desire most in this world.

The women come and go, my darling, but it is sometimes possible to hear a sound that is the sound of *you*; a sigh that could be yours; and so imagine your presence.

A couple of weeks later I wrote again in the diary:

17th February, 1878. Cefn-Ydfa.
My beloved:
I have just read the rubbish I wrote on the 3rd. Put it down to the alcoholic phantasies of a lunatic; I didn't intend so to desecrate my emotions, yet because I deserve your final judgment of me, I leave it to you to make what you will of it.

My real intention was to tell you that I am leaving Dai, Old Bid and the two girls here to run Cefn-Ydfa and am moving myself to Swansea; largely because I have reason to think that Karendeesh is about to make another move – such is the political turmoil in Kabul these days – and also because it is necessary for my own sanity to be out of your vicinity. Oh Jen!

Of late, obsessed by longing for a sight of you, I have been riding over to the Russian Villa and there secreting myself in the hope of a glimpse as you walk in the garden; or move your shadow on a drawn curtain. It is ridiculous for a grown man to behave in this manner, but I cannot help it: better I keep what little dignity I have left, and go out of your world, which, I know, will always be for Davie.

Having given myself up to this self-pitying twaddle, I then left the stables of Cefn-Ydfa, mounted the trap mare, and went at a trot over the snow-bound country towards the Russian Villa.

It was a bitter winter, one that constantly enforced its iron will on the freezing workers of Maesteg. Corpses were being fished out from the poverty cellars where the poorer than poor congregated, huddled together for warmth. The Ivorites and Benefit clubs did their best with their soup kitchens on the Pneumonia Corners, headed by the Quakers, always the first in and last out when evil threatened their perfect God. The Church of England pulpits warmed people up with promises of everlasting fire.

She was a fine little mare at the best of times, this one, and now free of the trap she broke into a sprightly canter across the mist laden fields, until I came to the coppice in front of the Russian Villa; here I dismounted and walked her into cover. My hopes were faint; it was the fourth time I had come to the place without so much as a glimpse of Jen; but, turning as I tethered the horse at my usual tree, I saw a little lace handkerchief lying on the grass; picking it up I held it to my mouth, savouring its perfume.

Left on purpose by somebody passing?

My heart thudded against my shirt.

"Well, I never," said Jen, and came out from behind the tree.

My eyes must have threatened to drop from my cheeks, and instantly my hands went out to her; as quickly, Jen backed away.

"Don't touch me, Tom, I couldn't bear it . . ." she said.

She was dressed in a long woollen coat that reached to her feet, a black hat with a peak in the front, and gipsy black was her hair. Like a woman in mourning black was she, but her lips were red, as if she had been eating wild berries, and her cheeks were bitten red with the frost.

Speechless, I stood before her beauty; in three years I had seen her only from a distance, one as insubstantial to me as Ann Thomas who moved in shadowy places. My eyes drifted over her and our breath moved between us as live smoke; I said with an effort:

"So . . . so much to say, Jen; now nothing. How is Davie?"

"Hanging on . . . bless him."

"Still in Switzerland?"

"In the nursing home. God, Tommy, he has gone to a skeleton!" Tears sprang to her eyes and she blinked them away.

I bowed my head before her misery. She said:

"Isn't fair! He never did any harm to anyone. He was a fine man – he still is – and sticking it, you know Davie." She shivered in the cold: I thought she was going to cry and I gripped myself in the readiness; had she cried I would have held her, and she didn't want that.

"Dead or alive, Jen, he will be remembered."

Covering her face with her hands, she put a fist against her mouth, shuddering with inner sobs.

"We . . . we so wanted to be 'appy, ye understand?"

For a moment her accent was Romany.

"Of course."

"You . . . you heard about the baby?"

I had heard, but was trying to forget it.

"It died. I mean, I lost it, ye know. Anyway, it would only 'ave been half alive, they said. It was a boy."

"Sorry, Jen."

Suddenly she shook her head, her tears brimming, and they loosened and dropped upon the black wool of her coat. Sunlight shafting down through overhead leaves glinted upon them, turning them into diamonds. Her eyes opened wide and she clung to me like the last man living, gasping against my throat, "Oh, Tom, hold me, just hold me!"

She was in my arms again, and I was reborn. I tried to kiss at her tears, but she averted her face, whispering, "No, darling, please no! Just hold me . . ."

There was no sound in the coppice but our breathing and the faint winter birdsong; then, distantly, came the strains of martial music. Laughing in tears like the old Jen, she held me at arm's length, and dashing a hand at her eyes, cried:

"A pair of old miseries, eh? And down town they're livin' it up with the Benefits!" Then her eyes saddened. "He's dying now, they tell me. Davie . . . is dying!"

"Yes, I heard."

"Queer old life, ain't it? He used to say that, remember? One moment up, next moment down, like old Peg Cuddle's petticoats – mind, he could be a rude old beggar as well!"

"Neither of us went for the priesthood," I said, and we laughed, suddenly clinging together again. Again the silence of embarrassment, and I said after a deep breath, "Whatever happens, Jen, good or bad, you've always got me."

She was on top of it now, drying up in laughter and wet eyes, as women do in grief, and she said, "Good old Tommy, innit?" (She was taking off my Welsh accent.) "Given the chance he always do bring home the bacon, eh?"

"Ay ay, I'm Welsh, an' don't ye forget it, missus. Any spare bacon around, boyo, and I brings it home."

We did not speak more: suddenly turning, Jen left me, and I was alone again.

The mare stretched the length of her tether and nuzzled my hand as if in consolation.

Chapter 28

Surely Aphrodite, the Goddess of Love, was at the graveside when the Grey family met to pay their last respects to Davie, their adopted son.

I was there only by Jen's request.

Very beautiful is a woman in grief, and of all the women there – and scores came from Maesteg, from dignified lords and ladies, the owners of the tin trades, to the ragamuffins of the town – Jen was the loveliest.

Little Bronwen Williams were there in her Sunday dress and pinafore, though her hair was still tied back with string; with her was Mrs O'Leary of Bowrington Street, she whose man lost his legs down the pit they called Croker's Double: blind Mrs Rhys Evans was there with her cat in its basket, as was Mrs Twp Jones, who came in to do Tom Williams on the chamber, but who these days wasn't quite the ticket. Scores of Chapel and C. of E. people came, good folks all, who were not recorded by *The Cambrian*; they being labouring tinplaters and of smaller consequence.

Cushy Cuddlecome and Peg her sister were present, of course, it being good publicity for the living to know that despite the general opinion, publicans are with us in death as well as life; and naturally, Swillickin' Jock and Hambone, her two big minders, were well to the fore – smelling of Tanyard Light even at that time of the morning. Naturally, such as these preserved themselves against the blank stares of the Good and the Great by standing in a group apart; which befits those of a different social class.

*   *   *

Others attended Davie's funeral whom he could have done without, such as a few old Revivalists left over from Dafydd Morgan's inspirations, and they sent up their biblical chants to accompany the dirge of the clergyman's orations; all of which must have bored Davie stiff, for I knew his views on organised religion.

Old Bid and Dai Dando were present, of course, the former bulging like a rhino in black and weeping buckets on Dai's shoulder; but Dozie Annie and Angharad were back in Cefn-Ydfa with Ann Thomas.

Ay ay, they put my friend down with pomp and circumstance, and folks naturally believed that this was the end of him, but it wasn't, for he, Davie, had the last word.

The Grey family had brought the body back to lie in state in the Russian Villa. But only the Church of England vicar knew the contents of the letter he had received from Davie, written two days before he died, and posted to the vicarage from Berne.

Therefore, when the service was over and Davie was in God's little acre and people about to disperse, this vicar, a man much respected in Maesteg, raised an arm and cried:

"Stay, good people. Stay, please! I received from our friend Davie Grey a letter written before he died; and it is his request that it be read by me at the graveside; this, with the permission of the Grey family, I will do now."

The sun burned down in smells of worsted cloth and mothballs. Unfolding the letter, the clergyman waved it aloft for all to see, and in that moment I saw Jenny standing alone on the other side of the unfilled grave. As our eyes briefly met, she smiled as if in the knowledge of what was about to happen – something we shared – Davie's belief in essential goodness. And then the vicar's voice floated above us:

"'Relatives and friends.
This message is the voice of all men of good intentions.
In their name I call upon you to aspire to nobler ambition

210

than commercial profit, and turn your eyes to the greater vision – that of the ideals outlined by the great Sir Thomas More, which beg for the creation of the perfect state.

This is an ideal that once prospered in Robert Owen's community of New Lanark in Scotland.

From this beginning, with God's help, free men will build such communities, their leaders sharing with their work-people the profits received from their labour, individually and collectively, as one.

To this end I leave all I possess in this world to the two young friends named in my Will, in the hope that they will add to this their own wealth.

Owenism is a worldwide movement: in France Count Saint-Simon and his friend Fourier have advocated its benefits; in Germany a new scientific socialist movement is being sponsored by Karl Marx, its creed outlined by his friend, Engels. Call it by any name you will, but assist my friends, wherever industrial fairness is discussed, in sowing the seeds of this great Beginning in the hearts of men and women who know that such is pledged by the God before Whom I stand today.

David Grey.'"

The clergyman lowered the letter. A little wind ruffled the hair of bareheaded men and tugged at the black ribbons of bonnets; we stood in a pin-drop silence, contained by memories of a friend. When I opened my eyes I saw Jen again.

In this unusual advocacy from the grave he had bound us closer than ever. Aphrodite, I thought vaguely, makes her contribution to lovers in the most unusual places.

But this, of course, was Davie's time, not ours, and I think Jen realised it, too, as we turned away to continue our individual lives.

With Dai and Biddy beside me in the trap, we went back to Cefn-Ydfa.

Chapter 29

Old Bid was getting beyond herself.

"Are ye sober, young maister?" she asked, shaking me into wakefulness.

"As a judge," I answered, pushing her away.

"*Jawch*, me darlin', you're like a dog a few weeks old – ye don't know what bone you're after."

"You mind your tongue!" I sat up.

"And you your soul, for that Devil's spawn Cuddlecome is after ye – sent a message from Swansea for ye to go there straight away."

"Swansea? You mean the Rose and Crown down town?"

"No! The woman's moved house. Peg Cuddle's handling that hell-hole now – Swansea, I said – down on the docks there – and she calls it the Cuddlecome Inn, and back to ye own beds at six o'clock in the mornin'."

"Talk fair, Bid – she's not that bad!"

With an impatient toss of her head she left me, then at the bedroom door she turned and with her hands over her face began to cry in gasps and wheezes.

"Aw, come on, Biddy!" Instantly out of bed, I held her and she pulled down her hair and began an Irish keening guaranteed to rouse the neighbourhood, saying between stuttering sobs:

"Sure to God, the place has gone to winter rags since ye lovely feyther popped 'is clogs; with you on the Devil's dew and me 'usband chasin' fast women, I don't know if I'm on me arse or me elbow." And since it was not like Old Bid to talk that way, I held her, rocking her into silence, till she said:

"As for that Peg Cuddle, she's a woman of the pave, and

212

if she lays another finger on me man, I'll be killin' her though death lays a chill hand upon me brow."

"Ach, you're stupid, woman! He wouldn't touch that Cuddle with a six foot barge-pole!"

"Then will ye tell me who broke his nut last night if it weren't a Cuddle wooer, for I found him this cock-crow near Corn Hwch wi' his boots in the air and Satan comin' to collect him."

"Dai's hurt?"

"Aye, and bumptious and cocky no more. He's abed. Come and see him."

Dai Dando looked as if somebody had been at him with a pickaxe, with two black eyes and his jaw tied up; said he, when Old Bid was distant, "It were four of 'em, Maister."

"That'll teach you to side-step Peg Cuddle," I replied.

"Ach no, sir. I never went near the trollop. Sober as a judge I was and fetched up the sods while returnin' from a Bible reading. Foreigners, too, and rattlin' on in a heathen lingo while they kicked the tabs off me."

"Foreigners?" I was instantly serious.

"Aye, for in the dark they thought I was you: very gentle with me at first, and please come quietly, sir, and it'll be easier for all of us."

"They said that?"

"But when I cut up rough, like, two held me and the others hit hell outta me."

I pondered this, and Dai added, "Then they eased up and asked me where you was, and I said you wasn't home, but gone off to foreign parts to bury your feyther." Dai paused for breath. "You remember that Ransit fella who came here once?"

I nodded.

"He was one of 'em, for I saw 'im in the moonlight – the others were big hulkers wi' jaws like iron, for I broke me fists on a pair of 'em."

I got up from the bed. "You've been lucky, Dando. And you're right – they mistook you for me. If there hadn't been a full moon last night you might have woken up this morning on

213

your way to Afghanistan." And I added, "Meanwhile, keep away from Peg Cuddle!"

"Great milking tits!" exclaimed Dai. "Me? Sure, Old Bid would 'ave me knackers off for a wink, never mind a fumble."

Clearly, it was again time to move out of the Afghans' sights, for Karendeesh had not yet given up his quest for a pretender king.

Meanwhile, Cushy Cuddlecome, like the witch she was, appeared to have anticipated my intentions to the hour, for that very morning I received a letter from her with the postmark "Swansea". It was written in a copperplate hand – certainly the work of an official letter writer, for as far as I knew Cushy couldn't even spell her name. The letter read:

"Your Honour,
Following your esteemed instructions, I have succeeded in finding an appropriate firm for your consideration to buy. The Upper Forest Tinplate Works, built in 1845, recently acquired by the bank, is now the property of Edward Bagot; it ceased trading a year ago and is now on the market.

Be good enough, if you are interested, to call at my new Swansea establishment known as the Cuddlecome Inn, Number Thirteen Wind St., Floating Dock, Swansea, where overnight accommodation and requisite facilities are readily available.

Fraternally yours,
Miss C. Cuddlecome."

Even entertaining thoughts of Miss Cuddlecome in legal procedures would have been considered madness by the lawyers; but such was the iniquity of the existing system, that it would have been a greater risk to employ a legal shark, and the words of the old Chartists rang in my ears:

". . . the pimps and ponces of the landed estates and their hundred thousand wrangling lawyers; they patronise a

214

Church Established, they wage unnecessary wars, they pay unmerited pensions to half-wits in plumed hats in the Army, Navy and Courts of Law; they live in a profusion of luxury maintained by those who live in misery . . . !"

And Dada, after a couple of whiskies, would pronounce their legal wickedness from *Genesis* to *Revelations*.

Cuddlecome at least repaid by personal service a little of the usurer's gold.

So, with her letter in my pocket, I caught the 4.32 p.m. train from Maesteg, and that evening alighted from a cab outside her hostelry in Wind Street, Swansea, knowing by the racket coming from within that this was the Cuddlecome establishment.

There was more going on in Cushy's that night than in The Whore of Jerusalem; lamplight and smoke hit me as I opened the street door.

The low-ceilinged taproom, lifted from a century before, was crammed with the riff-raff of Swansea Docks. Bull-necked sailors of half a dozen nationalities barged one another for room at the tap, where floss-headed barmaids, full-bosomed and slink-eyed, were pouring ale and totting out gin measures with professional flourishes; while Cushy, with one fist holding a rum bottle and the other beating time, roared out to the music of a melodeon:

"They come down from Yorkshire
over mountain and dell, for
drinkin' an' wenchin' wi'
the Cuddlecome gel! Hey-ho
for the Cuddlecome gel!
Hey-ho for the
Cuddlecome gel!"

And she pranced out through the bar flap, pulled up her skirts to show her red garters and kicked up her fat legs in a light fantastic, while the clients, sodden with ale, beat on

215

the tables with their mugs. In whoopees and bawled jollities she danced in obese tomfoolery, her great breasts shaking, until her golden wig came down, and seeing me, she came to a stop.

"Why, me darlin' – why didn't ye say?" she demanded, and stood breathless. "What are ye doin' in this neck o' the woods?"

"How do, Cushy?" I gave her a wink. "You wrote, remember?"

Respectful of the stranger, the customers dropped into silence.

" 'Tis me opening week, don't ye see?" said Cushy, "and we're wettin' the baby's bottom . . ." The men clustered about us, intent upon her business: young chaps with the bright eyes of children; old men with broken faces, bulbous and blue-nosed; vain, arrogant of features some, their eyes holding their Cairo dreams of distant places where the seas roared to the windjammers' songs; Eastern eyes, mostly, slanted in yellow cheeks, and the teak-brown glances of the lowly Lascars, the refuse of the seas.

For this was Cushy's place and Cushy entertained her lonely men, downstairs and upstairs, anyone she pleases, and she ain't pleased too often, neither, said Hambone later, "For she's like my cricket, mate – anything she can't sink wi' a word she gets her fist to."

"And when Cushy hits 'em, son, they stay hit," said Swillickin' Jock, coming up; and, "Ain't I seen you before somewhere, me son?" he asked me, shoving Hambone aside, his chin bristling.

"That's right," I said. "We fell out no end a few months back, so I laid ye out cold. Do ye want the same again?"

For this was the way you handled things in Cushy's, and hearing this she hooted in joy, shouting, "Lads, this is me new friend, a gent from Maesteg, and he do speak my language, so anyone gettin' across him has gotta see to me first – this way, me big handsome fella." And she fetched Swillickin' one in the chops that would have dropped a donkey. "Away out of it, ye big oaf – don't ye know a gent when ye see one?"

216

Barging a path through the customers and towing me with a fat hand, she led me into the quiet of an adjoining room.

"Now then, ye gorgeous thing," said she, "how gets?" And she sprawled in a chair, facing me. "Ye got me letter, ye said?"

"This morning. How much?"

"How much what?"

"The Tin Works – Upper Forest – what's the asking?"

The game over now, she eyed me, rubbing her chins, and I said:

"Now cut it close, girl – you make the running but we'll both tell the truth. Fiddle me some and you'll end up short."

"Jesus, you're a tough one!"

"When I'm dealin' with the likes of you. Now come on. We'll talk turkey after."

"Bankrupt stock, mostly," she said.

"That's more like it – go on!"

Violin music, an old Irish air, stole into the room and momentarily contained us. She said, "I rook the crooked bastards, mind, but I deals square on me friends. Eighteen thousand."

"All in?"

"Don't be daft!"

"What, then? Come on!"

"Twenty-two thousand five all in, and that includes spares, but it's goin' cheap, because the bank's got it."

"What bank?"

"Swansea and District – private – High Street." And she leaned towards me. "It's a good 'un, Tom Mortymer: sixteen tin mills, five sheets, four O-H Siemens furnaces, and they don't come cheap, they tell me. I got an old client in 'ere who give me the low-down. Knows the trades backwards."

"Output?"

"Don't know, but they say it's a dream at fifteen thousand basic boxes o' tinplate, two thousand tons of bars and five hundred or so black sheets. Them Siemens alone are worth ten thousand of anybody's money."

217

"The O-H patent? Outdated, girl. God, they take you easy! Is it clean?"

"Like a new pin. Take it or leave it."

"You're on," I said with finality. "I can get reconditioners for the Siemens from Germany, so I'll look the place over."

"And my cut?"

"Ach, you're a marvellous lady, Cushy. See ye after midnight."

"I can get that anywhere and talk's cheap – what's the cut?"

"I'll leave ye a bob on the mantelpiece," I said, going out, and bowed to her at the door.

It was the language she understood. "Bless me soul to hell, Tom Mortymer, you're a man o' me heart. Give Hambone a kick in the arse as ye leave."

At the door I said, "Leave it to me, Cush – ye won't lose by it."

"An' I won't gain much, either, I'm thinkin'," And she smiled.

It was the way she smiled.

I decided to keep an eye upon her; cunning being a woman's substitute for claws.

But this is when I learned that she was innocent, for when I said, "Me lovely, don't tell me you know anything about tin making, so who's been briefing you?" she answered readily:

"He's waitin' outside." And opening the door she put her fingers in her mouth and whistled shrilly. An inconspicuous old man entered; yet about him there was an air of authority, his tired eyes drifting over me with obvious scepticism.

"From him – all from him," said Cushy. "Gaffer Adams, meet Tom Mortymer – he's the gent who's after a Works."

The old man nodded. "If he's got the money."

"They've all got money, mate – trouble is they won't part with it. Say your piece." And he took my outstretched hand.

"I'm lately the foreman there – Upper Forest," said he. "But the debt overtook its capital and the bank closed us down. You interested?"

"If you're prepared to go back in charge," I answered.

"Scarcely know me, mister – you're taking a chance!"

"I'm prepared to; time's the essence with me – now or never. You know the trades?"

"Like the back of my hand."

The three of us paused, eyes switching. I said, "Listen, Mr Adams, I need a gaffer and you're as good as any since you know Upper Forest. How about its labour?"

"Still unemployed, sir. But if I whistle, it'll come running. Women, mostly – girls, I mean; some bring their childer and sit 'em outside in the sun."

"How many do you need to fire up Upper Forest Works?"

"Give me twenty and we could fire up tomorrow, and I'll also want a trained 'bossman', a 'doubler' and a 'first-helper' – you know these terms?" He was testing me now and Cushy interjected:

"Don't bother, boyo, he's made tin an' all."

The foreman said, grinning, "Five make a mill-crew, as you know – twenty would give me four shifts – twenty-four hour working."

"Nobody works at night," I replied. "You heard about Robert Owen?"

"Aye."

"You'll be working his routes – I hear you've got a ditty, you bloody lot – 'Eighty boxes on the sheet, fifty on the tombstone' – but that won't apply to us. So sign on three shifts straight away, which is fifteen, and we'll see how they go – another two shifts later, if it works. If it doesn't, you're out, understand? I'll give you three months, Adams. Break me even – no profit involved – and you can manage the lot: no back whispering, no dirty tricks . . ."

"It's goin' to cost you, sir, you realise?"

"Leave the money to me, you make the tin."

Adams looked astonished.

"Didn't I tell ye, son?" asked Cushy.

I added, "Have the three shifts here for this time next Friday, in working clothes – I take it they've got their own leathers. Can we use your Long Room upstairs?" I asked this of Cushy.

"At ye disposal, your worship. Ten bob an hour."

I nodded. "Upstairs then, Mr Adams. Next Friday, all of them, for I want a word with all my labour before we start."

"On Owenite principles?" He made a face. "That's somethin' new for employers round here!" He rubbed his face. "They won't like it, ye know."

"That's a bloody pity," I said, and when the foreman had gone Cushy gave me a fluttering glance and a wiggling come-hither.

"Dear me," said she, "ain't you masterful! Where're ye stayin' the night?"

"The Mackworth, if I can get in."

"You're welcome 'ere, mind."

"Business before pleasure," I said.

Chapter 30

I had a nightmare in the Mackworth Hotel, which was but a few doors down from The Cuddlecome; for me it put the stopper on the landlady's claim that it was the best in Wales.

Drooping between sleep and wakefulness, I awoke to a Gregorian chanting outside on the landing; astonished, I saw my bedroom door open slowly and expose a procession – Cushy in a white sacrificial nightdress with Swillickin' one side of her and Hambone on the other – being escorted to the nuptial feast; a virgin bride to a rapacious husband.

I was halfway out of the bedroom window before I realised it was a fifty foot drop to the cobbles below.

Thereafter, the days proceeded in orderly fashion.

Before midday on the following Friday the bankrupt Upper Forest Tinplate Company was mine, the deal signed legally.

Thereafter I dined at the Mackworth in the company of gentility, then repaired to Cushy's establishment. She accompanied me upstairs to her Long Room, where Mr Adams and his engaged work force were awaiting me, as promised.

Here was a ragtailed, bobtailed selection of dismal humanity if ever there was one.

The manufacture of tin, perhaps more than any other commodity, does more than produce tin, it manufactures skeletons. And it brands its servants with the lethargic movements of those on the road to death.

Statistics already told us that the tin trade had kinship with furnace working, where the life expectancy of the average puddler was fifty years; the onset of blindness probably arriving before that.

Merthyr Tydfil had the dubious honour (while under the lash of the Crawshays and Guests) of producing not only the finest iron in the world at that time, but also a life expectancy of about twenty-two years but that included the statistic of cholera, since the iron and coal masters took most of the drinking water for their Works: not so with the tin makers. Water was scarce too, but endemic fever outbreaks were few in the Llynfi Valley by comparison.

No, it was the manufacturing processes in tin making – the fumes rising from its pickling – that affected the lungs and increased the coffins; and such was the effect of septicaemia from the multiplicity of cuts and abrasions that the death-rate peaked from this alone.

The girl-women workers, often slender, having "slipped from girlhood into womanhood without experiencing a little of life's romance" (this according to one historian), faced all the blemishes of life without any of its saving sunshine.

Such a worker, scarcely in her teens – and the majority employed were females – dressed in her thick leather apron and two gloves – would seize the newly rolled iron plate, strike it a blow and rip it into sheets with the skill and dexterity of a conjurer, layer after layer being stripped off by hand; dealing with hot iron as one might peel off the layers of a scalding onion.

Now they sat like ragged statues on the forms provided in Cushy's Long Room: unmoving even when I entered.

These, many in the grimy bandages of their trade, were present now, not because of the natural wish to work but because of the driving needs of hunger. This alone brought them to the factory gates in summer when the temperature in the low-roofed sheds reached the blistering heat of 120 degrees, and in winter activated their worn bodies into speed to stop them freezing to death. Meals, summer and winter, could be cooked sizzling on pre-heated concrete floors.

And while a light accident was often welcomed – an arm cut to the bone (for tin making meant working with individual razors) might produce a respite by enforced rest – it also reduced the pay packet, which for labourers in the industry then was three shillings for a twelve hour shift.

So they sat unspeaking as I rose in the Long Room to address them, for I was a potential employer and therefore distrusted.

I began quietly, saying, "You may have heard from your gaffer, Mr Adams, who has selected you as my new work force, that I have purchased your old factory, Upper Forest, from the liquidator who brought about your recent discharge . . . Now it is my intention to re-employ you in the same capacity as you last enjoyed. You understand this?"

If they did, they made no sign of it, but raised their inexpressive faces. Among the women there I counted only three men.

They were the victims of a system that rewarded the rich and persecuted the poor. Many had wounds upon their hands and faces, others with limbs stained with factory grease; for the tin sheets often would unexpectedly fly out of the stack at any angle, cutting flesh to the bone. Such gashes were considered official only if blood was spoiling a tin sheet; otherwise first-aid consisted of slapping on a dollop of warm grease and wrapping the wound in sacking while continuing the work.

Any wound that meant a stoppage in the system caused the injured to be roundly cursed, since others had to do her work until she was healed sufficiently to return.

So the tinners' lives consisted of shearing and baling and stacking the hot loads, some of which exceeded half a hundredweight, hour after hour, day in, day out, working against the machines;"And if the rollers didn't get you, the Gaffer would," was the saying.

To be allowed time off to attend the toilet was considered a privilege.

I have seen men and girls soil themselves before daring to ask for this permission.

I continued, standing before them. "I want you to listen to me carefully, for you are about to embark on a manufacturing project differing entirely from anything you have yet undertaken.

"You will work in your trades in the usual manner, under a bossman and in mill-teams of five; doublers will continue to be doublers, a behinder will stay the same. What will change is your pay, which I will raise to a third above the rates paid by your previous employer. Every worker here will sign a contract with me, which, in due course – I can't change the system overnight – will entitle him or her to a worker's cottage; the building of such cottages will begin immediately . . ."

Slowly, my words raised them from apathy to attention, and now they moved their heads in whispered consultation.

I called, "Some here may have heard of Robert Owen, the Scottish employer who attempted to bring about changes in the social order – certainly, Mr Adams knows about him, and if you ask him will tell you more about this man whose views brought great success to the industries of New Lanark, where he formed a community for the common good of workers and employers alike.

"Robert Owen recognised that uncaring systems ring the death knell of the brotherhood of people; that the character of men and women is formed by circumstances beyond the control of the individual – do not look perplexed, for in fact it is a very simple belief – for who, sitting here before me, has had the smallest control over the cards life has dealt them?

"Isn't it true that, often, despite your efforts, you have seen your children die of malnutrition on starvation wages?"

I paused for breath and they stared at me, some with mouths agape in total disbelief.

"Do not suspect my intentions! I don't intend to trap you into any path you do not wish to take. I am a wealthy man with nothing to do with my money but begin an experiment in the Swansea Valley which, if it works better

224

than Owen's, will stand for all time as an example to employers.

"I confess to you that Robert Owen failed; that the land of heart's desire of which he dreamed did not come about, mainly because others failed to follow his beliefs.

"Men and women are entitled to enjoy the fruits of their labours. It is wrong for the clerk who doesn't soil his hands to earn more than he who earns it through sweat, and equally wrong that you should live in squalor while employers like me live in comfort for doing little but organise you into mill-teams, as I am doing now."

Now they were totally attentive.

Raked from their despondency, they began low murmurings of approval, with excited confirmation of the phrases I was now shouting into their faces. With a fist swinging before the front row, I bawled:

"Give me one good reason why such a brotherhood cannot come about, given goodwill on both sides and honesty of purpose?"

Now some stood up, calling assent. I cried:

"It may sound a dream, but it is not a dream! Reformers like Jeremy Bentham and the Quaker William Allen knew such hopes as facts, and put them into operation!"

They had now left their seats and were crowding around me, and I said:

"I have the money and I pledge it to pull down the filthy slums which the landlords call homes; to kill the vermin, clean up the cellars. And we will do this together, with you as shareholders in a common purpose, with no more than five per cent going into my bank, and no profit for me at all until we reach an acceptable social standard! Nor will I tolerate outside shareholders, for it was their greed that brought about the downfall of Robert Owen, and every social reformer who followed him. Are you with me?"

Forms and tables overturned in a rush to seize my hands, and when I had shaken myself free of them, I turned to the Long Room door to find Cushy standing there, her face expressionless.

"Sweet Jesus," said she, "that were wonderful, boyo, and I nearly believed it meself. But it were a parson talkin' to cannibals, mun. That lot? I know 'em: give 'em a month and they'll tear ye to bloody pieces."

Chapter 31

This certainly wasn't the case when I inspected the Upper Forest Works once a month, for three months later Gaffer Adams had got things organised in fine style, and I decided to leave him free of managerial interference for a month or two. For a long time now I'd nourished a wish to go off by myself somewhere on a brief holiday, so I fixed up the Wildflower caravan and set out on the road to the south in true Romany fashion.

Looking back, though lonely for Jen, it was one of the most contented and restful holidays I have ever taken, and the idea was sensible: the van, unused for so long, had grass growing up to its windows and its shafts disappeared in foliage. Now, cleaned out by Dozie and Angharad and painted inside and out by Dai, I polished its brasses so that they gleamed: yet nothing diluted the sense that this was once the home of a beloved; outside the van was the smell of new paint; within it was the scent of Jenny's hair.

Meanwhile, a more practical issue was being served. Adams was free to organise my Upper Forest Tinplate Company into an efficient, hard-working industrial unit.

On my slow tour around South Wales I gathered the knowledge required to implement my Owenite plan; at Bridgend my bankers assessed my credits and liabilities.

After selling up Dada's shares and the partnership in Grey's Llwydarth Works, I had amassed some £28,000 in addition to the estimated £20,000 value of the remaining diamonds: this an assessment by high-profile gem importers of Hatton Gardens, London, which took account of their elemental profit, usually twenty per cent.

Camping in the van outside Swansea, I visited a prominent architect and appraised him of my needs: to build outside the environs of the city, yet close enough to Upper Forest for the workers' convenience, a collective community housing a thousand people within six months; a complex complete with drainage, a water supply based on artesian wells (not Council mains) and served with the new phenomenon – lighting gas, recently available to Wales. We had this under the Llynfi Valley Gas Act of 1868, a commodity already known to Swansea; it was to be installed in my new houses and acquired property.

Work, I insisted, was to begin on a speculative basis at once, and planning had to proceed in advance of construction; speed being the essence of the contract.

My total liability for the envisaged complex, which the architect suggested should be called *Distributive Co-operative*, would cost me some £55,000 in immediate capital outlay, which meant a bank loan of about £7,000. This was available, supported as it was by the Upper Forest assets. Financiers instantly pestered the bankers for shares, but this is where Owen had gone wrong, and I would have none of it.

The bank loan was agreed at 1¾ per cent over a three-year period.

Signing away my capital, I returned from my tour revived and ready for the battle to make it work. There was no question of failure: if it did not work bankruptcy faced me; all that stood between that fate and success were my workers.

Chapter 32

As my father had immersed himself in his trade of irons, so I lost myself in a new and dignifying labour, the clattering sheds of the tin maker. Like him, stripping to the belt, I took my place as one of the mill crews of Upper Works, working in summer heat and winter cold.

Here, the only man I had to please was my behinder – he who seized the glowing bar from my pincers and fed it through first roll to second helper: and he, steering it over to his doubler, waited while the plate was folded back upon itself for the second roll.

With the company of mountain sheep (for try as we may we could not keep them away from the warmth of the open sheds in winter) it was a bedlam of activity and noise: two balling furnaces moaning and sighing like cows in labour to the surge of the compressed air bellows vying with the high-pitched shrieking of the rollers as the plates went through.

The clattering of blooming hammers and roaring of the furnaces combined to produce a hell of noise: a cacophony that rose from the sheds into the smoke-filled pluming sky, to sweep over a once perfumed valley; blackening the trees, coughing up men's lungs with its acrid stinks.

To add to the degradation, suicidal sheep, wandering in from the mountain, would seek the natural warmth, then finding it, react in a mad panic to the thundering processes in an orchestra of bleating and shrieks; to dash about haphazardly in search of escape from an unseen monster, and rush pell-mell for the furnace maws; to disappear, tails bobbing, into the red-hot fireboxes. It was a phenomenon I never understood; time and again this happened, instantly filling the air with the sweet savoury perfume of roasting mutton.

The old, nearly discarded Upper Works had, as if by the touch of a magician's wand, become alive again and we exported magnificently – black sheets for Portugal, Russian Rustless for the packing factories of Germany and France, tinplate for the cargo holds of a score of cargo bummers heaving out of South Wales Docks for the ports of the world.

The work was labour intensive and mainly female when discounting heavy loads: to see the girl-women seizing the "clacking" tin-sheets and ripping them free of one another for stacking, or dousing them in the pickling vats, was a lesson in dexterity. Most women, possessing long, slim muscles, are quicker than men with bulging biceps; also, few men can compete with the systematic rhythm of female tin makers from furnace to "boxing" for export.

Yet they worked with the utmost care these women, aware of tin's razoring cuts, for blood on a plate – and this was the important factor – automatically discarded it from use and slowed the system.

To shield themselves from time-delay accidents, the girls wore leather gloves and aprons, but nothing could protect them from badly stacked sheets with exposed edges waiting to slice the unwary hand or arm. Every woman in my Upper Forest sheds sported tell-tale scars on some part of their body; mainly chest wounds for a girl prominent in the breast: therefore some would bind their chests with layers of sacking under their aprons, despite the working heat. I have seen women with a breast sliced away, sometimes both; such women paying wet-nurses to feed their children while they were on shift.

Eye trouble attacked them all, the vaporous acid rising from the pickling vats as they bent above them, washing the tin before plunging the plates into clear water, the final process: within a year or so most had shrunken gums, the vat acid making them toothless fifty years before their time.

Men working in tin came different from any other trade, I noticed.

Usually diminutive for some reason, they spoke as did Gaffer Adams, with the monosyllabic slowness of the deaf through the machinery noise, expressing through symbolic gestures that which could not be heard.

Individually strong in character, they ruled by the fist; men of prized authority.

In many trades women were sexually exploited by men, who made their own laws when unhampered by authority. Not so the boss man in tin; his law had been formulated in the slicing cut and "Oh Jesus, Gaffer, our Girt has caught it, stop the bleeding!" Any boss man worthy of his salt could employ good "walking wounded" (for most accidents were above the waist) by getting them early first-aid.

No accident indemnity was paid, except by local Benefit Clubs, into which each worker paid twopence a week; no pension was paid on retirement.

In the earliest days of tin making, the cost of a plate spoiled by blood would mean a standard fine on the worker responsible. None of which applied to our working conditions in Upper Forest, where things were going like a dream. All my worries were coming from the usual direction: Afghanistan.

I see that I wrote a diary entry about a year after my new venture had begun:

Cefn-Ydfa House, Near Maesteg.
I give this address for convenience for I am now living at the Cuddlecome Inn, Swansea, on the waterfront; being aware that beef is available here for assistance, should I want it; having just received word that Ransit, who mistakenly attacked Dai Dando in the belief that it was me, has been making inquiries as to my whereabouts: these Afghans never give up.

Dai, hearing this, offered to come to Cuddlecome's place as a bodyguard, but I told him to take care of Old Bid and the girls; that immediately I had got the Works running in the way I wanted, I would return to Cefn-Ydfa. Which I did.

To tell the truth I am sickening of the mansion. It is falling into decay; the cellar is flooding now and most of the wines submerged in my absence; the servants' bedroom particularly is letting in rain. Even Ann Thomas, our resident wraith, appears to have abandoned us, for nobody has seen her lately.

The architect who designed the building of my twenty-five workers' cottages has suggested that he build me a small Georgian mansion within sight of the Works: but for whom? For a successful and still young speculator to live in alone, there to contemplate the amber slant of whisky . . . ?

If I possessed a wife this might be worth doing; to raise children and watch them grow to individual fulfilment, then to carry on the life's ambition propounded by Davie: such would be wonderful! But all my plans could fall at a stroke while this business of Afghan kingship still hangs above me.

Letters advocating this continue to arrive at Cefn-Ydfa; the same flowery prose, promises of everlasting wealth and of wives for the asking. It is all ludicrous.

Meanwhile, my love for Jen flowers with the years. Sometimes in desperation I write to her, but do not receive replies. I go to my secret coppice and, if lucky, sometimes see her move across a window . . . or pause at open curtains. I see her out riding, but she never comes near to Cefn-Ydfa, and I suppose she is still grieving for Davie.

She appears to be so utterly alone with the Greys in the Russian Villa; as if, now that his soul has fled, she is isolated and as imprisoned as Ann Thomas.

In my longing to seek in her my sons, I meanwhile lose myself in the building of the "Owenite dream".

And then, back in the mansion and remembering Davie and his *Songs of Travel*, I found the following, and determined to send them to Jen; so I carefully copied out:

"And this shall be for music when no one else is near,
The fine song for singing, the rare song to hear!
That only I remember, that only you admire,
Of the broad road that stretches and the roadside fire."

And by return of post I received from her:

"Give to me the life I love,
Let the lave go by me,
Give the jolly heaven above
And the byway nigh me.
Bed in the bush with stars to see,
Bread I dip in the river –
There's the life for a girl like me,
There's the live for ever!

"Low as the singer lies
In the field of heather
Songs of his fashion bring
The swains together.
And when the west is red
With the sunset embers
The lover lingers and sings
And the maid remembers . . ."

I was beside myself with joy: this is what Jen wanted – this and only this – not wealth or privilege; to return to her Romany roots. I cursed myself for my short-sightedness.

The joy snatched me up, propelling me around the mansion rooms, and on the way I knocked into Old Bid, sending her floundering, then steadied her, wrapped her in my arms and, turning her in circles, kissed her.

"Why, young maister, 'ave ye gone mad of a sudden?" And her lace cap came down over her eyes and her hair fell down, and while she was hunting hairpins in the hall, I came across Dozie and did the same for her, and ran out of the front door into the rain, for it was doing its nut in rainstorms that week. But I circled in the downpour with arms opened wide in greeting to it, and saw Mr and Mrs Thomas at their window, nodding and pushing, and look at that mad fella dancing in the rain!

But I didn't care: I cared for nothing, neither servants, neighbours nor Owenite principles: only Jen, Jen! She had snatched me up into new hope after the lonely years of waiting for her to forget her love for Davie, and remember the love she once held for me.

Caution then beset me, for the old adage ruled: never let the girl know you are too keen; the wise lover keeps his own counsel.

It was wise of me not to have moved too quickly, for my first intention was to race up to the Russian Villa and pull the girl out before she changed her mind. That, in view of what happened in the Cuddlecome Inn, could have changed the course of my life.

Meanwhile, the words of *Songs of Travel* beat in my brain:

"A red caravan, a Romany road and the moon like a Dutch cheese!"

Jawch!

Chapter 33

Christmas came and the whole shivering country from Bangor to Swansea was all over white like a Swiss ski slope, with the blackbirds turning down their mating tails in the frost, and Jenny Wrens cowering in the hedges without a twit between them. Only the Jinny Oolerts showed courage, giving the full moons something to go on with, and the rest of the curved beak brigade ripping and tearing up the neighbours for Yuletide dinners.

Sad was Wales that winter; the warm red sunsets had been replaced by the rainbow sun-downs of the molten iron factories, where men and women continued to labour in screams and scurries, and "Are ye all right down there, Joe, we'll have ye out directly," or, "For Gawd's sake, Alfi, what 'ave ye done wi' your legs?" For the pace of the Welsh Industrial Revolution, rather than slackening, seemed to quicken.

The export ports from Newport to Cardiff and Abercynon to Aberafon were packed with coasters and cargo-bummers, and the English Channel was full of empties coming in and loaders going out: and I had my share of the exports when it came to Upper Forest.

The end of the American Civil War should have brought respite to our factories, but the tempo of production was actually increasing, and up went the graphs of profit.

I was the envy of my competitors: with a workforce now topping fifty, and with sixteen tin mills, five sheet mills and four big O-H Siemen furnaces in full blast, I was sending out a happy average of 17,000 basis boxes of tinplates with 2,000 iron bars coming in and 800 black sheets going out on the trolleys. The trade names "Clarion" and "Koto" on my sheets and the now famous "Worcester" on our ternplates were a guarantee of quality, and with peace reviving it seemed that the world couldn't get enough of us.

Our storehouses bulged. New ranks of my company-owned cottages rose against the skyline to house the real assets of Forest Works – the workers who kept faith in bad times with Tom Mortymer, who was as good as his word.

I built a small Works Hospital with two wheeled stretchers for bad injuries and a third on standby; the married women had a creche and a supervising nurse for their children. A little dame school of older children followed – all on Owenite principles – and an infant school is going up even as I write this. Two official health visitors attended the cottages once a week.

I built a company store, its prices comparable with private shops in Morriston, and for the convenience of my workers, not a Truck Shop for amassing dubious profits.

In all of this the workforce responded: no firm in the Swansea Valley, never mind Morriston, was sending more tinplate to the world per worker than Upper Forest, and certainly nothing that had yet happened to South Wales could compete with what was now called "that damned madman of Upper Forest who, with his ridiculous social amenity schemes for his footloose and featherbedded workers, is riding for a fall. Watch it, lads! Sit quietly and watch it!"

The arguments rose to the roof in their Chamber of Trade and they cursed Robert Owen and everything he stood for and included the idiot, Mortymer, who had followed his example. And even while cursing us, one by one they went out of business.

Quoting the Chinese, they wrote in *The Cambrian* (and incorrectly, of course) the ancient adage: "He who rides on a tiger at sometime must get off."

The proof of what Robert Owen had to offer was in my bank statement.

In the past year of working Upper Forest it changed from a £7,000 debt to the bank to an £6,000 profit.

If employers are doubtful about the efficacy of signing up employees as working shareholders – I am not talking of foot-propping shareholders, remember, but people who make and therefore legitimately share in their own profits – look to Tom Mortymer who takes care of his workers who work for themselves. This is the result – they will load themselves with more profits than ever they thought possible.

But they did not take heed of it! So blinded were they by the streams of loveliness called "Gold" that they would risk bankruptcy rather than lose the early penny.

As Andrew Carnegie said, "Take a dollar off a working man and he starves to death; take a cent off me and I bleed to death."

Chapter 34

Meanwhile, the threats coming from Afghanistan by post to Cefn-Ydfa were increasing. These were caused, I concluded, by growing animosity between London and Kabul on arrival of the belated news of the deaths of two emissary officers, Colonel Stoddart and Captain Connolly, executed without trial by the Amir of Bokhara, a Kabul ally. Claims for compensation had been deferentially dismissed.

It is worth noting that no claim for compensation has ever been made in respect of the 17,000 British soldiers and their accompanying mercenaries who had been mercilessly slaughtered by Kabul during their bloodstained retreat into India.

But there was more to it than that.

Talk had it in diplomatic circles that a rift had arisen between London and Kabul, brought about by a political agreement between Afghanistan and Moscow, and conflict was again being threatened by London. A fourth Anglo-Afghan war would surely put an end to these constant threats to remove me to Kabul by force. In the interim the situation was of even greater sensitivity, and I determined to be upon my guard.

The opportunity for such an attempt came sooner than I expected.

Now it was midsummer and in Upper Forest Works the eve of a celebration – the opening of another fifteen workers' cottages, this time in Goat Street, Morriston; not new houses, true, but ones rehabilitated from virtual ruin.

The event was to be marked by Cushy at her suggestion. It would consist of a public meeting on the quay near Floating Dock when a red tape would be cut across the gangplank of the *Swansea Belle*, an ancient cargo-bummer, the first of my new fleet of ships bought to transport my "Rustless Russian" tinplate, and Karachi was to be my first choice for an Eastern export.

Had my intelligence served me better I would have realised the close proximity of Karachi with Afghanistan. A small draught vessel going up the River Indus to Kabul was but a five-day journey . . .

There are times in this life when in retrospect one wonders at one's patent stupidity: but at the time the arrangement of this bill of lading appeared as nothing out of the ordinary.

A little crowd of onlookers was awaiting me at the quayside on my arrival there, and the 1500-ton *Swansea Belle*'s funnel was already wisping up smoke in anticipation of her long journey.

The patriots of the Cuddlecome Inn were to the fore, and from them emerged Cushy all done up like the proverbial dog's dinner. With fat arms out she danced me in a circle to roars of approval, while Hambone, two sheets in the wind already, clapped the time with Swillickin' Jock.

Peg Cuddle was there from Maesteg's Rose and Crown, topped up with Mother's Ruin by the look of her, and down went the pair of them in curtseys on the arrival of the *Swansea Belle*'s captain; he having lodged overnight at the Cuddlecome Inn and looking a trifle delicate.

Potential combatants, too, were the order of the day, for deeper dusk (lamps were now blooming along the waterfront) was settling upon us, bringing Dai Dando, Dozie Annie and Angharad out of a carriage from Cefn-Ydfa. these, with Old Bid, took their place around the gangplank, the latter with looks to kill at Peg Cuddle.

Then came the Mayor of Swansea in the full regalia of his office, with attendant councillors bowing and scraping as the women went down in voluminous skirts and deep divides. After a lot of pushing and shoving, somebody found a chair and up on it went the Mayor, and read from a paper:

"'Miss Cuddlecome, Ladies and Gentlemen.
We are gathered 'ere tonight to pay tribute to Mr Thomas

239

Mortymer, better known to you as the Gaffer of Upper Forest Works, Morriston, the 'ighly successful Russian process tinplate works, which, as is well known locally, he is runnin' on what some are callin' communistic lines. Now gents, I ain't a communist which some call Bolsheviks, but I knows a good thing when I sees it, an' if it means that his product sells ten per cent cheaper and he pays wages that are ten per cent higher, then I says that 'is head is very much on 'is shoulders and not off his shoulders like some would 'ave it . . .'"

The dissertation rumbled on, but the gist of it was there – mayoral approval of my Owenite venture even if opposed by the local Chamber of Trade. It was a vindication of all Davie and I had hoped for during our distant planning; but even more, while in my lifetime such Utopian ideals could never be achieved, it seemed at that moment, with two thousand boxes of tinplate aboard ship bound for world markets, that I was on track. Indeed, looking around the eager faces on that dimly lit scene, I knew a faint surge of pride that Fate should have chosen me to continue the new precept in which Owen had failed: a business venture based on the labour of workpeople, and not foot-propping shareholders.

Thinking this, my mind turned to Jenny. It was a disappointment that she was not present to share in this, the culmination of my dreams: she alone knew the extent to which, as the sons of wealthy manufacturers, Davie and I had stuck to the ethos of our beliefs despite local antipathy and financial ostracism. And now that my success was no longer unreality, my world suddenly appeared insubstantial despite the knowledge that it was lying at my feet.

Only Jenny, I thought, could put the lasting seal on this success, and with me watch Upper Forest Works grow from minute beginnings into a prospect that would send its tentacles around the world.

The Mayor's eulogy rumbled on; people yawned, children fidgeted, but suddenly the crowd became intent, aware.

Turning, I saw to my astonishment coming towards the gangplank a group of ragged people – the tinplate workers of Upper Forest led by old Gaffer Adams.

They came three abreast and marching to a fifer, its piping music hushing all into silence. Twenty marchers I counted at first, then, as they rounded the go-down sheds, more – forty, fifty – a hundred and more they came, marching with fine precision; broad young men with their fists upraised to me in greeting, mothers with babies in their arms, and old men whom I had pensioned off into our Aged Courts, tottering along on sticks. Children danced along to the fife or turned cartwheels beside their elders.

The crowd at the gangplank turned; my workers faced them at the halt. The fifing ceased; it was so quiet that I heard the sea wind whispering in the ship's rigging.

From behind old man Adams a young woman emerged carrying a newly born baby. I recognised her at once, a young Jewess whom I had taken on as an apprentice behinder, and who, with her young husband, I had recently housed in a one-up-one-down cottage in Goat Street.

"Come to say God speed ye on the export, mister," she said, "and while I'm at it, will ye name our young 'un for me an' Ike, like ye do with all first-borns?"

I straightened before her as her husband came into view, and I took the baby. "A girl? Belle?"

"Ye know already?" She peered at me in the dim light.

I'd heard, but wasn't letting on.

"She do look like a girl, I'm thinkin'," I replied, speaking her idiom.

I pondered the name, while about me pressed tearfully Old Bid and the girls, with Cushy nearly breaking down and Peg Cuddle snuffling: even Dai Dando spared a tear for the scene, he said later.

Somebody helped the Mayor down and I held the baby up to the lamp, saying:

"I name this girl Belle, not only because all babies called Belle are beautiful, but because her parents brought her to see the *Swansea Belle* sail away with our first cargo of Upper Forest tinplate for India – the first of our tinplate to be exported to the East: the first messenger to carry the name of our Works so far away!"

This caused a palaver; hats came off and were thrown high, songs were started and everybody was hugging one another and happy congratulations. In the confusion Cushy arrived beside me just as I was about to cut the ceremonial ribbon across the gangplank which would send the *Swansea Belle* on her way.

"Is that right you're drinking a fond farewell toast aboard with the Captain o' this tub before she casts off?" And before I could reply, up came the Captain himself; and he was as Irish as the State of Killarney, saying, clapping me on the back:

"Ay ay, would ye be doin' me the honour, sir?" And he wiped the ale off his whiskers. "Sure to God I'd sail the thing that much better if I'd got the blessin' of a friend of Robert Owen in me whisky."

"Are you a Liberal fella, then?" I asked him in the pushing and shoving.

"I am that," said he, whispering confidentially, and so was his breath, for it was enough to take the shine off cassocks. "Sure, me pa fought in the '79 Rebellion and me Uncle Pat would have singed the tabs off Cromwell. Are ye ready, then?" And he stood aside as I mounted the gangplank.

"What about me, then?" demanded Cushy.

"What about you?" I asked, and Hambone and Swillickin' looked doleful.

"Am I left standin' with the Mayor and Corporation, to say nothin' of a hundred or so workers hopin' to wet their whistles?"

"Take them down to your place and wet the baby's head – the drinks are on me." And they must have heard the cheering in Swansea town as the mob of people, led by Cushy, made off along the quay.

"This way, Mr Mortymer," said the Captain, and escorted me down the companionway steps to the stateroom of the *Swansea Belle*.

"Ay ay," said Cushy later, "there's one born every minute, and I didn't trust that fella further than I could throw him.

Tonight he's a Liberal, last night in the feathers he was a Tory."

Afterwards I wondered if my father would have been caught so easily, because immediately the Captain had poured two whiskies the companionway door opened again and four men entered the stateroom; two black-jerseyed bruisers and the man Ransit whom I had met before.

Astonished, for I had just picked up my glass, I stood there, staring stupidly.

One man took up a position at the companionway to prevent my escape, the other two approached me. Recovering, I threw the whisky into the face of the first man and got the second with a left hook that dropped him like a sack.

"Easy, sir, come quietly, sir," cried Ransit. "We mean you no harm, remember . . . !"

For answer I head-butted the Captain and reaching behind me, got Ransit by the collar and pulled him over my head.

Inwardly seething, I was outwardly calm, but tripped over somebody on my way to the companionway steps; three after me now, slipping and sliding, snatching at me from behind, but I had a foot on the exit steps as a voice rang out:

"Right, Mortymer, that's enough!" And I turned, and there he was . . . *Karendeesh*, with a pistol in his hand.

I might have guessed it, I reflected later.

The others climbed to their feet, mouthing Afghan curses.

Strangely, standing there among them, I knew no fear; and heard nothing, I recalled later, but their breathing and a sudden inexplicable thumping . . .

Of course, the engines: the ship's engines had started.

Karendeesh said evenly:

"I truly regret having to take this violent course, sir, but really, did you leave me with any alternative?"

I answered without conviction, "You won't get away with it, you know. I've told you before, I've no intention of finishing up in Kabul or any other place!"

The engines increased their revolutions and the sound contained us. I made no protest as Ransit brought out a pair of handcuffs.

"Put them away, there's no need for that!" snapped Karendeesh. And as he said it the ship swung on her hawsers to the night tide and a confusion of commands came from the quay. They were casting off and soon we would be easing out into Swansea Bay.

For the first time the true reality of the situation struck me: they had won. Within an hour, accompanying our first major export from Upper Forest, I would be sailing for Karachi; and from there would be taken by ferry up the River Indus to Afghanistan.

Crammed together in the little room, we all stood uncertainly while a cacophony of shouting and ship's bells grew increasingly louder on the deck above.

Karendeesh, I noticed, had put the pistol away and I was just contemplating a go at him when heavy boots came clambering down the companionway and the face of a burly customs official appeared above us, peering down.

"Who's Tom Mortymer in this lot?" he demanded.

"I am," I said.

"Right. Upstairs, the lot of you. An official complaint's been made about a missing person, and the ship's detained for further inquiries." He prodded Karendeesh, the most conspicuous, in the chest. "Who are you, for a start?"

"I am the Grand Vizier of the House of Barakzai, sir, and I am warning you . . ." Which is as far as he got.

"Upstairs wi' the rest of 'em."

So much for the Court of Kabul when it came to British customs officers, I thought.

"Ach, I was worried about the drinks all round," said Cushy later, "for I've been caught like that before. D'ye realise it came to four pounds four-and-sixpence?"

"Mind, you was lucky, for she anna fond o' the slate, our Cushy," said Hambone, genially. "On the day she was eighty she hit ole Swillickin' up somethin' cruel for goin' over two and eightpence."

And right and proper, too, I thought; thank God for ethics, and for Cushy in particular.

On my way back to Cefn-Ydfa next morning, I called into Swansea Police Station as requested, and made a formal complaint; and that, I supposed, was the end of the affair. After all, I consoled myself, with diplomatic relations with Kabul at an even lower ebb since the Afghan War of a few years ago, Kabul would want no further truck with a half-Welsh pretender.

The most important thing now was to do something imperative about love, which was a bit thin on the ground these days.

Chapter 35

With the words of "Il Seraglio" running through my head, I
lost little time in returning to Maesteg to kidnap Jen.

> "When a maiden takes your fancy
> And you want her for your own,
> Be a hero in your wooing,
> Always kissing, always cooing,
> Never leave the girl alone . . ."

My failure to do this had been a major mistake, and I decided
to put an end to it.

The fact that there was a family celebration going on in
Mr Grey's Russian Villa didn't deter me. My woman was
in there yearning for a husband, and now that my mate had
gone, I reckoned I fitted the bill. Nor was there going to be
any diplomacy about it, such as, "Excuse me, Mr Grey, may
I have the honour of asking for your daughter-in-law's hand
in marriage?" and all that. She had been mine before their
son had set eyes upon her, so I was going into the family
home to hook her out of it.

But first there were a couple of duties I had to perform, and
one was settling up with Dai, Old Bid and the two girls.

The day after we had all returned to Cefn-Ydfa, I got them
round the kitchen table and set out my stall.

Very expectant was this lot; Dozie and Angharad holding
hands under the table, as shy and expectant as a pair of
brides. Dai with his eyes still glazed after last night's hop
festival down at Cushy's, and Old Bid well starched up in

246

the apron and polished severe, even at this time of the morning.

I began, "I have something important to communicate to you," and most formal I sounded, this being employer and servant stuff to be taken seriously, which opened Dai's eyes in wide expectancy.

"After careful consideration," I continued gravely, "I have decided to take a wife; for a gentleman of commerce, such as I am now, is like a comet flashing across the sky if he hasn't got a woman in the house."

Which formality didn't deter Old Bid, for she said, outraged:

"Ain't got a woman, young master? – you got three 'ere!"

Most interested in all this was Angharad, although I have scarcely mentioned her to date.

She was now eighteen and highly delectable since beginning to go in and out in all the right places; with lovely blue eyes on her and a rose-bud mouth slightly open in expectation. Astonishingly, she now fluttered me a wink.

"He do mean," growled Dai, looking evil, "a woman he can take to 'is bed – natural, innit?" And he turned his back upon them.

"Oh well," said Biddy, up on her dignity, "that comes different, don't it!" And Dozie, with no teeth in front at all now, presented me with a rhubarb grin of human understanding.

Hitherto, I had looked upon Dozie as one with a barren future, ending up a single maid who would content herself in a rocking chair with a memory or two to bring a nostalgic smile to her old age. Yet the opposite was the case, according to Dai, who lately whispered that while errant louts lounging around Cefn-Ydfa always gave the cold shoulder to Angharad, they almost begged for Dozie: she being a riot of femininity in a haystack apparently when once they'd got her going.

Strange about people, I thought later; at the time you think you know them, later you realise that you know very little about them.

Now, with a conscious effort, I said boldly:

"Well, there it is. With a commercial empire brewing, it's necessary that I produce a son to carry on the business after I'm gone."

"Oh Gawd!" sobbed Dozie, and burst into tears, and Old Bid looked daggers at me.

"Who you intendin' to cut and carry then, young 'un?" asked Dai.

I took a deep breath.

"Widow Jenny Grey of Russian Villa."

Old Bid's eyes, sudden orbs in her rosy cheeks, grew even wider. "Oh no, young master, you *can't*!"

"And why not?"

"Well, she's a Romany, ain't she?"

As has been said before in better places than Cefn-Ydfa, there are no greater snobs than the working class.

"That is why I am marrying her; also because I have loved her all my life. Besides, what was good enough for my father is surely good enough for me!"

Old Bid's mouth was now a little round button, for now she'd got her dignity well up her apron, and she said:

"Oh no, young master, there be a difference, ain't there? Didn't marry 'er proper, did he?" That delivered, she added, "Jumpin' over a broom is only a Romany marriage, ain't it?"

One of the difficulties of living close to people and giving them the licence of true friendship is that the qualities of caring and affection are often mistaken for weakness. Further, it instils in the unwary an assumption of superiority so that in moments of crisis, as now, those spoiled assume the role of command, and begin to tell you how to conduct your business. Power, they say, is always slipping away from the many to the few because the few are more vigilant: we in the rooms upstairs further assume that those downstairs are largely in the dark; the truth is that they do not miss a trick.

Therefore, being about to tell Old Bid that whom I decided to marry was none of her business, I paused, realising that mine was the fault, not hers: I had contributed to her dominance by my own familiarity.

248

Somewhat weakly I said, "Well, that's all I have to say. After leaving here with my wife-to-be it may be months before we return to Cefn-Ydfa. Meanwhile, you may live here on full wages, which will be paid every week by my Maesteg solicitors – just keep the place in order, and from time to time I will be in touch." At which Dai brought an end to the discussion by asking:

"Beggin' ye pardon, Maister – 'ave . . . have you popped the question to the lady in Russian Villa?" and he faltered. "I . . . I mean, 'ave you asked 'er?"

I hesitated, and he added, "Only last time I were over at the Grey place, 'nobbin' wi' my mate, the coachman, he didn't think you 'ad."

I returned his grin. "I think you can safely leave that part to me, Dando." His battered old face broke into a bunch of laughs and he shouted in his booming fighter's voice:

"Good for you, young 'un, an' when ye get her goin' – give it socks!" The meaning of which was debatable.

As I left them, he added:

"I brought the Wildflowers' caravan up outside like you said, and when you're ready for the off I'll bring the new pony from the stables and shaft it up directly."

"Thank you," I answered, and left them, staring, and to this day I'm sure that they didn't expect me to go. But of one thing I was certain, whether Jen came with me or not, I was going: the *Mortymer Co-operative*, as people were now calling it, had been substantially launched; for the next couple of months at least, there was nothing to keep me in Cefn-Ydfa.

Chapter 36

After packing my things into the caravan, it was dusk before I set out for the Russian Villa on foot, to give me time to contemplate my actions; and nearly summer dark when I entered the grounds of the Grey mansion.

In younger years, in the company of Davie, I had enjoyed a warm welcome in these rooms; but now I wondered what would be my reception. Davie was gone, and with him memories of childhood.

The Grey family and mine since those days had scarcely seen eye to eye; one of the many obstacles to a happier business relationship was my father's fundamental beliefs in the dignity of labour, and my abhorrence of their Truck Shop, a system long outlawed by Parliament. This had put the families on opposite sides of the political fence; and Jenny's obvious isolation in the family circle since Davie's death did nothing to moderate my concern for her.

This was to be no back door entry into a hostile camp: Mr Grey was a gentleman, and as such would receive me; but to ask for Jen's hand in marriage under such circumstances could only be called a confrontation.

Worse, as if intent on making a sensitive situation more difficult, Fate was taking a hand that night.

I had hoped for an unobtrusive entry; instead, as I reached the mansion I saw that a celebration of some sort was in progress; the main entrance being crowded with broughams and carriages; and music announced dancing.

People massed within under blazing chandeliers were

circling to a waltz, which ceased abruptly as if anticipating my arrival; a token of dislike?

Other sounds crowded my consciousness; the hedgerow secrets of night-birds, the scuttling of a dormouse – I actually saw his beady eyes watching me from beneath a shivering leaf.

Then I heard other music coming from distant Maesteg . . . the whispering of a brass band on the still air, while the puppets in gowns and evening suits paraded soundlessly upon the glass of the mansion's windows.

It was the music of a saint, General Booth; he who radiated kindness. The band was playing:

"Onward Christian soldiers marching as to war (Pom, pom, pom)
With the Cross of Jesus going on before (Pom, pom, pom)
Christ, our royal Master leads against the foe (Pom, pom, pom)
Onward into battle, see His banners go (Pom, pom, pom . . .)
Onward Christian soldiers . . ."

Yes, I thought, within my circumstance of arrival in an enemy camp, the man who was attacked by bishops and pelted by the mob was having a private word in my affairs; he who opened his first Citadel in Maesteg in 1889.

A buzz of conversation struck me as the door opened before me.

"Yes?" A butler appeared in the dim light of the hall, large of girth and countenance.

I said, "My name is Thomas Mortymer; I wish to speak with Mr Grey, please." And I stared at the man in disbelief.

"You have an appointment?" he asked, peering.

"I haven't. More, you know who I am. Bring him at once, or I shall come in."

"Kindly wait."

I was astonished: it was Bumstead, the bastard Dai Dando had kicked out of Cefn-Ydfa years ago; unknown to me, he was now butler to the Greys!

Vaguely I wondered if they knew his history.

There was little in David Grey's appearance to flatter his enormous success in industrial Maesteg; diminutive in personality and form, he nevertheless exuded a fine air of confidence which my father, in his time as a partner with him in tinplate, considered a little overdone; a man, said he, to be served with faint praise.

That he was a Christian went without saying; he attended with his family the Parish Church at Llangynwyd with unfailing regularity. His engineering genius was unquestioned, for in addition to founding the Llwydarth Tinplate Company, he owned the Caerleon Works in Monmouthshire; nor was· his benevolence doubted, for with profits made from his mining engineering (he sank the old No. 9 Duffryn Pit and had patents in the now famous "Greys" Pickling machines) he built rows of houses for his workers. Yet amazingly he was the perpetrator of the iniquitous system of Truck in the Llynfi Valley: an unforgivable act, and one which caused discontent and rioting – its goods being priced considerably higher than those available in the few local shops, as I mentioned earlier.

A worker tied to the Grey Tommy Shop (as they called them) had his job linked to Grey's Six Weeks' Bill; and this account, if not paid when presented, could endanger the worker's job, particularly were he of a labouring class.

True, the mists of time are forgiving to such employers, and Grey was a "creature of his time": but so were others: men like Robert Owen whose example I had copied. Even the hated William Crawshay of Merthyr Tydfil never descended to the economic torture of outlawed Truck, from which Grey received bulbous profits at a time of workers' distress.

So, while we have to endure vivid eulogies accorded to masters by our tame historians (who don't get paid unless they make the histories acceptable to descendants), let us also ring the bells of Truth, however discordant they may sound to unwilling ears.

"Ah, young Mortymer, how nice of you to visit us!" Grey offered his hand, which I took with less sincerity than his.

For while I commiserated with him in his loss of Davie, he had not done that which I had hoped – make Jenny feel as much at home in his household as would have been had Davie lived. It was now many years since his death and Jen was now more of a stranger than when Davie took her into the family as his bride.

Even now, looking beyond the anteroom door into the ballroom where couples were once again dancing, I could see her sitting alone.

Mr Grey was speaking, but I scarcely heard his words, being riveted by the sight of Jen the gipsy being ignored by prancing bucks doing the military two-step.

I said to Mr Grey, "Your butler, sir – haven't I seen him before?"

"Possibly, around town."

"He used to work for us when my father was alive."

Grey nodded. "I believe he mentioned that when I appointed him, but it is of small importance – he came with such excellent references." He folded his small hands towards me. "And now, young man, what can I do for you?"

"I would like to speak to Jenny."

"Of course, of course! Indeed, I've wondered why you've stayed distant so long; the families used to be such excellent friends."

"I have been busy. Getting a co-operative movement off the ground takes time. Also, it might have been indelicate to impose myself upon you after the death of Davie."

Grey nodded, lighting a cigar. "Ah yes – you and Jenny were friends before Davie came upon the scene – would it be fair to say that he took her off you?"

"It would." I returned his amiable grin.

"And now that he's gone you hope to pursue her?"

He wasn't making it easy: indeed, beneath the surface

of his friendliness he seemed to be trifling with me; and suddenly, out of context, he asked, "You . . . you propose to continue this . . . this co-operative business here and in Morriston?"

I nodded.

"You will find that it will meet with considerable opposition; I hope you realise."

"I expect it. All new ideas do, Mr Grey. When once people are on a good thing, the last thing they want is interference with profits."

"And you suppose that you can run this new movement on fresh air?"

"Workers' profit, sir, not rank exploitation."

He smiled, exhaling smoke. "Owen tried it, did he not?"

"And was beaten by greedy shareholders."

"You will have no shareholders, I hear."

"They are the last things I need!"

A silence came, accompanied by distant waltz music. He said portentously:

"Young Tom, your father's Liberal beliefs, which he took to ridiculous extremes, were the cause of discontent in our brief partnership. It would appear that you have inherited these and I'd like to say how delighted I am to be in opposition to you.

"However, you will be happy to know that the liberality of your new-found socialism – which some call communism – is not entirely confined to the working class which sometimes climbs our ladders.

"Robber barons – this you sometimes call us – can also compete when it comes to do-gooding." And he smiled up into my face. "You will be delighted to know that I am negotiating for a three-bed hospital in Maesteg."

"Too late, sir. I'm converting a three-bedroom house farther up the Llynfi into a six-bed casualty centre, with an adjoining room for chest complaints. It's a scandal that you have operated the Llwydarth for the past ten years with the nearest hospital as far away as Cardiff. This was one of Davie's complaints, if you remember."

"It would be best to leave Davie out of this."

"We can't! He is as much involved in death as he was when alive. It is because of men like him that things are better in this valley today, and will be better still when all of us are dead and gone with our profits." I was breathing heavily now, and although I fought to control my tongue the pent disgust of the past spilled out. I continued.

"You operate a system of Truck that is an abomination in this valley; through its debts you bind your workers hand and foot. As the price of tin goes down on world markets, so the price in your shop goes up; and that is not the economics of the madhouse, Mr Grey, but those of the greedy who can never have enough. But I tell you this. One day, through the co-operation of workpeople, we'll build a system worthy of the nation: we will have unions which will force people like you to spend until you hurt in the interests of labour – site homes where they can raise their families in decency – not the filthy, rat-infested alleys of Wales. You will be forced into supplying site first-aid, where a woman cut in the breast by tinplate can be patched up before hospital. Twice to church on Sunday, Mr Grey, may do something for one's soul, but little for the men of the lower coal galleries; and a pension of three shillings a week for a man with a broken back doesn't feed his children, who are left to scavenge from the bins of the rich like us." Now out of breath, I paused, staring into his face.

"Have you finished, Mortymer?"

"Of course not. I've only just started, but I know I'm wasting my breath." And I pointed a finger. "You are the best of the mob, Mr Grey. But you're in the company of the worst of them – men who pay starvation wages – non-resident bunkers like Charlotte Guest of Dowlais who scarpers every time the cholera comes to town. At least you stay put. Such names are blackened to the end of time, and unless you change your tune, yours will go down with them.

"Now then, may I see Jenny?"

"My God, you really are a fiery young man, aren't you!" said he.

I noticed the sudden pallor of his face – contrition or fury – I knew not. Picking up a little bell from a table, he rang it vigorously. The alacrity with which the butler appeared proved that he must have been listening outside the door.

"My compliments to Miss Jenny," said Grey calmly. "Ask her to meet Mr Mortymer." He added to me:

"This long recital to which you subjected me does nothing to contradict the notion that you must be off your head, Tom, for I've heard it all before, from such as you, and don't deny that you deserve that after the roasting you gave me."

I returned his grin.

"They also tell me that you imbibe, so let us toast the happiness of one whose interest we have in common – the woman my Davie loved, his Wildflower." And he poured two whiskies and gave me one. "In times of stress, young man, the elderly also turn to thoughts of love." He drank steadily, adding: "I bless your intentions towards my daughter-in-law if they are honourable; if not, I will come after you and find you wherever you are. You see . . ." – he played with his glass – "gossip abounds in a valley like this, and good subjects are not difficult to find. It appears that the good name your father enjoyed has been besmirched of late; when prominent women are involved, it bodes ill for a decent woman like Jenny . . .

"It won't work, son. Davie made her a good husband, and you'd be wise to follow his example. I doubt if your father would approve of you playing fast and loose with the daughter of the woman with whom he lost his life."

His expression changed as the door opened. "Aha," said he, "here she comes!"

Momentarily we stood, Jen and I, just looking. She was wearing a white gown that reached to the floor, I remember; her black hair in ringlets was down upon her shoulders, and her beauty would have tempted a saint. Unmoving, I said quietly:

"Well, here we are at last. The van is waiting up at Cefn-Ydfa and old Dai is lining up its pony. The summer and the open road is before us. I wonder what Davie would have us do?"

Mr Grey closed the door quietly behind him.

"Davie is dead, Tom," said Jenny, and stepped into my arms.

Got her!

And this time for good.

Aye, I thought, the open road!

The open road where the wind blows clear from the south and the cornfields wave golden under the summer moons: where no sulphurous fumes choke lungs in the pickling sheds, no blood is spilled on coal at the Farewell Rock and no child feeds from a lacerated breast.

All is milk and honey here, in the Land of Heart's Desire; the linen washes white, the water is sweet, the soil tastes good; no rancid stinks of violated earth exist in this heaven of the mind: no shrieks of machinery invade the ear; nothing but birdsong in the hedgerows and the shine of blackbirds, where you can linger in the sun and watch the cold moon-rise of kindly winters.

For this, my beloved, is our land as she used to be before the coming of the industrial boot, the hammer, knife and saw: the rivers themselves were of honey, the hills hot brown loaves straight out of the baker's oven – He the great Jesus who gave us Wales!

Will my country one day become revived and free of the savaging which men call Progress? Will the wind blow soft again, and the sun shine kindly beyond the furnace maw?

And I thought, as I prepared to pick up Jenny Wildflower, of a little poem out of our past. So many years had gone; so much laughter had been lost to us; so much loving would be forgotten:

"Does 'ere a one remember
The beautiful songs we sung,
When you were sixteen in April,
And I was lissom and young?"

Chapter 37

With our travelling cases aboard and Jen sitting up front beside me, I reined in and took the caravan down Corn Hwch lane to the Bridgend Road, but with one last look at Cefn-Ydfa.

It was a night of full moon and the woods about us were all over silver, with gossamer blowing in the wind. The big spit-bob spiders had been at it all night, thinking it was September, dew-fall last night having been as heavy as rain.

Just before I reined the little piebald around the mansion terrace, I turned to give one final look, and there stood a tearful foursome – Dai, Old Bid and the two girls. They were having a marvellous time of it in sniffing and wiping buckets: for wedding a Romany, said Old Bid, was asking for a blast on Satan's trumpet; not that I disapprove of the travellin' people, mind – handsome is as handsome does, I say, but 'is poor mither of royal blood would 'ave turned in 'er grave at the thought, bless 'er heart . . .

Oh aye? My poor mother didn't give a tinker's cuss for me, or ever did; and if my eyes were bright at that moment it was because I was thinking of my father.

It was thoughts of him that turned me for that last wave, which was responded to with sodden handkerchiefs; and it was then that I saw the Maid of Cefn-Ydfa for the last time before my return.

Before us was a wandering life, that which Jenny loved, for her Romany blood was tuned to the open road; one which had no fears of dark shadows and the chattering of wayside tragedies. The shrieking of an owl at the kill is one with the liquid libretto of the blackbird.

We did not speak, Jen and me, as I took the road to the north: nor did I bother to explain that we were going to the great ranges of Plynlimmon where the Roman legions had formed before the coming of the Barbarians.

In a self-imposed silence, one broken only by the clip-clopping of the pony, we went in the fierce moonlight of what was suddenly evolving into a world of absolute togetherness.

After the lonely years of hoping, the longing was at last diminished, and I put out my hand to her and Jen gripped it and settled it in her lap, so that I knew the warmth of her.

And still we did not speak; to have done so would have severed the chord of the total understanding that so rarely anoints the love of people.

When, long after midnight, which is a witching hour for Romanies, we came to a chosen place on the road to the Rhondda (which fervent Welshmen choose for the consummation of their marriages), a place, Dada once said, where, being Welsh, they are particularly good at it and ring the bell first time . . .

"We are stopping here?" asked Jen, and I did not reply, but reined the pony into a glade where the trees hung above us as a mantle against the stars; for what I had in mind wasn't the business of anybody, even the constellations.

The night was cold now and the wind, roughing the windows of the van for entry, had a bite in his uneven temper; for the wind, as all lovers know, believes it his right to know what is going on inside . . .

But the door of the van was locked and the pony was grazing outside in his world of chew and cud, as I took the nightdress off my girl.

Romanies, it may not be generally known, dress their brides in evocative nightgowns with more varieties of colour than Jacob's Coat, so that in the dark it's a job to know if the thing is on or off. And, while the world slept in its dreams of avarice, I went into my girl with such a joy to us both that Jen said she thought it was the end of the earth: and did so again and again, until the sky was blushing in the east and

259

fingers of gold crept in under the door of the caravan. In that love-making Jen called a name once only:

"Tom!" she said, deep in her throat.

Earlier I had been fearful that at such a moment she might have called for Davie, her joy in him revived in the love for him that was once so splendid.

But no. She called to me.

"Tom Mortymer," she said then, sitting up, "you are very good at this. If I didn't know you better, I'd have thought you'd had a little practice . . ."

I did not reply; there are times when a man answers such questions and when he does not.

Instead, I kissed her into silence, seeing in my mind's eye a vision of one whose love had not been so sanctified: and it was strange that I should see her at a time like this . . . poor Ann standing at the window of Cefn-Ydfa, one hand upraised to me as I left her to her lonely vigil for, unlike mine, her lover Wil Hopcyn . . . did *not* return.

It was like the closing of a chapter in the book of my life. Yes, the ending of a chapter, but not the book; for that has not yet been written.

Yet, *Amen* is still the word for this one.

Meanwhile, Jen had gone to sleep on me; something that had never happened to me with any other woman . . .

Amen.

Evidence of Children in the
Mines – Nineteenth Century

Little has been written by modern historians on the condition and labour of children working in the mines and ironworks of nineteenth-century Britain; indeed, such history was virtually undiscovered until recently: the result of this dilution of historical fact is that claim and counterclaim as to the veracity of modern statements were invariably challenged. Establishment historians have lied by omission.

Testimony of Phillip Phillips, aged nine years (his face badly scarred as a result of an explosion). Questioned by the Inspector of Mines, Mr H.W. Jones, he said: *I started work when I was seven. I get very tired sitting in the dark by the door* [ventilating door] *so I go to sleep. Nearly a year ago there was an accident and most of us were burned. It hurt very much because all the skin was burnt off my face, and I couldn't work for six months. I have seven brothers and sisters, but only five of us can find work; none of us have ever been to school.*

Testimony of Mary Davis, aged six. She said, when found asleep: *I went to sleep because my lamp had gone out for want of oil. I was frightened, for someone had stolen my bread and cheese, I think it was the rats.*

Susan Reece, also aged six and a doorkeeper, said: *I've been below six or eight months and don't like it much. I come here at six and leave at six at night . . . I haven't been hurt yet.*

Such young doorkeepers often rolled on to the line in sleep, and were run over by oncoming coal wagons.

Testimony of John Fuge, aged eleven: *I began work when I was seven, cutting slates in Cornwall; came to Wales two years ago. This is a very wet mine, our feet are never dry. Pumping is hard work, so we only work eight hours at a time. Sometimes I get so tired I don't care about eating. When I'm thirsty I drink the mine water, and I earn thirty pence a week; I work every day, so I can't go to Sunday school.*

Richard Richards, aged seven, told the Inspector: *I was six when I first came below. I work for about ten hours a day with my father; sometimes he lets me cut coal in his stall.*

William Richards, working underground, appears to have been a character; he said: *I don't know how old I am, but I've been below about three years. When I first came down I couldn't keep me eyes open, but now I sits by the door and smokes my pipe. I smokes about 2 ounces a week, and it costs me twopence. I don't know what tobacco is made of.*

Another lad, the son of a clergyman, working in the same colliery, said: *My name's Josiah Jenkins, and I'm seven. Been down eighteen months and get threepence a day, but I haven't been hurt yet*; and Jeremiah Jerimiah, aged ten. His father was dead and he had a badly disfigured face, caused by an explosion when he was five, and his friend, William Skidmore, aged eight, had a badly crushed hand – caused by a roof fall.

Ben Thomas, aged eight, hauling skips of coal – a 'very pitiful little fellow' said the Inspector, and Ben said: *I've been down here a year helping my brother to haul skips [sledge carts] of coal. Sometimes I get oatmeal broth before work, which is very hard and I am running all day. None of the boys in this pit wears shoes* – and Edward Edwards, who was aged nine, described how . . . *I've been working down here three months dragging carts loaded with coal from the coal face to the main road underground; there are no wheels to the carts [skips again]. It is not so well to drag them as the cart sometimes is dragged on to us, and we get crushed often. I have often hurt my hands and fingers and had to stay home.*

One of the doorkeepers was Zelophila Llewelyn, aged nine, who told the Inspector: *I eat bread and cheese down there. I don't often lose my food to the rats, but they do sometimes steal the bags of bread and cheese from other lads.*

Finally, Tom Jenkins and his tram partner in the hauling,

John Hugh, told the official: *We have no dinner time under-ground; I eat when I can; sometimes I get into the tram while my butty is hauling, and eat in there; he does the same when I push. My father is dead and my mother has seven children; one of these is aged seven and drives a horse. The trammers beat him and the others with whips when they do not mind to get the coal out quickly.*

Commissioner's note:
The boys are called Carters. Their occupation is to drag the carts or skips of coal from the working place to the main road underground. In this mode of labour the leather girdle passes round the body and the chain is between the legs, attached to the cart, and the lads drag on all fours.

This is the history that has been side-stepped in our time by 90 per cent of our Establishment historians; it is to be wondered if the crimes committed against the children of the Industrial Revolution are not being repeated, in a different guise, against the bodies of the children today.

Further Reading

Ty'r Llwnyi: Some Historical Notes of the Town of Maesteg. David Davies.

The Old Parish Public Houses Past and Present. John Lyons.

Tinplate. W. Robson Brown.

The Swansea Guide: 1851 (Hotels, Lodging Houses – Maps). John Lewis. (Glamorgan County Council – Facsimile edition – 1989.)

The Story of Swansea: Districts and Villages. Norman Lewis Thomson.

The History of Iron and Steel: Tinplate and Other Trades of Wales. Charles Wilkins.

Tinplate Through the Ages: The British Steelmaker. Frederick Evans, MBE, MA.

Chronology of the Tinplate Works of Great Britain (1944). Edward Henry Brooke.

The Llwydarth Tinplate Works. Thomas Bevan. A Dissertation on the Industrial Developments of the Llynfi, Ogmore and Garw Valleys.

Glamorgan Gazette (Maesteg fifty-seven years ago). An extract dated 7th October 1927; Truck: "Lagos".

The Cambrian (newspaper). 23rd May 1856 – Cefn-Ydfa.

The Hard-Earned Penny. Leisure Hour – June 1870 – Anon.

Encyclopedia Britannica. Brief biography of Robert Owen (1771–1858).

White Wheat (the story of Cefn-Ydfa). 1947: Michael Gareth Llewelyn. Publisher John Murray.

History of the Llynfi Valley. Brinley Richards, MA, 1982. Publisher D. Brown and Sons Ltd, Cowbridge, South Glamorgan.

Commissioners Reports, Commission of Enquiry into State of Children in Employment (1847) in Wales. An official Government Commission document of the utmost prejudice; one that indicts the Welsh people for degraded morality; referring to Welsh women as 'evil, savage, slatternly and rude and with scarcely a ray of spiritual intelligence'.

Such is the temerity and malicious bias of these reports that when the industrialists are reluctantly taken to task for the exploitation of their workers, the true facts of the social conditions of the time emerge with unparalleled significance; despite the efforts of 'tame' historians who could not get their work published without diluting the irreducible truth.